Please REMEMBER Me

JACOB Z. FLORES

Dreamspinner Press

Published by
DREAMSPINNER PRESS

5032 Capital Circle SW, Suite 2, PMB# 279, Tallahassee, FL 32305-7886 USA
http://www.dreamspinnerpress.com/

Please Remember Me
© 2015 Jacob Z. Flores.

Cover Art
© 2015 L.C. Chase.
http://www.lcchase.com
Cover content is for illustrative purposes only and any person depicted on the cover is a model.

ISBN: 978-1-63216-779-8
Digital ISBN: 978-1-63216-780-4
Library of Congress Control Number: 2014952119
First Edition February 2015

Printed in the United States of America

This paper meets the requirements of
ANSI/NISO Z39.48-1992 (Permanence of Paper).

To Tere Michaels. Thank you for the plot bunny!
To Mike Zimmermann. Thank you for the inspiration.

Prologue

"DID YOU hear my question?" Dr. Beth Anglin asked. She peered over her chart at my fiancé lying in his hospital bed while I stood behind her, wringing my hands. It had been two weeks since Hank's accident, and this was the first time I'd seen his baby blues in far too long. It took every bit of self-control I had not to leap across the room and take him in my arms.

I needed to feel his warm skin against mine, the brush of his calloused hands gliding over my cheeks. It was how he'd greeted me for the past three years. A gentle caress followed by a kiss that always left me breathless and wanting more.

If Dr. Anglin had not been in the room when Hank regained consciousness, I would have done exactly that, even though she'd already warned me that all might not be as it once was.

Hank's head trauma had been severe.

"Yeah," Hank answered. His deep voice rasped. It reminded me of sandpaper scratching across cobblestone. "I'm Henry Burton. But everyone calls me Hank."

The hope I'd tried to keep from swelling too high surged forward. Hank's answer was a good sign. It was how he always introduced himself to new people, and they were the words Hank had first spoken to me all those years ago.

Dr. Anglin nodded at Hank's reply and scribbled something on the chart. "Can you tell me where you are?"

He made a show of scrutinizing his surroundings, as if in deep thought. He did that whenever asked a question with an obvious answer. "I'm gonna go with a hospital." Not even being in a coma for the past fourteen days could squelch Hank's penchant for being a playful smartass. It was one of the many things I loved about him.

"What city are you in right now?"

"San Diego, I hope."

Dr. Anglin paused before jotting down more notes.

San Diego? Hank hadn't lived in southern California since he moved to Houston to be with me. That couldn't be good.

"Where were you born?"

"Don't you have all that information on my chart there?" he asked. The knock to his head hadn't made him a better patient. Despite thinking he lived in San Diego, he was still the man I'd fallen in love with.

"I do," Dr. Anglin answered with a smile. "How about you indulge me anyway?"

"Well, all right, then. I was born in Los Angeles." He glanced over her shoulder at me. When his gaze lingered upon mine, I almost melted. "How am I doing so far?"

"Good," I replied with a hopeful sob lodged in my throat. "*Real* good."

"Can you tell me what's the last thing you remember before your accident?" Dr. Anglin asked.

That question caught Hank by surprise. He studied her carefully, almost as if she had just materialized out of thin air. "Accident? I don't remember an accident."

In response, Dr. Anglin scribbled more notes.

"Am I okay?" he asked me once he realized that the doctor's attention had been momentarily lost.

"I think you're doing splendidly," I replied. I smiled real big, trying not to let Hank see my concern. But since Hank usually knew me better than I knew myself, I didn't count on the smile working.

When Hank nodded and refocused his attention on Dr. Anglin, the flood of hope within me ebbed a few feet.

"What are your parents' names?"

"Henry and Sharon," he replied. Hank's tone hardened as it typically did whenever he was faced with something he didn't know what to do with. "Just what the hell happened to me?"

"I promise to answer all your questions," she said. "Before I do that, though, I just have one more question for you."

"And that would be?"

"Can you tell me who this man behind me is?" She stepped aside to give Hank a clear view of me.

My knees began to shake, and my hands grew cold. I had to shove them in the pockets of my jeans for warmth. Suddenly I wondered what I must look like. After two weeks sleeping in the most uncomfortable chair God had ever created, I was certain I looked like Medusa's ugly sister.

After a five-second once-over, Hank returned his gaze to Dr. Anglin. He shrugged. "I've never seen him before in my life."

CHAPTER

One

DURING THE summer of 2011, I took my first vacation since I graduated law school at Rice University in Houston, Texas. It wasn't that I didn't enjoy vacationing, although I hated driving long distances with a passion. I just didn't have time. I was too busy making a name for myself at Canales, Crenshaw, and Emerson. But a few years of working seven days a week started to take their toll. To make matters worse, my best friend, Jill O'Neal, turned into a real nag on the subject.

"You really need to get away," Jill said as she stretched out on the chocolate brown leather couch in my living room. She'd brought me dinner while I worked on a case Mr. Canales had handed over to me.

"Can't," I said while poring over legal textbooks at the same time as I scarfed down my lemon chicken. "Busy."

"That's your answer for everything," she complained. "All work and no play makes Santi Herrera a dull boy."

"Actually, you're referring to Jack," I corrected with a twisted grin. "Jack is the dull boy, and before you argue with me, there are years of documented records on that little tidbit all over the place. I would be happy to Google it if you need verification."

"Don't you get all lawyery on me," she said with an arch to her newly pierced eyebrow. When it came to piercings and tattoos, Jill was obsessed. "Or I'll punch you in the arm. Remember what happened the last time?"

How could I forget? The last time I went all "lawyery" on Jill, as she so eloquently put it, was when I saw her glove compartment full of unpaid moving violations. She loved speeding more than she loved the awful horror movies we enjoyed watching together. Unfortunately her lead foot had resulted in at least a dozen citations. I tried explaining the ramifications of not paying the tickets. Instead of heeding my advice, she punched me in my arm. Her fist hit like a pile driver and resulted in a purplish bruise that lasted over a week. "I remember," I replied and then scooted farther away from her on the couch.

She laughed. "That's right. You better be scared."

"Of you?" I asked. "Always."

"Seriously, though, you need to slow down. You've been going ninety to nothing for a while now. You need to take better care of yourself."

"I take excellent care of myself. I eat right and go to the gym five times a week. That's better than most of the lawyers at the office."

"There's more to taking care of yourself than living a life as bland as a bran muffin."

"My life's not a bran muffin," I grumbled. I hated bran muffins!

"Oh really?" she asked. She sat up and locked on to my gaze. This wasn't good. Jill only did that when I unexpectedly walked into a trap she'd slyly set for me. "When was the last time you even got laid?"

I had to stop and think. I hadn't been on an actual date in at least three years. Romance required work and commitment, and I had already committed myself to making partner. Nothing was more important to me.

"That's right," she said with a smile of smug satisfaction. "You can't even remember, but I do."

I wasn't going to get any work done as long as Jill was set on this current path, so I placed the legal pads and books to one side and faced her. "Enlighten me."

"Last year at the office Christmas party," she said. "You got drunk and went home with Wyatt."

Damn. Had it really been that long? Since I could recall no other man since I practically bent Wyatt Perry in half in the back seat of his Mercedes, I had no other choice but to nod in agreement.

"That's way too long to go without a nice stiff one," she added.

Jill was right again. How had I gone that long without sex? My romp with Wyatt had been pretty damn good, and Wyatt had wanted a repeat performance. He'd made that abundantly clear since last year, frequently asking me out for drinks or dinner. I'd been interested, but work somehow always stole my attention.

Wyatt understood. He was a lawyer too and just as busy as I. But no matter how disappointed he was when I brushed him off or how fine his body looked in the tailored suits he wore, I still turned him down until he stopped offering.

"What the hell's wrong with me?" I asked. "Wyatt's pretty fucking hot, and those blue eyes of his. Damn!"

Jill nodded before she scooted over to me and put her arm around my shoulders. I rested my head against her and sighed. "You love your job and you're a workaholic. Those aren't necessarily bad, but when you turn down a hottie who's obviously into you and who has blue eyes that you typically cream your undies for, well, it just proves my point: you need more fun in your life and a bit less lawyery stuff."

"And a lot more sex."

"Fuck yeah," she said with a fist pump to the air. "Sex is better than milk. It does the body good."

Jill didn't get any arguments from me.

TWO WEEKS later Jill and I landed in San Diego. She made it her mission to see that I had a good time and had pretty much mapped out every hour of our weeklong stay. We went to the San Diego Zoo, the Presidio, and SeaWorld. We ate lunch in Balboa Park and rode bikes along the beachfront. We hiked through the mission trails, and, of course, we went shopping. While I bought some new club shirts, Jill pierced the cartilage of her right upper ear for the fifth time.

"What do you think?" I modeled my new club attire for Jill in the hotel room. I was nervous. I hadn't been to a gay club in years, so I had no clue if what I'd purchased was the "gay fabulous" Jill had insisted I find. I was even more apprehensive about where we were going. Jill had managed to talk me into going to something called a stripper circus. What the hell did that even mean? I pictured gay men spinning on stripper poles that were lit on fire. Evidently it was a standard event at Rich's, one of the more popular clubs in town. At least that was what Jill told me.

"Santi, are you sure you're gay?" she asked as she rose from the bed and crossed over to me. Her black boots clicked against the hardwood floor of the five-star hotel room she'd made me book. "I ask because you dress like a Republican." She sighed in exasperation.

"What's wrong with my outfit?"

"Where do I begin?" she asked as she walked circles around me. "First of all, you don't tuck in your shirt when you go clubbing. Or wear a work belt." She unbuckled my belt and slid it free of the loops in one quick jerk. She then shoved her hands in my jeans and pulled out my shirt.

"Hey! At least buy me dinner first."

She rolled her eyes. "If only you were that lucky."

"Do I pass muster now, oh wonderful Wizard of Oz?"

Jill snorted. "Did you have to buy a long-sleeve button-down shirt? We aren't going to a deposition, you know?"

"The saleswoman said it looked perfect for an evening out."

"Let me guess. She was over sixty and wore bifocals."

How the hell did she do that?

"No need to answer. Your slack jaw tells me I'm right." She unfastened the first two buttons of my shirt and peeked inside. "Are you wearing an undershirt?" she asked with an eye roll.

"Well, yeah. I always do, especially when I wear white. You can see my nipples through the fabric. I'm not pasty-fleshed like you. I've got a natural tan."

"So what if your nipples show?" she asked. She pointed to her chest. The low-cut blouse proudly displayed the tattooed blue swallows at the swell of each ample breast. "You can see mine, not that anyone at Rich's will notice."

"Aw, come on!" I protested. "I don't want to see your nipples."

"Okay, you are gay." She sounded relieved. "Now take off the shirt."

"What?"

"Take. Off. The. Shirt."

"Why?"

She eyeballed me. "Do you want me to punch you? Because I will."

I sighed and did as Jill requested.

"Now *that's* what I'm talking about!" Her lips parted in a salacious grin. "Wifebeaters are hot."

"Who doesn't get a woody from a man beating his wife?"

"Can it, smartass," she said as she spun me around. "Look at yourself in the mirror. You've got good muscle definition in your arms, which the muscle shirt shows off nicely. Plus the ribbed material makes your flat stomach look even tighter. And with those tight jeans displaying your bulge and tight ass, you'll definitely be getting some play tonight."

I stared at myself in the mirror. Was she serious? I couldn't look any more ridiculous if I tried.

"Just one more thing to do before the look is complete."

I glared at Jill's reflection. "What's that?"

She ran her fingers through my slicked-back dark hair and messed up the perfect do I'd managed to create. "Hey!" When she was done, I looked like I'd just rolled out of bed.

"Perfect!"

"Seriously? Bedhead is perfect?"

"It's casual," she said with a nod. "And hot."

I was wrong. I looked even more ridiculous now than before.

Jill then smacked my ass. "Now, let's get to Rich's and get you laid."

I stared at my reflection. Who in their right mind would want to have sex with this mess?

WHILE WE stood in line at the club, waiting for our turn to pay admission, Jill gave me instructions on how to catch the eye of a hot man. "You've got to pretend that you're an old pro at this clubbing crap. Don't stand around with your arms folded across your chest. It makes you look bored and stiff, and not in the good way." She eyed me until I uncrossed my arms. What was I supposed to do with my hands now? Standing with my arms crossed was my thing. "You also have to project confidence, not desperation. All men, especially gay men, hate that. If you look like you don't give a fuck if anyone talks to you, then you'll have your pick of the dogs to take you to pound town. Also, try smiling. You've got nice teeth and sexy lips, so wipe that grimace from your face."

"What I want to wipe is you from the bottom of my shoe."

"As if you could," Jill said with a smile. "Don't be afraid to chat up some hottie either. If he talks back, see where it goes. If he doesn't, it's his loss. Just move on and don't let some stuck-up prick get you off your game."

I stared blankly at her. "I have no game."

"No truer words have been spoken," she said with a nod.

"Bitch."

"Cocksucker."

We broke into hysterics. We always did that whenever we called each other by those names. They were terms of endearment that only Jill and I could use. When the laughing fits ceased, Jill continued on with her advice as if she'd never stopped.

But I had stopped listening. Someone new had my full attention.

Crossing the street toward the club was the most attractive man I'd ever laid eyes on. He had to be well over six feet tall, since he towered over his two friends on either side of him, and he was built like a brick shithouse. His broad shoulders stretched the fabric of his red muscle shirt, which, for some reason, had Hello Kitty across the front. He packed a pair of amazing guns. Green ink from a tattoo design I couldn't make out in the dim light trailed around the biceps of both arms. I'd never been into tattoos on guys before. I had always preferred the clean-cut, professional look, but on tall, tanned, and blond, the body art somehow made him look professional, rugged, and forbidden.

My cock agreed. It fattened and lengthened within the uncomfortable confines of my tight denim.

"Are you listening to me?" Jill asked.

"Not a word," I replied as I stepped out of the line.

"Where are you going?"

Where the hell was I going? I'd never approached a man in the almost thirty years of my life, but here I was walking toward someone I'd just laid eyes on. What had come over me?

The answer was easy enough. *He* had.

Something about him yanked me from my usual complacency and spurred me into action. It was as if I had to talk to him or I'd regret not doing so for the rest of my life. As I drew closer to where he had stopped to chat with his friends, the man became more stunning. His blond hair was clipped short, and his sideburns descended into a dark blond beard that cut a manly swath across his tanned, rugged cheeks. But the rough appearance and the fact that he could probably break me in two didn't fool me. The light of his smile and the twinkle in his blue eyes as he laughed with his friends told me this man wasn't some asshole prick.

His hard exterior hid the gentle lamb he truly was.

"Hi," I said as I reached his side. "I'm Santi."

His lips spread into a smile that was warmer than my parents' house on Christmas Eve. "I'm Henry Burton," he said as he extended his hand for mine. "But everyone calls me Hank."

When Hank's big, rough hand closed over mine in greeting, I had to stifle a moan before it could escape my throat. "Nice to meet you, Hank."

"Same here," he replied. When he didn't immediately withdraw his grip from mine, I realized that this tall hunk of man flesh might like me too. How incredible was that?

HANK AND I sat at one of the farthest corner tables we could find to escape the swirling crowds and loud music. I'd been worried that we wouldn't be able to hold any sort of conversation whatsoever. Animated voices and guys screaming "whoot whoot" on the dance floor filled the entire building with a constant thrum. There were people everywhere.

Bare-chested guys with more muscles than clothes paraded through the club, strippers danced for dollars on top of tables and the bar, and for some reason, drag queens walked around with bunny ears on their heads. The oddest sights, however, were the people dressed in circus gear, pretending to tame guys dressed as lions, or performing aerial maneuvers on sheer pieces of fabric that hung from the ceiling.

Was this a gay club or Cirque du Soleil?

But once Hank returned with our drinks, a Cape Cod for me and a Red Bull for him, the chaos that churned around us turned into barely discernible background noise.

"Thanks," I said as I took the drink. Our fingers brushed. My cock sprung to life and could have flipped the small circular table where we sat.

He flushed, and his gaze briefly darted away. "No problem," he said in a rasp. Had Hank developed a super boner too? I'd never wanted to crawl under a table more in my life.

"I hope your friends don't mind you talking to me," I said with a nod to the two men he'd been standing with in front of Rich's. They leaned against the bar, drinks in hand, surveying the crowd. One had long blond hair that made him look way too much like a young Dakota Fanning, and the other had short curly dark hair that made him look way too much like Annie.

Hank chuckled as he nodded to his friends, who grinned back at him. "Nah, they're good. Mitch and Darren may be my roommates, but they're not my keepers."

"How long have you three lived together?"

Hank's forehead wrinkled in thought as he surveyed the ceiling for an answer. "Mitch and I have lived together since we were sixteen, so that's just over ten years. Darren joined us about four years ago."

Well fuck. "Oh, so you're not just roommates. You're what? A trio?"

Hank about busted a gut. His eyes sparkled like topaz reflecting the sun. "Oh God no! We're just roommates. That's it." He shuddered as if he'd just taken a bite out of a lemon. "Well, Mitch and I were boyfriends for a few months in our early twenties, but God! That was ages ago. We're more like brothers now. The thought of either of them naked in bed turns my stomach."

I couldn't help the smile that stretched across my face or the blood that surged back to my dick. "That's good to hear."

11

Hank's laughter sputtered, and my cheeks burned hot. Had I really just said that? From the wicked grin that slid across Hank's lips, I had, and he evidently liked that. "I'm glad." He reached across the small table and took my hands in his and leaned into the space that separated us. The scents of mint and musk clung to the air around him. "How about your friend?" he asked.

"Who?"

He chuckled as he nodded over my shoulder to Jill, who smiled at me and gave me a thumbs-up. Did she really have to be so obvious?

"Oh, her," I said with a shake of my head. "Jill's the bane of my existence, as all best friends somehow seem to be."

"I know what you mean. I've known Mitch longer than anybody, and he drives me absolutely batshit."

The crowded dance floor erupted in cheers when the DJ started spinning a dance track of Britney's latest single, "Hold It Against Me." Hank excitedly squeezed my hand and started dancing in his seat. "I love this song."

I stood up and tugged Hank toward the dance floor.

BY THE time Britney's song ended and Rihanna started singing about S&M, I'd surprised myself by pulling Hank's tee from his body. I now had a close-up view of a broad, muscular chest covered in dark blond fur, pierced nipples, and the tattoos that covered his arms and torso.

On his right arm extended a jungle backdrop that started at his shoulder and descended down to above his elbow. What appeared to be a design of the universe covered his left pectoral. The planets and their stars orbited up his collarbone and shoulder cap and down his side in a swirl of green and purple. A huge tree with a blazing sun had been etched into the skin along his left shoulder cap.

The designs were gorgeous and made his already stunning body even more spectacular.

He grinned wickedly down at me and tore the shirt from my body. After gazing appreciatively at my tanned, smooth flesh, he growled low in his chest. I wrapped my arms around his sweat-slick body and pulled him close. I slid my fingers up and down his massive back as our groins rocked and ground against each other.

The thick hardness in his denim scraped against my throbbing dick. As our cocks rubbed, Hank enveloped me in his embrace. He reached his long arms around my shoulders, following the curve of my spine until he dipped his fingertips just beneath the waistband of my jeans. When he rested them there, I sighed and leaned my head against the moist blond mat of hair that covered his pecs.

In my life, I'd never behaved this way—strolling up to a man, introducing myself, and dirty dancing half-naked. I'd always been far more reserved and much too stubborn to just abandon the reins of control I used to direct my life. Every step I took was planned and meant to follow a carefully charted-out path. It was how I had pulled my way out of poverty and into the comfortable life of a pretty successful lawyer.

But right now, I had discarded the bridle and spit out the bit. I didn't know where I was going or even which way was up. And I didn't care. All that mattered was this moment and the man in my arms, who filled me with desire I'd never experienced before in my bran-muffin life.

"You're driving me crazy," Hank muttered. The loud music couldn't drown out his deep voice. In fact, Hank was about all I could hear. He pulled back from the embrace and gazed down at me. His face lit up brighter than the strobe lights that flashed around us.

"Tell me about it," I replied.

We stayed that way, staring into each other's eyes like two serpents mesmerized by a snake charmer. Our swaying bodies moved in sync with the beat as our fingers strummed across the other's flesh. It was as if we were in tune not just with each other, but with everything around us. As if our souls had suddenly opened up to encompass everyone.

When the first few notes of Lady Gaga's "The Edge of Glory" filtered through the speakers, Hank moved his hand from the swell of my butt up to my cheek. He traced my jawline with his fingertips, gingerly scratching a path across the stubble I had yet to shave away. He rested his other hand on my chest, directly over my rapidly beating heart.

He then palmed my face with both hands before craning down for a kiss.

When our lips touched, I groaned into his mouth, and the lyrics of the melody exploded around us. I thrust my tongue between Hank's lips, coaxing his tongue out of his mouth and into mine and tasting the sugary sweetness of the energy drink he had purchased earlier. Our tongues danced as our surging passions crested, threatening to drown us beneath their endless waves.

Hank pulled out of the kiss, panting. I had no breath left to exhale.

"Fuck!" he said.

I could only nod in reply.

A strange look came over Hank's features. "What's wrong?" I asked.

"Nothing whatsoever," he replied immediately. "I was just wondering if... well, if you might want to get out of here or something." Hank's lips parted into an uncertain yet mischievous grin.

I laced my fingers around his neck and rose to meet his lips. "I've never wanted anything more." Then I molded my mouth against his once again.

ABOUT THIRTY minutes later, Hank and I arrived in front of the three-story house he shared with his roommates in Hillcrest, a predominantly gay area in San Diego. He took my hand in his after we exited his Ford F-150, and we giggled like schoolkids on recess as he fumbled the front door open.

On the other side sprawled an interior courtyard with grass so lush I could still see its greenery easily in the moonlight. A low bark grabbed my attention. On the front porch sat an English bulldog that eyed me, a tongue lolling out of the corner of his mouth.

"That's Picasso," Hank said as the dog lumbered over to us and wagged his cute brown butt. I knelt down so Picasso could sniff my hand. When he'd determined I had no plans to harm his house or his master, he presented me with his butt for a good scratching, which I heartily doled out.

"What a cute boy," I said as Picasso snuffed.

14

"Cute?" Hank said at Picasso's other end. He squatted to take Picasso's big squashed head roughly in his hands. "He's my handsome boy!"

"Very handsome," I replied, looking now at Hank and not Picasso.

Hank grinned at me before kissing the top of Picasso's fuzzy head. "Come on, boy. Follow Grandpa inside for a treat."

At the word *treat*, Picasso scrambled after Hank and through the front door of the house.

"Grandpa?" I asked as I followed them inside. The interior was all hardwood. The front hall led to a small dining room with a patio just beyond. Outside extended a panoramic view of the city and Mexico just beyond. It was breathtaking.

"Yup, Picasso's my grandbully," Hank said after reentering the dining room from what had to be the kitchen off to the far right. "His mother was Gracie. Since I don't have kids, I considered Gracie my daughter, and since Picasso is one of her pups, that makes me his grandpa."

I nodded. I'd always believed it was strange when adults treated pets like children, but with Hank I found it too adorable for words. "Where's Gracie?" I asked, looking around for another bulldog hiding in the shadows.

"She passed a few years ago," he replied. The joy that had effused from him since we first met flickered. A profound sadness now descended upon him.

"I'm sorry," I said, crossing to him and rubbing my hand along his hairy forearm.

He smiled at me appreciatively before pulling me back into his embrace. Just like that, his rakish smirk returned. "Don't be," he said as he nuzzled his face into my neck. I clutched his arms as he sniffed and lapped at my skin. "There's something about your smell that drives me fucking crazy."

Normally I wouldn't have understood that comment. I'd never had a really good sense of smell, and my allergies typically drove me crazy around guys who slathered on cologne. But no such artificial scent clung to Hank. It was all natural and all man. He seemed to be pure musk and pheromones that made my cock harder every time I caught a whiff.

I inhaled his scent, and my body trembled. "All I can smell is you," I replied. "And it's pretty fucking incredible."

Hank rested his forehead against mine. "I'm glad you like it. I made it myself."

"What time will your roommates be home?"

He shrugged. "They'll be back when they're done tricking. What time do you need to head back to your hotel?"

I mimicked his shrug. "Jill's my hag, not my keeper. Besides, she was so happy when I told her I was leaving Rich's with you, she practically shoved me out the front door."

"So we have as long as we'd like?" Hank asked before pressing his lips against mine.

"For as long as you'll have me," I replied into the kiss.

Hank caressed my cheek with his big hand. It was a sweet gesture, one that I could spend a lifetime getting used to. "Be careful with what you say around me. I consider words to be powerful things."

"And?"

"Well, I could imagine having you all night."

I rose on my tiptoes and he brushed his lips against my forehead before bringing my mouth to his. "That doesn't sound like a bad deal to me."

AFTER SECURING Picasso in Mitch's room, Hank led me to his bedroom and closed the door. Pictures from his past covered his walls. There were photos with younger versions of him, Mitch, and Darren at various locales—beaches, the Golden Gate Bridge, and the Grand Canyon. Scattered between them were pictures of his family. Based on the photographs, Hank had two sisters and a brother. There was only one picture of his parents, though.

Hank suddenly wrapped his arms around me from behind. He drew me against his hard body and sniffed at my neck before letting out a contented sigh. No one had ever held me like that before or seemed so happy to be with me. For two men who had just met, this was a little strange. I loved it anyway. "What are you looking at?"

"Just your family." I leaned into his embrace. Since he was about six inches taller, my head rested against his muscled chest. "You obviously love them."

"I do. We've had some tough times together, but who hasn't?"

"That's right, Effie. We've all got pain."

Hank laughed. "*Dreamgirls* is one of my favorite movies."

I turned around in his arms. "I wouldn't have thought that such a big, rugged guy like you would be into musicals."

"There's lots of things about me that might surprise you," he said with a playful nip to my nose.

"Really? I'm intrigued now. Name one."

"Well, for starters, I'm a pretty ravenous power bottom."

I *was* surprised. I figured Hank to be a merciless top, what with all the muscles and the manly swagger. I'd been a little apprehensive about how hard he was going to pummel me, especially considering I hadn't had sex in over a year. "Wow. Really?"

He nodded. "Most guys think I'm a top because I'm so tall and big. Don't get me wrong, I can top for the right guy, but I prefer bottoming." He hesitated for a moment before outlining my lips with his index finger. "That okay with you?"

"That's more than okay." My asshole was suddenly relieved, and my cock grew harder in eager anticipation. "I don't really tend to bottom much anyway."

"Then I guess we're a perfect fit."

I nodded before running my hands through his short blond hair. I grabbed a handful at the back and forcefully but gently tugged, making Hank reveal his thick, muscular neck. I kissed and gnawed on his sensitive flesh as he moaned. In one quick motion, I removed the shirt he'd put back on after we left the club, and I nibbled a path from his neck to his pierced nipples. I flicked my tongue around the pebbling flesh and gently bit down.

"Fuck!" Hank groaned in appreciation. He grabbed the back of my head and pushed me harder onto his nipple. I'd been right. Hank liked it rough, and for some reason, he brought out the dominant side of me that had never existed before this moment.

I placed my hand on his chest and gently lowered him back onto his California-king bed. Hank scrambled up on the mattress, giving me room to join him. I pressed my body on top of his and proceeded to sensually torture both of his nipples with gentle kisses and more aggressive nibbles. I even managed to capture his sensitive flesh between his piercing and my teeth. Hank undulated underneath me, and he clutched at the sheets.

"You like that?"

He glanced down at the hearty bulge in his jeans. "Do you really need to ask?"

"Yes," I replied with a firm grab at his crotch. I squeezed his junk and tugged to cause the pain that obviously gave Hank pleasure. "Now answer me."

Hank gritted his teeth and thrust into my grip. "Fuck yes," he cried. "I love it."

"Good," I responded before clamping down hard on his nipple while yanking on his balls at the same time. The combination caused Hank to whimper and his breathing to turn ragged. When he started to gasp for air, I released my hold and immediately descended on his lips.

Swept up in the frenzied passion, we pushed our tongues in and out of each other's mouths. As we kissed, our hands developed minds of their own. I clawed at his hairy chest while he kneaded my ass. I slid off him so we lay side by side, and I gripped his hardness, still confined in his denim. Hank pinched my nipples and rolled them between his fingers. I shoved my hands down the back of his jeans and clutched at his meaty ass, and he dove his hand beneath my waistband and took my cock in his grasp.

I pumped my dick into his fist and grabbed his chin, forcing his mouth open for another series of deep kisses. Hank then took my bottom lip in his mouth, sucked on it hard, and then bit down. The slight pain in conjunction with the wild look in his eyes and his hand jacking my cock almost made me come right then.

I had to slowly pull my lip from his jaws and take deep breaths to calm down.

"You okay?" he asked. "Did I hurt you?"

"I'm fine," I said between pants. "It's just been a while since I've done this, and, well, you've got me so turned on I almost blew my load."

"We can take a breather. I can get us something to drink."

"Oh, we're not stopping," I told him as I unfastened his jeans. "We're just switching focus."

Hank kicked his high-tops from his feet, and I tugged down his jeans. Freed from the denim, his thick, pierced cock flopped onto his belly. I'd never been with a man with a Prince Albert before. In truth, they'd made me a bit queasy, but nothing about Hank diminished the desire that burned within me.

Everything about him just added more fuel to the blazing inferno.

But it didn't mean I knew what to do with a cock that had a two-inch ring sticking out of it. Did I swallow the piercing along with the cock? Would it get stuck on my tonsils if I did? That was a 911 call I didn't plan on making. Not that I'd be able to talk with a dick lodged in my throat.

"You can take it out," he said with a grin.

I laughed in embarrassment. "I've never actually worked one of these before."

Hank reached down, popped the small metal ball out of the ring that kept it in place, and then tugged the piercing free of his cockhead in about three quick gestures. I watched in amazement.

"Does it hurt?"

He grinned at me. "Not at all, but then again, I like a bit of pain."

"So I noticed," I replied before grabbing his hard cock at the base. "How about a little of pleasure and pain right now?"

Hank's eyes grew big and dreamy. "Yes, please."

I circled the head of his cock with my tongue, lapping up the precum that oozed out of the slit at the tip and the hole from the piercing. Hank's juices tasted sweet like his Red Bull kisses on the dance floor. It made me thirsty for more, so I swallowed his cock to the base and tugged on his ball sac at the same time.

Hank arched his back off the bed. "Damn, Santi," he gasped. "It's like you know exactly what my body craves."

He was right. I instinctively did know what he liked. I swirled my tongue around his head when I came off his cock and then used it to tickle the base when I once again took him to the hilt. With each slobbery pass I made on his dick, I fondled, pulled, or twisted his nuts until Hank couldn't keep still. His limbs flailed and shook as if he had no control over their movements whatsoever.

"I don't know how much longer I can hold out," he muttered. "You've got me so fucking close already."

I came off his cock long enough to say, "Good." Then I sucked him back into my throat. As I slid up and down his hardness, I jacked his shaft in rapid circles with one hand while tickling and torturing his cum-heavy balls with the other.

Hank's panting grew more ragged, and low whimpers escaped his throat. His big, muscled body shuddered, and his chest heaved rapidly. "Holy shit," he mumbled. His hard cock turned to steel before flooding my mouth with his sweet spunk, which I greedily swallowed.

"Dammit!" he muttered between wheezes. "I've never come that hard in my life."

I wiped the spittle from my lips and smiled. "Glad to be of service." I kissed a trail from the nest of blond pubic hair up his furry belly and chest until I could linger upon his lips once again.

"Just so you know," he said as he gently pushed me on my back, "we aren't done here. Not by a long shot."

"What*ever* do you mean?"

In reply, Hank unzipped my jeans and pulled them and my underwear down so quickly it was almost as if they were on fire. He tossed them over his shoulder and then pressed his mouth to mine. As he slipped his tongue between my lips, he took hold of my erection and slowly milked my dick in his rough palm.

"Damn!" I said when he circled his finger around my cockhead, teasing a pearl of liquid from the slit. "That feels amazing."

"And we're just getting started," he replied before chewing on my lip and then biting his way down my chin, around my neck, and toward my nipples. He took each one in his mouth, catching the taut flesh between his teeth before lapping at the sensitive skin with his tongue.

While he chewed on my chest, he slowly jacked my rock-hard cock until it leaked a steady stream of clear liquid.

Hank rubbed his fingers in my precum and then brought his hand to his lips. He sucked each finger dry before returning for more. He continued the mind-blowing slow hand job and then licked a trail down my smooth, tanned skin before burying his face in my thatch of dark pubic hair. He inhaled deeply and growled. "Fuck! Your smell makes me want to devour you whole."

"Who's stopping you?"

He grinned up at me before swirling his tongue around my shaft. He flicked it all the way up to the cock head, where he slurped up the juice he'd coaxed from my throbbing prick. After having his fill, Hank grabbed my dick at the root and slowly took me into his mouth.

The world spun as his hot, wet mouth closed around me. He sucked and bobbed as his tongue swirled and flitted around the head and base. Every few strokes, he pulled off my dick and rubbed my sensitive cock along his facial hair. His scratchy beard made my cock jump with each pass, and then he swallowed me all the way down to the base.

"I'm getting real close," I told him through measured pants.

Hank immediately released my cock and sat on his haunches.

My dick pulsed in protest. "Why'd you stop?"

He reached into his nightstand and pulled out a condom. "Because you're gonna fuck that load in my butt, not my mouth. I'm a ravenous bottom, remember?"

I grinned. The smile that slinked across his lips made Hank look both innocent and devilish. My heart, which had been pounding in my chest, swelled. I wasn't sure exactly what the emotion was, but it was the best feeling in the world. "How could I forget?"

Hank rolled the condom down my shaft and then lubed up his butt before kneeling on the bed. "You ready?"

"Are you kidding me?" I asked, shaking my rigid dick at him.

He grinned like a naughty schoolboy and sat down.

When the head of my cock penetrated his flesh, we both gasped. Hank slid his hands over my chest, and I gripped his waist to help ease

21

him farther down. Slowly, he slid all the way, opening his body to take my full seven inches up his butt. When his ass rested against my pubic hair, his eyes rolled back.

"Damn, you feel so good," he said.

I shook my head. "It's you that feels good."

He smiled, and the joy in his expression was unmistakable. For some reason I could tell it wasn't just because the sex was good. Something else, something unexpected, seemed to be happening between us, and it made being in bed together far more intimate than a one-night stand.

"Well, then I guess it's both of us," Hank said as he moved up and down on my cock.

When he sat on my dick, he squeezed his ass muscles tightly and rode my shaft that way all the way up. With just my cockhead in his ass, he relaxed and then slid all the way back down before repeating the process.

"Holy shit!" I cried, clawing at his thighs and waist. "That's fucking amazing."

"I'm glad you think so," he said as he tortured my cock with his hot ass.

Within a few minutes, sweat dripped down Hank's chest and forehead, and I surfed my hands across his chest and down his body as he rode my cock. I thrust up hard into him in conjunction with his slow rise. Every time I slammed against him, his cock got harder and his whimpers became more pronounced.

"You're hitting spots in my body that no one else has," he said with a delirious grin. "That curve to your cock is fucking wonderful."

I grabbed Hank's shoulders and used the leverage to force him down harder. I pummeled his ass with deep, long upthrusts until his cock throbbed to life and he started to pump it in his palm.

"I think you could make me come again."

"Oh yeah," I whispered. "I want to see you shoot while I fuck you."

"You do?" he asked. His eyes looked dreamy and far away as he tugged on his dick, and I slammed into his ass.

"Yeah, I do."

He nodded and bit his lower lip as he furiously jacked his cock. I worked my hips like a piston, forcing my way in and out of his butt in strokes that measured from fast and deep to slow and shallow. Hank's mouth hung open in evident ecstasy as he worked his cock in his hand and my dick in his ass.

"Don't stop," he pleaded.

How could I? I was too close to stop. My balls had pulled up into my groin, and we were so slick with sweat that our bodies collided in moist thwacks. Our moans, the musk and perspiration, and Hank's blond, furry, muscular body riding me brought me quickly to the edge.

"I'm going to come," I said.

"Fuck, me too," Hank replied.

After one more tug on his dick, Hank sprayed my chest with a volley of white spunk. His powerful orgasm caused his ass to clench around my dick. The sensation took me over the edge as I flooded the condom in his ass with my semen.

Spent, Hank collapsed on top of me. His body still shook with the aftershock of ecstasy, and as I cradled him in my arms, I craved more. I wouldn't be satisfied with just this one night.

HANK AND I had sex two more times before drifting to sleep in each other's arms. Standard tricking protocol dictated that I should leave after busting the final nut of the evening, but I made no move to leave his bed, and Hank didn't seem to want me to go. Even though I'd spent the past two hours on top of his back, when it was over, he turned around and pulled me into his arms.

Shortly after I rested my head on his sweat-soaked chest, he began to snore. Typically, I needed peace and quiet to drift off and usually couldn't spend the night with someone who sawed wood as loudly as Hank, but the noise, the comfort of his flesh against mine, and the warmth his body generated sent me off into the deepest slumber I'd experienced in years.

I was also surprised to find myself still asleep on his chest the following morning. Usually I didn't wake up in the same position I fell asleep in. I was a wiggle worm, as my mother called me in my youth. I apparently flailed and flopped around all night, but lying with Hank somehow calmed the restless sleep I'd lived with all my life.

That was why I didn't want to move. If I did, I might wake Hank, and then the peace I'd somehow found in the past few hours would shatter and fall away. Even though it was inevitable, I wasn't quite ready to cope with reality.

"I know you're awake."

So much for that. I lifted my head from Hank's chest and rested it on the pillow beside his. "Sorry about that. I was too comfortable to move."

"I didn't want you to move," he said. He wrapped his arm around me and drew me closer. I nestled my head into the crook of his neck, delighting in the lingering scent of sweat and cum that still clung to him. "I just wanted you to know I knew you were awake."

"As amazing as you smell, I might not ever leave this spot right here."

Hank laughed. "I think I might look funny heading over to the jobsite with a full-grown man attached to my neck." He fell silent for a minute. "But it's not like everyone doesn't know I'm gay, so who cares, right?"

"I like the way you think, Mr. Burton," I said after reluctantly withdrawing my nose from his neck. I settled my head on his shoulder.

"Aw, you remembered my name," he teased before lacing his left hand in my right.

"I've got a great memory. It helps me be all lawyery and stuff." It bothered me that Jill's annoying term had worked its way into my vocabulary, but there was nothing I could do about that now, it seemed.

"Well, I've got probably the worst memory in the world," he admitted with a sigh. "It drives Mitch and Darren crazy. They can tell me something one day, and by the next, I've completely forgotten about it."

"Are you telling me you've forgotten my name?" I asked, pretending to be insulted.

Hank pulled me on top of him and wrapped his arms around my waist, resting his hands once again at the swell of my ass. That seemed to be his favorite place on my body. He placed them there when we danced and when we slept. "I could never forget you, Santi Herrera. The man who entranced me with his dazzling smile and his hot body. You're one sexy fucker, you know that?"

I'd never been called that before. I wasn't ugly, but I'd never really considered myself all that attractive. I certainly didn't think I was sexy. I figured I was slightly above average, but Hank gazed into my eyes as if I were a falling star he'd happened to pluck from the heavens. "Well, I appreciate the comment," I finally said. "But I'm nowhere near as hot as you are."

Hank snorted. "Please. You're like ten times hotter. At least."

"Than who? Mr. Bean?"

He smacked my ass. The sting caused me to gasp and my cock to grow rigid. "Stop that!" he said. "Someone as beautiful as you shouldn't be so hard on himself."

I placed my hands under his knees and raised them to Hank's chest, resting my throbbing cock against his still-slick ass. "How about I be hard on you instead?"

Hank grabbed his ankles and beamed at me. "Now *that* you can do!"

AFTER THAT morning, Hank took a short break from work and we spent the rest of my time in San Diego together. I'd been worried that Jill might feel neglected, but she practically shooed me out the hotel door every time Hank came to pick me up. She was a big girl who could take care of herself, she told me.

So I no longer fretted over the time Hank and I shared. He took me to the Presidio, and even though I'd already been there with Jill, eating lunch on the lawn and then napping on Hank's stomach in the sunshine beat the short visit Jill and I had there, hands down.

Plus, we learned a lot about each other.

"An only child?" he asked. "That sure must've been nice having everything to yourself. Since I'm the oldest, I always had to share."

I repositioned myself on his stomach so I could gaze up into his eyes. "I guess it was okay, but I envy you having a brother and sisters.

My parents were great, but it got lonely sometimes. And since my parents were only children too, I didn't have any cousins to play with. It was always just me."

"That does sound lonely," he replied, cupping my cheek.

I leaned into his palm. "Yeah. But my mom and dad were always there for me."

Sadness drifted across the blue ocean of Hank's eyes. "I wish I could say the same thing."

"What do you mean?" I rose from his stomach and sat up in the grass to his left.

After letting out a deep sigh, Hank sat up as well. He wrapped his hands around his knees and stared down at his toes, which peeked through his sandals. As usual, they were coated in red nail polish. When I first noticed it, I'd been surprised, but as I spent more time with him, I realized that Hank incorporated something flashy in his wardrobe whenever he wasn't at work. He was a strong, confident man who knew who he was, but with the mention of his obviously troubled childhood, that man gave way to the unsure boy who lived inside. "My dad kicked me out of the house when he walked in on me and my best friend Josh making out in my bedroom."

"Holy shit!" That was a difficult concept for me to understand. My parents had always been loving and accepting. When I had come out to them, it was no big deal. "How old were you?"

"Sixteen. That was where I first met Mitch. On the streets of San Diego. He'd been kicked out of his house too."

"You've got to be kidding me. That's way too young to be on your own."

Hank nodded. "But that's just what I did. After my dad screamed at me for being a sissy, he told me that fairies didn't live under his roof, so I grabbed my shit and left."

I stared at him in silence. I really didn't know what to say.

"We don't speak to this day," he continued. "My mom gave a few halfhearted attempts over the years, but she's too scared of upsetting my dad for it to be genuine."

"And your sisters and brother?"

"They do their best to include me, but they're too busy with their own fucked-up lives. My sister Cally is on her third marriage, and my other sister, Taylor, just got out of rehab. My little brother, Joe, doesn't do all that much except mooch off whatever woman he happens to be living with at the time."

Maybe Hank was right. Being an only child did have its advantages.

"Still want siblings?" he asked.

"I still do," I replied. Despite having their share of problems, a brother or a sister made life less lonely. "Especially now that my parents are gone."

"Jesus." He took my hand in his. "When? How?"

"Car accident. Senior year in college."

Instead of offering sympathies through words, which I never believed were sincere, he offered me comfort through touch. He trailed his fingers across the back of my hand and leaned his forehead against mine.

"I've been on my own ever since. It's probably one of the reasons I push myself at work so much, to prove to my parents that I'm a success. That everything they did for me wasn't for nothing. At least that's what Jill tells me. Maybe if I had family, I wouldn't work as hard. I sure as hell wouldn't spend all my time at work."

"I feel like shit now."

"What?" I asked. "Why?"

"I've been bitching about my family, and yeah, they suck sometimes, but they're still here at least. I guess I've been taking that for granted, huh?"

"A little. But you've been through a lot with them. It makes sense. But it also makes sense to try and fix what you can when you can, right?"

"How'd you get so wise?"

I shrugged and stared up into the sky as if the answer were obvious. "Just born that way, I guess."

Hank chuckled before he laid me back on the grass and rested his body on top of mine. "You're being Silly McSillyson."

I laughed. "I'm being what?"

27

"You heard me," he said before brushing his lips against mine.

After Hank's kiss, which made me feel drunk and unable to walk a straight line for a few minutes, we left the Presidio and strolled up and down Hillcrest. Every few feet, we ran into someone who knew Hank, and he always introduced me with a big smile on his face. Some of his friends stared at our joined hands, no doubt wondering what was up. We also ran into quite a few men who were either disappointed or pissed that Hank no longer appeared to be on the market.

Jerry Robles was one of the worst. Shortly after being introduced to me and seeing my hand in Hank's, he did everything he could to pull Hank away from me.

"I want to tell you something," Jerry said, motioning for Hank to follow him into a Starbucks.

"Well, say it," Hank replied. He made no attempt to move or let go of my hand.

"It's private." His wicked leer made the subject quite clear. He wanted to arrange a hookup for later. If I had had an iced latte in my hands, I would have poured it all over Jerry's face. Not that I had any claim to Hank. After I left, he might take Jerry up on the offer, but I didn't want to think about that.

"Well, then, text it to me." Hank pulled me close, and his hand immediately went to my ass. *Take that, you bitch*, my big, satisfied grin told Jerry. "We've got things to do."

Jerry replied by turning around and walking into the coffee shop.

"Sorry about that," Hank said as he led me back down University Avenue.

"What do you have to apologize for? It's not your fault you're so popular."

"Yeah, right," Hank replied with a roll of his eyes. "Jerry's nice, but if I had a type, he wouldn't be it."

"Really?" Even though Jerry seemed to be a real prick, he was six feet of lean muscle.

Hank nodded. "Don't get me wrong. He's a pretty hot guy, but he's a fucking asshole. It's a real turnoff."

That comment made me like Hank even more.

"Not into assholes?" I asked, wiggling my eyebrows.

Hank laughed and then grabbed my butt. "I like yours."

"Yes, I know." How could I not? Whenever Hank rimmed my ass, he grunted and turned into an animal rooting around in his favorite spot. "So you're not one of those guys who is attracted to the bad boys?"

"Oh, I like bad boys," Hank said. "But there has to be some good in there too. It's a fine line, and Jerry waved bye-bye to that line a long time ago. I've been there and done that already."

Now Hank's dislike of Jerry made sense. "So how long were you two together?"

He gazed down at me as if I needed to be fitted for a straitjacket. "Oh hell no. Jerry and I have never been together. I was referring to someone else." Hank then turned away, and the faraway look in his eyes told me he'd been transported to an obviously painful past.

"What was his name?"

"Karl McClure," he said with a long exhalation.

"Bad breakup?"

"Bad everything." Hank's posture had changed considerably. His sparkling blue eyes grew muddy, and the smile that had lingered on his lips all morning stretched thin.

"You must've loved him a lot."

He nodded. "The first and only man I'd ever fallen in love with."

My inquiring mind longed to know more, but now wasn't the time. "Maybe someday you'll tell me the story."

"Maybe." He attempted a smile, but he hadn't quite recovered from the Ghost of Boyfriends Past. "But only if you share your first heartbreak with me."

"I'm afraid I can't do that."

Hank stopped in the middle of the sidewalk. My answer evidently threw him. "Why not?"

I tugged him by my side, and we walked on. "Because I can't share something that hasn't happened."

He stopped dead in his tracks again. "You've never been in love?"

I shook my head.

"But you've had boyfriends before, right?"

Not really. Did that make me a loser? Or worse, a commitment-phobe? I'd never actually given it much thought before. I never had the time. What was Hank going to think when I shared that bit of information? I could always stretch the truth a little, make myself sound less like a complete douche, but one look in his surprised blue eyes made that idea fly right out of my head. How could I lie to that face? "No. I haven't."

He shook his head in disbelief and then started walking again. "Wow," he said before grabbing my hand once again in his. "Do you just not do relationships?" The disappointment in his voice was hard to miss, and I couldn't help but smile.

"I don't know." And that was the God's honest truth. My life had been paved by career goals since college. Nothing else had mattered. "I'm not averse to them. I've never really made the time. I guess that's part of the reason I'm here."

"What do you mean?"

"Well, Jill worries that I'm not living my life. That I'm spending too much time at work. She wants me to get out there and find someone. At the very least, she wants me to get my freak on."

Hank chuckled. "That definitely helps keep the stress down."

"I've certainly not been stressed ever since I met you."

He smiled down at me and pulled me into a kiss. "And there's no one back home?"

"Not really. There's this one guy at the office. Wyatt. He's interested. Or at least he was."

"What's wrong with him?"

"Nothing really. He's a nice guy and very attractive."

Hank gazed at me out of the corners of his eyes. "But?"

I shrugged. "I just don't feel it, I guess."

He nodded as if he completely understood. As we crossed the street, Hank pressed his hand once again to the small of my back. My heart fluttered, and my insides bounced around as if they were filled with Mexican jumping beans.

That was certainly something I'd never felt before.

WHEN MY last night in San Diego finally arrived, I was shell-shocked. I'd grown extremely fond of Hank and didn't know how I was going to handle suddenly not having him in my life. I was definitely going to miss him as well as Mitch and Darren.

They were good guys, if a bit odd at times. Mitch was a hairdresser who fancied himself butch. But if he was butch, then so was Richard Simmons. Darren was the complete opposite of the flamboyant Mitch. Darren was very reserved and quiet. He stuck to the periphery, preferring to sit and watch television than hang out on the patio and talk. Most people might mistake his behavior as stuck-up, but I didn't. Darren was simply painfully shy. As a socially introverted lone wolf, I spotted that right off the bat and made extra effort to engage Darren in conversation, which he seemed to appreciate.

I'd also grown particularly fond of Picasso, who usually accompanied us on our outings. I'd become so accustomed to the life Hank had brought to my world that I didn't know how to behave or find the right words to say, so on our last dinner at Harvey Milk's, an American-style café in Hillcrest, I sat in the booth beside Hank in silence.

"What are you going to order?" he asked over his menu. Today he wore a yellow muscle shirt that featured a smiling bear face. The word "Growl" had been printed in pink letters above the bear's face.

I had no idea, and I also had no appetite. "Any recommendations? I'm not really all that hungry."

"Me either," Hank said as he placed his menu on the table. "You'd think we'd be ravenous with as much fucking as we've been doing."

I snickered and nodded. "Well, I am thirsty," I said before taking a drink of my iced tea. "I've lost a lot of fluids."

Hank growled. "I know it!"

Silence once again descended as we both returned to studying our menus. When the waiter came, we decided to split a Cobb salad.

"So what are your plans when you get back to Houston? Are you gonna jump headfirst back into all your lawyery duties?"

I grinned. It seemed Jill's phrase had worked its way into Hank's vernacular as well. "That's what I do. When do you think you'll be done with your latest project?"

Over the course of the week, Hank had revealed that he owned his own business as a building contractor. He called it Gracie Designs after his deceased English bulldog. His company had been working on a lucrative condo remodel that was proving to be a tad difficult because of a nitpicky client.

"Once my client settles on paint colors, kitchen cabinet styles, and bathroom faucets, maybe a few weeks. She's changed her mind at least four times. I finally told her I couldn't do any more work until she made some decisions."

"Do you think you might want to come visit me in Houston sometime?" The question flew out of my mouth before I could wrangle it in. I immediately felt stupid and embarrassed. Even though we'd had a great few days together, it wasn't as if it changed the reality of our situation. I lived about fifteen hundred miles away, and everyone knew long-distance relationships didn't work. Someone eventually grew tired of the separation and wound up in bed with the next best thing. I'd been a fool for even entertaining the idea, much less vocalizing it.

Hank's answer surprised me. "I'd love to!" He perked up in his seat, and the dazzling smile that had been eclipsed by my impending departure suddenly returned.

"Really?" I asked. The hopeful astonishment in my voice was unmistakable.

"Of course! I'd been thinking about how to ask you if I could see you again, but I didn't want to assume you *wanted* to see me again. Or appear needy. I mean, we *did* just meet."

I scooted in the booth next to him and took his hands in mine. "You're right, we did just meet, but it doesn't feel that way for me at all. If you don't mind my saying, it feels like I've known you my entire life. I've never been this comfortable this quickly with anyone before."

Hank withdrew his right hand from my grasp and caressed my cheek. God, I loved when he did that. "I feel the same way. Not to be inappropriate or anything, but I've been with my fair share of men, and I've never felt like this before. I'm not really sure what it is, but it's not something I'm ready to throw away. If that makes any sense at all."

I leaned into his touch and smiled. "It makes perfect sense because I feel the exact same way."

Hank closed the distance between us and delivered the sweetest, most loving kiss to my lips. It completely took the breath from my body. "It's settled, then. This isn't a good-bye. We will see each other again."

When the waiter returned with our salad, we sent him back for burgers and fries. Suddenly our appetites had returned, and they were voracious.

FOR THE next few months, Hank and I took turns flying out to see each other. He'd spend a week in Houston between construction projects, but I usually couldn't afford to spend more than a long weekend away from the office. The demands of being all lawyery required a great deal of time, and billable hours were definitely important in order to be made partner.

Fortunately Hank's schedule proved more flexible, and his time in Houston became more extended. Then the greatest thing happened. His parents, who'd recently moved to Lufkin, Texas, had hired Hank to build them a house on the new sixty-acre property they had purchased.

Their troubled past didn't seem to matter now that they needed his services. Although Hank worried what further strain working for his parents might put on their relationship, he took the job in order to be closer to me for the next nine months.

By the time Hank had finished building his parents' house and patching up their relationship, I'd managed to slyly introduce Hank to clients and colleagues, who all just happened to need remodels of one kind or another.

His nine-month stint in Texas turned into a year and a half, and I'd never been happier. Naturally Hank lived with me for the interim, and he became such a part of my daily life that when all his Texas projects were completed, I was sick at the thought of Hank needing to return to San Diego. It resulted in one of the biggest fights of our relationship.

And one of the most memorable nights of my life.

"I have to go back." Hank ran his fingers through his blond locks and sighed. He only did that when he was at wit's end. "I have to make money, you know?"

"No, you don't. I make more than enough to support us both."

He looked at me askance. "I'm never going to be a kept man, Santi. Not even for you."

"I'm not asking you to be a kept man. I'm just saying you don't have to rush out and always find new projects. You can work as they fall into your lap. I can take care of the rest when you have dry spells."

Hank didn't appreciate my response. He blew out a lungful of air before speaking. "My work makes me happy. I feel productive and useful. I'm not about to lie around waiting for jobs to fall in my lap. Not when I can be in San Diego and pick up where I left off. I've got clients begging me to do work for them, and the work they want me to do is good."

"What about getting a job somewhere here? That way you can work regularly and then do your contracting jobs when they pop up."

"And where do you think I should work?" He surveyed the condo as he typically did when asking a question he had a smartass answer for. "Home Depot? I'm not gonna do shift work for ten dollars an hour when my going rate is over a hundred. That's a step down, and I'm not going to take it. I could just as easily ask you to move to San Diego. There are plenty of law firms you could join there. You'd still be able to practice law, make the same amount of money, and we'd be together."

I crossed my arms over my chest. "You know I can't do that. I've spent almost a decade at my law firm. In a few years, I can be a partner. Moving to a new state invalidates the hard work I've been busting my ass doing these past few years. You know that."

He nodded. "I do. That's why I'm not asking you to give up your livelihood for me. I respect you too much for that. I wish you'd respect me and my work the same."

Suddenly I felt like the biggest dick in the world. "I *do* respect you and the awesome work you do." I crossed my living room to him and rubbed my hands across his arms. Even though he was still upset, his posture relaxed, and he melted at my touch. It was an effect we had on each other. No matter what crap storm blew our way, the slightest touch erected a rampart that nothing outside the two of us could reach. "I just love you so damn much. I don't want to be without you for one single day."

Hank held my cheeks in his palms. He caressed the corners of my mouth with his thumbs as he gazed down at me with love and utter devotion in his dazzling blue eyes. Whenever Hank looked at me that way, I felt like I was the most important person in the world. "And I love you too. The thought of not sleeping next to you is ripping me apart, but I've got duties and obligations back in California. I know you hate hearing this, but Mitch and Darren are my family, and we own a home together."

He was right. I didn't enjoy this part of his life. Whether it was right or not, it made me jealous to think that Hank had already built a life and a future with two other men he was neither related to by blood nor in love with. I should be the only one he had such strong ties to, but that was not the case.

"Besides that, Picasso's getting older. He doesn't have much more time left, and I've only seen him a handful of times this year. He's probably forgotten all about me."

"How could anyone forget you?" I asked before burying my face in his chest. I inhaled Hank's soothing scent, and the aroma brought tears to my eyes. I wouldn't smell him every day anymore, and though his scent lingered in my condo and on the bedsheets, eventually that would fade. I'd be left with nothing but a memory and a longing for his return.

"And I won't forget you or our love," Hank said. "I hope you realize that. You're a part of my life. A part of my soul. I spend more time thinking about you every day than I do anything else."

"But you have to go," I said.

He stroked my back and kissed the top of my head. "Yes. But I will be back. And you will come see me in San Diego. It's not ideal, but it's the reality of our situation." He placed his thumb under my chin and forced me to meet his gaze. "And remember, this is just temporary. Things will work themselves out, and you and I will be together for the rest of our lives. That's my goal, and I hope it's yours too."

"It is," I replied. "Which is why I need to ask you something."

"What's that?"

I led him to the couch, where I motioned for him to sit. When he sat down, I got down on my knee and pulled a small felt box from my pocket. "Ever since I met you, I've been drawn to you. You've brought so much joy to my life that I sometimes feel like I'm going to burst from the happiness. And holding you every night, feeling your skin against mine, is all of heaven I need to know. I know we're going to be dealing with a long-distance separation for now. That's just the way it has to be. But I'd like to ask you, Henry Gale Burton, if you would do me the honor of being my husband."

Hank sat in silence, staring at the silver band I held in my hand. When he settled his gaze on mine, fat tears fell from the corner of his baby blues and a huge grin spread across his lips. "Of course I'll marry you," he said. "Nothing in the world would make me happier."

He leaped out of his seat and into my arms, sending us both crashing to the floor. We ripped the clothes from each other's bodies, but before I entered him, Hank placed the ring on his finger. Then he slipped me inside him, and the two of us once again became one.

"I'll never forget this day for as long as I live," Hank muttered.

I held him close, easing myself in and out of the man I loved more than life itself. "I plan on holding you to that promise."

He smiled before kissing my lips. "I'd be upset if you didn't."

CHAPTER
Two

IT HAD been almost a month since I last saw Hank, and I missed my man terribly. We talked at least four times a day, and we texted about every two hours. Still, it wasn't enough. Nothing could replace his rough skin against my smooth flesh, his scratchy facial hair marking me with beard burn, the low rasp of his voice as he spoke, or the deep bellow of his laughter when he watched *Family Guy* or *Robot Chicken*.

I missed the sweet Red Bull kisses, the daily trips to Starbucks for his latte, and his scent lingering on the air and everything he touched. When he and I were together, I was complete. Without him, an emptiness I'd never known opened up inside me.

Though we lived separately, Hank was very much a part of my life. As Hank had said, our situation wasn't ideal, but it was far better than *not* having him in my life. That just wasn't an option. I'd do anything and everything to make the long-distance relationship work.

And so far it had.

We had some bumps in the road. I got a little pissy when Hank, Mitch, and Darren drove to Palm Springs for a long weekend. Hank got grumpy when I was being lawyery all day and not available to talk or text as frequently as we'd grown accustomed to. But after we talked or used FaceTime on our phones, the pissy and the grumpy faded away. It just wasn't important once we realized the root of our bad moods was the simple fact that we wanted to be together twenty-four seven.

Being together however we could manage it was all that really mattered, and it was why I impatiently waited for Hank to FaceTime me. We had missed our morning video chat because I had an early deposition, and since Hank was two hours behind me, I was at the office by the time he climbed out of bed.

We had already planned for the interruption in our schedule. I would eat lunch in my office, and we'd talk for the whole hour. A quick glance at the office clock told me that I only had ten more minutes of lunch, and with a client scheduled to drop by at one thirty, Hank and I wouldn't get the hour we had planned.

Where the hell was he? I'd called him at noon, but his phone went straight to voice mail. Fifteen minutes later I tried Mitch and then Darren, and the same thing happened. I'd initially shrugged it off, but now I was starting to get a little worried.

Had something happened?

"I thought you would still be on the phone."

I glanced up from my phone, which I had been willing to ring, to find Wyatt Perry leaning against my open office door. A smile hitched his lips up to the left, and he stuck his right hand in his trouser pocket. It was Wyatt's standard pose that made all the girls in the office want to bear his children.

He was an exceptionally attractive man with the dark hair styled to perfection, the bushy eyebrows, the piercing blue eyes, and the always-present five o'clock shadow. Wyatt's looks belonged on the cover of *GQ* more than they did in the courtroom, but as a lawyer, he was sharp and cutthroat.

But no matter how many good qualities Wyatt had, there was one big downfall. He wasn't my Hank.

"Yeah, me too," I finally answered.

"Trouble in paradise?"

Although Wyatt meant for the comment to sound casual, I heard it for what it was. He was just biding his time. "Not at all," I replied with a firm shake of my head. "Something must have come up."

Wyatt's slow nod told me he suspected another man. I wanted to throw my crystal paperweight in his face, but I didn't. The resulting litigation wouldn't be pretty. Besides, I couldn't take Wyatt's attitude personally. He practically chased me for a year, and after one vacation, I'd come back with my heart set on someone else.

That had to be a blow to any man's ego.

"Probably a client," I said. "Hank's got three projects going on right now. We both know how clingy clients can be."

Wyatt nodded. "Speaking of which, what time is Mrs. Trevino coming in?"

Sarah Trevino was our new client. She was currently married to a state representative and had caught him screwing one of his interns. It was quite the public scandal, and the newspapers were eating it up. Mr. Trevino had tried his best to make it go away, but his wife was pissed and going for the jugular. Since the case was so high profile and promised to bring in some good money for the firm, the partners had teamed Wyatt and me together to handle it. "She'll be here at one thirty."

"You ready to do battle with Representative Trevino's lawyer?"

I raised one eyebrow at him. "When aren't I ready?"

He nodded and laughed. "I know. That's why we make such a good team."

The smile on Wyatt's lips faltered. We were good together professionally, but Wyatt had wanted more. I felt like an asshole. He was a good guy and a successful lawyer. He needed to focus all his energy on some other man who'd appreciate him. I opened my mouth to offer some words of encouragement when my phone rang.

It was Hank.

"I'll talk to you later," I said as I accepted the FaceTime call. Wyatt slowly closed the door behind him.

When Hank's face appeared on the tiny screen, I immediately grew alarmed. His eyes were bloodshot, and he was wiping his nose. "Hank, what's the matter?"

"Picasso's dying," he said before breaking down into soul-shattering sobs.

"Oh, Hank," I said, caressing the screen. What we both needed was actual physical contact.

He took several deep breaths and held his hand to the screen on his end. We might not be able to touch physically, but the psychic connection was unmistakable. "What happened?" I asked after Hank gained some semblance of control.

"I had trouble waking him up." He sniffed. "And he's been extremely lethargic. He wouldn't even eat bacon." That *was* a big deal. I'd seen Picasso scramble off Hank's bed in two seconds flat at the first sizzle of bacon in the frying pan. "We finally took him to the vet when his breathing became labored. The doc says that it's just old age."

I nodded. Picasso was twelve years old, which was an advanced age for his breed. "How is he doing?"

"He's not in any pain that I can tell." Tears welled up in his eyes. "We have him back at home, and he's resting in my lap. I don't know how long we have. Maybe tonight or tomorrow morning. I don't know."

"I'll be out on the next flight," I said as I stood up and gathered my things.

"Santi, you can't. You have that meeting in a bit for that high-profile case."

I raised the phone as close to my face as I could, so Hank could see that arguing with me would get him nowhere. "I don't care about the Trevinos or their fucking divorce. I love you, and I love Picasso. I want to be there for you both."

Though there were tears in his eyes, he smiled. "Are you sure? You won't get in trouble?"

"They can sue me," I said. "I'll call you when I'm at my gate and let you know what time I'll be arriving."

He nodded. "God, I love you."

"And I love you."

I ended the call, grabbed my briefcase, and darted out of my office. My secretary was still out to lunch, so I dashed into Wyatt's office and filled him in.

"You're leaving?" he asked. He evidently thought I was crazy. "For a dog?"

"He's not just a dog," I replied. "He's part of the family, and Hank needs me."

"What about our meeting?"

"Tell them the truth or make up an excuse, I really don't give a fuck."

"And what do you want me to tell Mr. Canales? He's the one who assigned us this case."

"I'll call him on the way to the airport," I yelled over my back as I ran through the office toward the elevator.

SEVEN HOURS and one phone call to my boss later, my plane landed in San Diego. Fortunately Mr. Canales was just as big a dog lover as Hank. He made sure to tell me to give Hank his sympathies and assured me that Wyatt would be just fine on his own. I grabbed my backpack, which contained some random clothes from my closet, from the overhead compartment and exited the plane. I got a cab, and twenty minutes later I was knocking on the front door of Hank's house.

Darren answered. He looked as miserable as Hank had. "How's Picasso?" I asked after giving the smaller man a hug.

"He's fading pretty fast." He sniffled as he pulled out of the embrace. "Mitch is in his room. He said he couldn't watch this."

"And Hank?"

Darren answered with only a downward glance. Since I knew what that meant, I charged past Darren and into the house. "Hank!"

"In here," he mumbled from the living room.

I sprinted toward the direction of his voice and found Hank sitting on the leather sectional that sat in front of their seventy-inch television. Picasso lay across his lap and opened one eye to stare at me. He immediately lifted his head and managed a wag of his butt before resting his head once more on Hank's lap.

"Such a handsome boy," I said to Picasso as I knelt before him and gave him a kiss. He snorted in appreciation and sniffed at my cheek. I gazed up into Hank's red-rimmed eyes and the look of absolute torture etched on his face. More than anything, I wanted to take away the pain that mangled him from the inside. "How's my love?"

He smiled at me and reached out to caress my cheek. God, how I missed that! "I'm better now that you're here," he said. "But I'm still pretty fucking miserable."

"I know." I slid onto the couch next to him and wrapped my arm around his shoulders. He rested his head against mine and took my hand in his as he continued stroking Picasso's back with the other. "But I'm here for you. Anything you need, just ask."

Hank gazed up at me. Even though sadness deeper than the Mariana Trench filled his eyes, his lips parted into the smile he always wore when he looked upon me. "You're here. I don't need anything else."

FOR THE next several hours, the three of us sat on the couch together, Hank in my arms and Picasso in his. It was the family we had created, and though we were reunited for a very sad event, we were there to show our love and dedication in the final hours of Picasso's life.

Somewhere around six in the morning, Picasso woke us up.

He whimpered, and his body shook as if he was having a bad dream. But when we gazed down at him, his eyes were open and looking at us.

"He's in pain," Hank said. He bent over Picasso. He rubbed his body and spoke gently into his ears. "Grandpa's here. Don't worry. Grandpa's here."

In reply, Picasso wagged his butt, but the whimpers continued.

"What do you want me to do?"

"Call the vet," he replied. He turned to look at me with tears streaming down his face. "I can't have him in pain. Make the call and tell him to get over here now."

I nodded before getting off the couch. I got Hank's phone, found the veterinarian's number in his contact list, and hit the dial button. Dr. Culberson answered on the first ring. "Hank, how's Picasso?"

"This is Santi Herrera, Hank's boyfriend. Picasso's not doing well and Hank asked me to call you and—"

"I'll be right there." Dr. Culberson then ended the call.

I woke Mitch and Darren, and twenty minutes later, Dr. Culberson knocked on the front door. A short fiftysomething man wearing a robe and fuzzy slippers stood on the front porch.

"Santi?" he asked before stepping inside. "I'm Dr. Culberson."

"Nice of you to come here so early," I said after ushering him inside.

"Don't mention it. I've been with Hank since Gracie was a pup." He stopped in the hall and touched my forearm. "I'm glad you're here for him. He's gonna need you."

I nodded and then led him into the living room, where Picasso fidgeted and whimpered in Hank's lap. When Hank saw Dr. Culberson, the dam broke. The sobs he'd held back burst free. There was no more delaying the inevitable. This was it.

I rushed to Hank's side, wrapped my arms around his big, shuddering body, and kissed his neck. Though my eyes were wet, I had to be strong for the man I loved.

"He's in pain, doc. Please help him. I can't have my boy in pain."

Dr. Culberson nodded. He reached into his black bag and brought out a syringe and a vial. As he prepared to deliver the injection that would ease Picasso's suffering, Mitch and Darren crossed over to Picasso. They kissed his face and rubbed his belly one final time before heading out the patio door and gazing out into the sky.

"Should I wait for them to come back?" Dr. Culberson asked.

Hank shook his head. "No. They've already said good-bye, but I'm not going anywhere. I'm staying right here with my boy." He rubbed Picasso's head and kissed his nose. "Grandpa loves you."

Picasso gazed up at him before wagging his butt.

"He loves you too," I said, through the sobs caught in my throat.

"I know he does." Hank sniffled.

Dr. Culberson injected Picasso and then patted him on the head. Then he walked out of the room to join Mitch and Darren outside. I held Hank tightly while he stroked Picasso's back and ran his hand over his head. Picasso stared back at us, his adorable doggie smile etched on his face. He snuffed at us, giving us one final good-bye, before his eyes closed and his labored breathing stopped.

Hank collapsed on top of Picasso, his body racked with sobs. I leaned against his back, my tears falling onto his shirt. I held him tight to tell him that I loved him and that I was there for him and that I was never *ever* going to let him go.

HANK BURIED Picasso later that morning in the backyard. I wanted to help, but Hank said he needed to do it alone. I stood in the kitchen with

Mitch and Darren. They drank their coffee in silence as we observed Hank rip off his shirt and begin digging the hole.

"Right next to Gracie," Mitch said with a sniffle.

Darren nodded. "That's where he belongs."

"I wish he'd let us help. Or at the very least be out there with him."

Mitch patted my back. "Bubble doesn't deal well with loss." That was Mitch's nickname for Hank. He called him Bubble because of Hank's perky butt. "He may be strong physically, but when it comes to matters of the heart, these kinds of things tear him apart. Isn't that right, Grandma?"

Darren nodded. He had earned his nickname by being the hermit of the group. Unlike Hank and Mitch, Darren lived a far more reclusive life, preferring to sit at home most nights of the week and watch television. "Hank likes to tackle these things alone. When Gracie died, we barely saw him for weeks. He'd just come and go to work, and he usually ate dinner in his room. The only one he'd let in with him was Picasso. Now that he's gone, I'm not sure what he's going to do."

"Well, I might not be Picasso, but I'm here."

Mitch eyed Darren before speaking. "And he's glad you are. But I wouldn't be surprised if he shuts you out. That's just how he copes. He hides behind his walls until he feels it's safe to come out. Don't take it personally."

I mulled over what Mitch and Darren told me. I'd give Hank as much space as he needed, but I'd do it right by his side. If he wanted to shut me out, that was his call, but it wouldn't change a thing. I'd be right there, waiting for those walls to crumble so I could climb over the rubble to the sad little boy on the other side.

"I won't." I headed toward the outside kitchen stairs that led down to the backyard.

"Where are you going?" Mitch asked.

"To be with Hank."

"But—"

"Trust me, Mitch. Whether or not he realizes it, Hank needs me." Before Mitch could respond, I walked out the door and down the stairs.

As I made my approach, I watched in amazement as Hank's muscles flexed as he dug the hole that would eventually be Picasso's resting place. My lover's physical body definitely housed enough

44

strength for three men, but the Hank on the inside needed the kind of love and support only a lover could provide.

"How's my love?"

Hank stopped digging and gazed over his shoulder at me. Though his eyes were still puffy and red, the tears had stopped for the moment. "Pretty fucking miserable," he said while leaning against the shovel. "How's my love?"

"About the same as you," I replied. I crossed into his space and leaned against him. His body trembled under my touch. "I wish I could do something to take away your pain."

He let the shovel drop and wrapped his sweaty arms around me. "I know, but having you here means the world to me. I hope you know that."

I nodded. "I just wish there was more I could do for you."

He stroked the back of my head. "What you're doing is more than enough. I usually have to handle things like this by myself, but I don't have to do that anymore. Because now I have you."

I nodded as I smiled up into his big, beautiful eyes. Even though they were swollen from crying, they were still the most gorgeous sight I'd ever seen. "Yes, you do," I replied with a grin. "For as long as you'll have me."

"Forever it is, then," he said.

"I'm good with that."

"Then it's settled."

I surveyed the backyard. "What can I do?"

He nodded toward the garage. "There's another shovel in there if you want to help."

"You got it," I said before walking away. I'd made it halfway through the yard before Hank's voice stopped me.

"Santi?"

"Yeah," I said after turning around.

"Have I told you how much I love you?"

"Not in the past few hours."

"Because I really, really, really do."

"And I really, really, really love you too."

A FEW months after Picasso's passing, the greatest event since my proposing to Hank occurred—he moved to Houston and moved in with me. The only way to celebrate, of course, was to throw a party officially welcoming my fiancé to Houston and introducing him to all my friends he had yet to meet.

I reserved the pool area at our condo for the event. Not being much of a decorator, I enlisted the aid of Jesse and Mario, two friends I recently made after expanding my nonwork horizons since living with Hank. They happened to throw parties as often as they enjoyed inviting one or two other men to share their bed.

I spared no expense, and Jesse and Mario took full advantage.

My friends managed to line the pool area with tiki torches, hang balloons that arched diagonally across the pool, and set up a disco ball that skimmed the surface and reflected its light on the bottom. The lounge chairs were covered with white linens, as were the tables set up at various locations around the perimeter. An assortment of brightly colored place settings that incorporated all the colors of the rainbow decorated the tables.

As for food, Mario settled on barbecue, catered from Salt Lick, which was one of the best places for ribs in town, and Jesse made sure the bar was stocked with the best liquor money could buy.

When Hank and I arrived, Jesse waved with a flourish at the spectacle he and his partner had created. If he could have managed it, he'd be patting himself on his back. "What do you think?"

"Good God," Hank mumbled. Tonight he wasn't wearing one of his gay graphic tees. He traded his usual attire for a skintight black V-neck and tight black jeans. He refused to abandon his need for bling, however. Sparkly studs decorated his belt. After taking everything in, he settled his gaze on mine. "You went to too much trouble."

I rose on my tiptoes and brushed my lips to his. "You're never too much trouble."

"Aww," Mario said after taking his place by his man. The two of them looked almost identical in their matching polo shirts and white shorts. They were often mistaken for brothers since they usually dressed alike and had the same dark features and matching buzzed haircuts. "How sweet."

"Sweet? That's fucking hot." Jesse raised one eyebrow at us before asking, "Are you sure you two are settled on being monogamous? Because we could have a fucking good time."

I'd already warned Hank about my friends' extremely flirtatious and inappropriate behavior. Fortunately their offer didn't bother him one bit. He smiled at them before wrapping his arm around my waist. He dipped his fingertips beneath the waistband of my khaki shorts and rested it at the swell of my ass. "While I'm sure we would, my body is Santi's playground only."

I leaned into Hank. "Sorry, boys," I said while staring up into Hank's smiling eyes. "We are off the market. Permanently."

Hank nodded while Jesse and Mario teasingly scoffed.

"All right, break it up, bitches!" a voice behind us said.

Only one person in the world could cackle at us in that manner. I turned around and smiled as Jill entered carrying a small ice chest. Although we had plenty of alcohol, Jill never arrived to a party without at least a two-pack of her favorite—Kingfisher Premium Lager.

When Hank saw Jill, his handsome, bearded face parted into a big grin. "Jildo!"

Every time he addressed her by that nickname, I snickered. Jill loved the fact that her nickname rhymed with dildo, especially since she had quite the collection of assorted plastic phalluses. Hank, who had brought a Rubbermaid container from San Diego that housed his impressive dildo collection, had immediately bonded with Jill over their shared love of meat substitutes.

Jill grinned at Hank before saying, "How ya doing, Butt Munch?"

"Great!" Hank said before taking the cooler from Jill's hand and delivering a peck to her cheek. "Especially since I just finished eating Santi's ass fifteen minutes ago."

"Hank!" My cheeks burned.

Jill hooted and gave Hank a high five. "My boy has always enjoyed a good rimming."

"Who doesn't?" Mario asked.

"I know that's right," Jill announced. "First in the pink and then in the stink is my motto."

"Are you trying to gross me out?" I asked Jill after I gave her a big hug and kiss. As usual, she dressed in a low-cut blouse that proudly displayed her breasts and her tattoos.

"What? Only you gay boys can talk about sex?"

I nodded. In reply, Jill punched me in the arm. How in the hell did her tiny fist deliver such a powerful punch? I was going to have another bruise later.

"Well, think again," she said. "I've listened to more stories about you boys taking it up the ass or sucking cock than I can count. It's about time I returned the favor."

"Please don't," I pleaded.

Fortunately, more party guests arrived before Jill could launch into her latest sexual escapade, and since I was the host, I left Mario and Jesse to Jill's story and took Hank with me.

Hank bent down and whispered in my ear, "Thanks for the save." His breath rushing against my neck instantly made me hard. I almost led him past the latest arrivals and upstairs to our bedroom for another round of sweaty sex.

Hank glanced down at me and wiggled his eyebrows. He must have caught on to my arousal. Either that or my erection was tenting the fabric of my shorts. Either way, I knew what the gesture meant: Hank was telling me that later, his ass was all mine.

I'd never wanted a party to end faster than I did right then.

WHEN HANK'S parents arrived, I was pretty nervous. I'd only met them once during the time Hank was building their house, and the meeting had been coolly cordial. His father, Henry, didn't fully approve of his son's "choice of lifestyle," and his mother, Sharon, behaved according to her husband's expectations. Although it was clear that Sharon loved her son no matter what, Hank had been right. She didn't fully show it.

I'd initially considered not inviting them to the party. Being surrounded by so many homosexuals might make them feel uncomfortable. Throwing Jill into that mix only increased the potential for disaster, but there was no way I could exclude them. I sent the invitation and hoped for the best.

"Mr. and Mrs. Burton, I'm so glad you could make it," I said after shaking Henry Burton's massive hand. Henry muttered a barely audible hello as he nervously eyed the male guests in skimpy swimsuits, splashing in the pool. He was even taller and broader than Hank, and there was no doubt where Hank got his chiseled good looks. At almost sixty, Mr. Burton was a striking and imposing figure.

After withdrawing my hand from his, I gave Sharon a quick hug. She had a mousier appearance than her husband with her dull brown hair and dark eyes, but a genuine friendliness hid underneath the mask of meekness she wore.

What the Burtons all had in common, though, was height. I was like a pygmy walking among giants.

"Mom!" Hank said suddenly behind me. He stepped into his mother's open arms and gave her a powerful hug. He then turned to his father, the big, hopeful smile never once faltering from his lips even though I knew how on-edge Hank's father made him. Ever since our talk on the streets of San Diego, Hank had changed his attitude toward his parents. He released the anger and resentment, hoping to foster mutual love and affection. "How are you, Dad?"

"I'm good," Henry said as he shook his son's hand. His eyes remained glued to the festivities. "Quite a party you've got going on here."

Hank nodded before wrapping his arms around my shoulders. "I know, right? Santi sure knows how to throw a party."

Henry arched his eyebrows at me. "So I see."

"Well, I think it looks lovely," Sharon said, coming to my aid. She drew a scowl from her husband but managed to shake it off. "Thank you for doing this for our boy."

"No thanks necessary, Mrs. Burton. I love your son."

At that, Henry walked away and headed straight for the bar.

Sharon watched her husband order a drink and sighed. She then turned back to me and said, "Call me Sharon. The two of you are going to be married, after all."

"Thank you, Sharon. I'd like that."

She beamed. Away from her husband's scrutiny, her unconditional love couldn't be more obvious. "Why don't you introduce me to your new friends?"

"I'd love to," Hank said after taking his mother's hand. They proceeded to walk away. After a few steps, Hank gazed over his shoulder at me. "You coming?"

"I'll be right there," I said.

Hank nodded and walked off with his mother while I headed over to the bar to talk to Henry Burton.

"What are you drinking?"

"Whiskey," he said after downing the contents and ordering another.

"Make that two," I told the bartender, who brought us our drinks.

Henry turned on the barstool and stared at me. "I figured you'd prefer something fruitier. With an umbrella."

I ignored the intended insult and said, "I prefer stiffer drinks." I then emptied my glass.

He seemed impressed. "Are your parents coming?"

I shook my head. "They died a few years ago. Car accident."

Henry slowly nodded. "That's right. Hank told us. Sorry about that." He then ordered us another round.

"It was tough. I loved them a lot, and I miss them every day."

"Any brothers or sisters?"

"No. Just me."

"Too bad," he said. "It sucks to not have family."

I couldn't agree more. "That's why I'm hoping that you and I can be close." Henry stared at me out of the corners of his eyes. "I miss being a part of a family. My parents were everything to me, and since they've been gone, I've kinda been on my own. I mean, I've got friends, but it's not the same, you know?"

He nodded but said nothing.

"It's never been easy for me to make friends. I've always been more of a loner. Probably the only child syndrome, I guess. Most of the friends I've made have been through my best friend, Jill. She's a social butterfly and hasn't met a stranger yet. Having her in my life has been a lifesaver." I was rambling, but I didn't know how to stop. What happened to the eloquent orator I made my livelihood as? Apparently he'd hightailed it out of there as soon as Henry Burton showed up. "But like I was saying, I miss being a part of a family, and I'd really like to be a part of yours if you'd have me."

Henry motioned to the bartender for another drink.

"I know it's been tough for you having a gay son, and if you say yes, well, I guess you'd have one more. But I do love Hank, Mr. Burton. And I plan on making him happy for the rest of my life." He swallowed his drink in silence. "Well, I just wanted you to know that, I guess." I sucked down my whiskey and pushed away from the bar.

"Santi?"

"Yes, sir."

"I'm not a man of words. My son and my wife will tell you that. Words don't mean a whole hell of a lot to me. Actions are what count. So let me tell you this: I'm not happy that my son is gay." He paused, as if speaking the word caused him physical discomfort. "But I'm here, and I'm hoping that tells Hank everything he needs to know."

"I'm sure it does."

"So don't tell me you're going to make my son happy. Just do it. That will tell me all I need to know about you. Understand?"

I swallowed hard and nodded. Henry then patted me once on the shoulder before walking over to where Hank was introducing Sharon to Jill.

I wasn't quite sure what to think about our discussion. I'd hoped being frank and honest with him might earn me some brownie points. Whether it had or not, I wasn't really sure. All I knew for certain was that it was going to take more than just one conversation to get in good with Hank's father.

As I watched Hank laugh at something Jill said to his father, I couldn't help the smile that stretched across my lips. Fortunately I had a lifetime with his son to prove that I was a man of action as well as a man of my word.

AFTER THE guests had left and we said our good-byes, Hank and I got undressed and crawled into bed. This was the moment I'd wait all day for, when I could hold Hank's naked body against mine, feel his hairy legs wrap around my waist, and fill my nostrils with his scent, which made me both horny and drunk.

"Thank you for the party." Hank kissed my lips and pulled me on top of him. As much as I enjoyed lying on him, his eyes practically rolled back in his head every time I pressed against him.

"I hope you had a good time." I nuzzled my nose into his neck and gently bit at the sensitive flesh. He inhaled sharply and gripped my ass tightly.

"Of course I did," he said. He moved his fingers from my butt and traced the curve of my spine up to my neck. He then followed the slope of my shoulders down to my biceps until he found my hands, which he laced with his own.

"Do you think your parents had a good time?"

He pursed his lips in thought. "It's always hard to tell with them," he admitted. "My dad's always been a Grumpy McGrumperson." I grinned as I usually did when Hank spouted one of the silly names he often created. If I was being pissy, I was Pissy McPisserson. It was a strange and playful personality quirk I still found endearing. It was also one I'd started adopting, much to Jill's displeasure.

"I don't know," I said. "I think there's more to your dad than just being grumpy."

"What do you mean?"

"Well, we had a talk tonight."

He nodded. "I saw that. I've been dying to ask you about it, but I figured you'd tell me if you wanted me to know."

"Of course I was going to tell you, Silly McSillyson."

Hank grinned before kissing my lips. He liked that I copied him.

"I know your dad isn't very comfortable with the gay thing."

"That's an understatement," he said with a roll of his eyes. "He forced me to pack up and leave at sixteen. That sure told me a lot about how he felt about having a fag for a son."

The pain and animosity from that point in Hank's life remained a raw nerve. Only time and effort on both parts could dull the ache. "But I think you need to give him some credit."

Hank's eyebrows stitched together. "What do you mean?"

"Well, no matter how he feels, he was here, right?"

"I suppose so."

"What does that tell you?"

Hank shrugged. "That my mother made him come."

I smacked the side of his ass, which made Hank growl in want. He then dove upon my lips and began thrusting against me. Although I didn't want to, I pulled out of the kiss. We needed to have this conversation before our bodies took control and made anything more than grunting and moaning impossible. "How easy is it to make you do anything?"

"No one can make me do shit," he said quite proudly.

"And who do you think you got that from?"

"Hmm," Hank uttered. "I guess I get that from my dad."

I nodded. "Right. So if your mother didn't make him come, then why do you think he came?"

"To show he loves me?" He obviously wasn't sure that was the answer.

"That's what I think. Your dad's not a man of words. He's a man of action. That's pretty much what he told me. You just need to remember that. Has he made some mistakes in the past?"

Hank snorted. That answer was obvious.

"But don't focus too much on that. We all make mistakes. Look at his actions now and what he's trying to tell you today. I know sometimes cutting our losses is what we need to do to get over the pain, but I don't think that's the case here. He's trying, and he's the only father you've got."

"You're right," he said with a nod.

I pretended to be exasperated. "Of course I'm right."

Hank tickled me, and since he was much stronger, there was no way I could stop the torment. I struggled as I howled in protest, but he held my hands fast and wrapped his legs around my waist, making squirming off him almost impossible. When he finally relented, I was exhausted.

"Thank you for everything," he said. He pressed his lips to mine and, as usual, stole all breath from my lungs. "You're such a sweet, beautiful man for everything you've done for me."

"You're the one who moved halfway across the country to be with me," I said before I parted his lips with my tongue and drank in the sweetness of his kiss. "It was the least I could do."

Hank panted, blowing hot bursts of air across my face. He unlaced his fingers from mine and then charted a path all the way back to my ass. When he arrived at his spot, he used his muscular legs to push me harder against him. "That's true," he said with an impish grin.

I smirked at him before running my hands down to his sides, where I proceeded to tickle him mercilessly. Hank thrashed and screamed underneath me. It was like riding a mechanical bull in a country-and-western bar. I just had to hold on and hope for the best. The longest I'd been able to torture him had been about four seconds before Hank had managed to either buck me off or use his strength to restrain my hands.

That night he did both.

He rolled over, pinning me under his bigger body, and held my hands above my head. "No tickles!" he said. His eyes were wide, as they typically were after I tormented him.

"But I like to tickle you," I complained.

Hank clamped down on my nipple. I cried out as he chewed and bit at the sensitive flesh.

After a few seconds, though, the pain turned to pleasure. I moaned and forced my chest up against his face. He regarded me with a sexual frenzy that turned his blue eyes into twin flames of desire.

I easily interpreted the look. It was the one he gave me whenever Hank the Bottom became Hank the Top.

I scratched my fingers through his facial hair and spread my legs for him. He grinned up at me and growled. He placed his hands under my knees and brought them to my chest. I held them tightly to my body while Hank reached across the bed to fish the bottle of lube out of the drawer.

After removing the piercing from the head of his dick, he coated his big cock and my ass with the lube and then aimed his erection at my twitching center. Hank had ridden me hard the last time he fucked me a few months ago. He had practically rammed me into the next condo.

I'd been sore for at least a week, but it had been well worth it. Based on the look in his eyes, my ass was in trouble.

"Are you ready?" he asked as he pressed his hardness against my butt.

I held on to Hank's shoulders and nodded.

As he entered me, Hank whimpered, and I bit my lip. I wasn't the best bottom in the world like Hank. It always took me more than a few minutes to get used to the huge cock shoved up my ass, but as always, Hank caressed my cheek and kissed my lips as he gave me time to adjust to his girth lodged inside me.

Far sooner than I expected, the pain disappeared and a wonderful fullness spread throughout. Not only did I have Hank in my heart and in my soul, but my body now housed his. His hard cock spasmed inside with each rapid heartbeat.

It turned my already blazing lust into a raging inferno.

I moved my hips up to take the rest of him. As Hank's shaft was pulled farther inside, his mouth hung open, and I took his lip between my teeth as he worked in and out of me.

I gasped and clutched his hips. "Harder," I begged him after releasing his lip.

Hank growled and thrust against me. Every muscle in his body tensed, and I surfed my hands all over him. I flitted my fingers through his chest hair and rolled his pierced nipples. Every time I pinched them, he dove inside me harder and faster. I craned my neck up and he leaned down to me as our mouths molded together once again.

Our tongues found each other, and we drank the sweetness of our kiss. As our tongues wrestled, I inhaled every ragged breath Hank panted, and he stole all the oxygen from my lungs.

"Fuck!" Hank said. He slid his hands from my sides to my hips, where he could gain further leverage for his powerful thrusts. "You feel so fucking good."

"Oh God, you too," I moaned as Hank's balls slapped against my ass. "I want to feel you come inside me."

"Oh hell yeah," he said. His eyes turned dreamy, and his body became tense. Hank was close.

I palmed my cock and jacked it to match Hank's rhythmic hips.

"Shit," he said. "Here it comes!"

Hank's body spasmed. Whenever he topped, his orgasm took complete control of his body. He cried out at the top of his lungs as his cock exploded inside me, filling my butt with his spunk. As he came, Hank shivered, his head rolled back, and he sometimes stopped breathing for a few seconds.

Seeing him that way, lost to the pleasure my body had given him, and feeling his cock flooding my insides, always pushed me over the edge. I shot my load across my stomach in five white volleys of spunk that left me almost as breathless as Hank.

When we recovered, he collapsed on top of me, sweat dripping from his body onto mine.

"Have I told you I love you?" Hank panted in my ear.

"Not for the last few hours," I replied.

He leaned his head against his hand and gazed down at me. "Because I really, really, really do."

"I'm glad," I replied with a kiss. "Because I really, really, really love you too."

And ever since Hank moved in, that was how we said good night before drifting off to sleep in each other's arms.

CHAPTER
Three

I WENT from being the happiest man in the world to the most annoyingly cheerful pain in the ass in existence. Although Jill couldn't have been happier for me, she had her limits when it came to perkiness.

"I'm going to punch you if you don't wipe that cheesy-ass grin from your face," she told me over lunch. "I'm trying to eat here."

I tried to tone down the smile, but thinking about going home to Hank only made it worse. We'd been living together almost a year now, and the newness of it all had yet to wear off. I seriously doubted it ever would. "I can't help it. I've never been this happy in my life."

"I know," she said before patting my hand. "But please try. Because I'd really hate to hurt you, and we both know I'll do it."

That was no lie. "Fine, Grumpy McGrumperson."

Her hand tightened around mine. "What have I told you? No cutesy names or I'll really hurt you."

"How about bitch? Does that work?" I bared all my teeth at her in utter satisfaction.

She nodded. "Much better, cocksucker."

We snickered, and when Jill was content that I'd floated down a few levels from cloud nine, she released my hand and returned to her burger and fries. "So Hank's business is doing well?"

When he first moved, it hadn't gone well at all. He had called the clients he'd worked for after building his parents' house, but none of them had any work for him. I introduced him to people I knew, but that only resulted in a few handyman jobs. It brought in some money, but it wasn't what Hank was accustomed to. He'd been concerned relocating to escape the memories of Gracie and Picasso had been a hasty professional move, but six months ago, Hank struck gold.

He met Consuela Sifuentes, a wealthy widowed Houston socialite, at one of the charity events my firm cosponsored for the Houston Zoo. After chatting about classic automobiles, which was a passion for both Consuela and Hank, she asked him what he did for a living. Hank met with her the next morning to discuss redoing the garage where she housed her antique car collection.

Hank not only got the job, but Consuela passed on his name to all her friends. He was now booked solid for the next sixteen months.

"Really well," I finally said.

She chomped on her fries before answering. "Good. I guess making friends with the hoity-toity can pay off." Jill had an aversion to the super wealthy. She believed they were the scourge of society and would ultimately cause its collapse because of greed.

"It sure doesn't hurt."

"And the wedding plans?"

I glared at her. "You're like the worst best man ever!"

"That's because I'm the best *woman*," she said with a jut of her chin.

"Semantics," I replied, waving a cherry tomato from my salad at her. "*Any* best woman worth her salt wouldn't have to ask one of the grooms such a question."

"And why would I bother with the details?" she asked before popping a french fry in her mouth. "You've practically shanghaied the whole wedding. You've made all the arrangements and haven't delegated jack shit to anyone but your poor secretary."

I couldn't argue with that. Jamie was the most efficient assistant I'd had in years. She knew what I needed before I did. Although she already had a full plate with her duties at the firm, she'd been glad to take on some of the wedding details. She'd be getting a big bonus from me this year. "Jamie doesn't complain. Besides, she's not absentminded like some people I know."

"I'm gonna tell Hank you said that," she said before flipping me off.

If this were any other circumstance, Jill would be correct. Hank had probably one of the poorest memories I'd ever encountered. He never forgot how to fix mechanical problems or tear apart houses before restoring them, but when it came to details like where we ate lunch last week or what I'd asked him to do before coming home, he just couldn't keep such information in his brain. But for once I wasn't talking about Hank, so I decided to throw one of my cherry tomatoes at Jill to drive home my accusation. "I'm talking about you."

Jill grimaced at the tomato, which landed amid her fries. She had an aversion to all vegetables and refused to eat them. "Gross! Your tomato is touching my fries!" She flicked the offending veggie off her plate. It rolled off the table and underneath the seat of the man sitting to our left.

"Classy," I said, raising one of my eyebrows at her.

"This from the man who hurled his food at me?"

"Trying to switch subjects won't work, you know?" That was one of Jill's favorite diversionary tactics. "You aren't very detail-oriented and you know it."

She harrumphed. "I'm detailed enough to know you're an anal-retentive Hun who doesn't like to relinquish control about things that are truly important to you." She brushed aside the french fries the tomato had touched. "And let's face it, there's nothing more important to you than Hank and this wedding."

She had me there. In a few weeks, Hank and I would travel to California and get married. I couldn't wait. "Fine," I said. "You win."

She gazed at me as if that should have been obvious from the get-go. "Now, fill me in on what you've done since you booked the Presidio, hired the caterer, and finalized the reception menu."

"You *do* listen to me!"

Jill smiled at me. This time all traces of playful mocking disappeared from her expression. "Of course I do. This wedding is important to me too. I love Hank, but most of all I love you. And I haven't seen you this happy in all the time I've known you. That's all I ever wanted for you." Her lips hitched up at the right, signaling the return of her usual good-natured disdain. "I just wish the two of you weren't so fucking perfect for each other, because it sometimes makes me hate you."

"There you go. Being Grumpy McGrumperson again!"

She picked up her ketchup-drenched french fry and gazed at it, and then at me. She was obviously contemplating hurling it at me. The devious glint to her eye revealed that quite clearly, but we both knew she wouldn't waste it. When it came to her fatty foods, Jill ate every bite. Finally she popped it into her mouth instead. "I'm going to strangle Hank for teaching you that shit."

"Can you wait 'til our fiftieth wedding anniversary?"

She sighed in exasperation. "Fine!"

For the rest of our lunch hour, I told her about the wedding. How I'd arranged to fly in all of Hank's siblings, who didn't have much money, for the festivities. That I'd finally settled on the menu for the reception, an assortment of finger foods that were both classy and casual since Hank didn't want anything too formal. And that I'd managed to get Hank's father to agree to walk his son down the aisle.

It was going to be a glorious event, one that we'd remember vividly for our lifetime together.

AFTER LUNCH I drove over to River Oaks, one of the most expensive neighborhoods in Houston. Hank was working for one of Consuela's dearest friends, who needed a kitchen and bathroom remodel as well as some exterior work on the home. I'd promised to bring him lunch since he was going to be busy breaking in some workers he'd never worked with before, and then we had to make a quick trip to Saks for our final tuxedo fittings.

I couldn't wait to see my handsome man all decked out in his wedding duds. He looked scrumptious in his muscle shirts and shorts. I could only imagine how delectable he'd be in formal attire.

I just might have to take him right there in the fitting room. The image of Hank's half-naked body pressed against the wall, with his shirt pulled up, his pants around his ankles, and his bare ass sticking out for me made me hard. I imagined his ragged breathing and muffled moans as I thrust in and out of him, the shuddering of his body when I touched him, and then the eventual grunts of our climax.

Yeah, we'd definitely be doing that later. My hard cock throbbed in agreement.

But first I had to actually drag Hank away from the site, which was sometimes difficult to do. Once he started working, he didn't stop until the day was done.

I parked in front of the three-story house where Hank was working. I couldn't see him, but his truck sat in the driveway, and the sound of hammering and other whirring machines I couldn't identify emanated from the backyard.

The house was exquisite and certainly didn't appear as if it needed any work whatsoever. The front façade was a combination of stucco and brick. The brick covered the lower half of the building while the stucco extended up to the roofline. A huge stone chimney crawled up the side of the house, and the windows on the first floor were enormous. They practically spanned the entire height of the first story.

Hank and I would never be able to afford one of the multimillion-dollar homes in this area, but I couldn't help but imagine the kind of home we'd end up buying together. I pictured something small and cozy like a cottage with a huge garden out front. It needed to be bigger than the condo we'd quickly outgrown, and we needed enough yard for the English bulldogs that were in our immediate future.

While Hank wasn't yet ready to own another pup, he would be soon enough.

"There's my love!"

I tore my gaze from the structure to Hank, who was coming around the side of the house. He was wearing his usual work clothes—a short-sleeved gray-and-white Gracie Designs shirt and jeans—and my body quickly reacted to his presence. My breath caught in my throat, my heart pounded in my chest, and my cock practically sprung out of my pants. "And there's *my* love." I crossed the lawn to meet him. We engulfed each other in an embrace and our lips and tongues quickly found their mates.

When our groins pressed together, my hard cock rubbed against Hank's erection. I'd definitely have no problem getting him naked in the fitting room later.

"Someone's happy to see me."

Hank leered down at me. "Always."

"That makes me happy."

"Me too, love."

"Hank!" a voice from behind us called.

Hank turned to his left but made sure to keep his arm around me, resting just above my ass as usual. Everyone, including his workers, knew Hank was gay. He wasn't shy about admitting who he was or that he loved me. He took great pride in both. I'd initially worried that Hank's carefree approach to life and his sexual identity might prove problematic in south Texas, where being gay wasn't necessarily okay.

But so far no one had batted an eye, not even any of the men who worked for him. I couldn't tell if it was because they truly didn't care or if Hank's size and intimidating appearance made them not care.

Whatever it was, it worked.

"What is it, Felix?"

Felix placed his hands behind his head and sighed. "Pork Chop is at it again."

Hank cursed under his breath. "I'll be right there."

Felix nodded. "Good to see you, Santi."

"You too," I replied with a wave before Felix disappeared around the house. I turned to Hank and asked, "Pork Chop?"

"The new guy I was telling you about. He eats pork chops for lunch every fucking day."

I laughed. "Okay. So what's he done now?"

"Who fucking knows?" Hank asked before grabbing my hand and leading me around the side of the house. "He's a moron, and this might just be his last day on the job. I have to show him how to do something every ten minutes, which is fine, we all have our weaknesses, but if I've already shown you how to do something twice, I expect you to remember."

Hank was easygoing away from the job, but when it came to work, he was professional and a perfectionist. If something wasn't done to his standards or if someone wasn't pulling his weight, he had no trouble trimming the fat.

When we entered the backyard, still hand in hand, the sheer opulence took my breath away. A tree-lined perimeter shaded half the yard, which also contained a stone patio and a crystal-clear rectangular pool with a hot tub inset. A wall about eight feet high stood over the far end of the pool, and water cascaded down its rocky front and splashed rhythmically into the pool.

"Wow!"

"I know," Hank replied as we made our way to the men working on the rear exterior. A huge three-level scaffold had been erected along the south wall, where men were reframing the structure for newer and larger windows.

"Where's Pork Chop?"

Hank nodded to the top of the scaffold, where a guy stood staring back and forth between what he held in his hand and the building before him. He definitely looked like someone who might not know his asshole from his elbow.

"Pork Chop!" Hank called up from the bottom of the scaffold. "What *are* you doing?"

When Pork Chop saw Hank, he grinned. It made him look slightly like an idiot. He didn't seem to realize he was in trouble. The man couldn't be more clueless if he tried. "Hey, Hank! I'm just trying to remember what you told me to do."

Hank sighed and then glanced over his shoulder at me. "I need to go up there, and then we can go."

"Take your time, love," I said as I lay back on the lounge chair facing the pool. "I'll be right here."

Hank blew me a kiss before climbing the ladder to the top of the structure. Even though I had the beauty of the outside paradise to keep me company, I could only focus on Hank. Nothing was more beautiful or precious to me in this world, and I could watch him twenty-four seven.

As I observed Hank instruct Pork Chop on his task, I couldn't help but notice that Pork Chop was doing something Hank was not: he was wearing a hard hat. It was a long way down from where Hank now stood, and when he once again stepped onto the stone deck that

63

surrounded the area, I planned on scolding Hank into wearing his helmet.

"Almost done!" Hank yelled down to me. He leaned against the rail while Pork Chop walked backward on the scaffold carrying a huge box.

"You should really be wearing your helmet." I made a pretend angry face to let him know I wasn't amused.

"I'll be fine," he said.

"You may be," I said while nodding to the struggling Pork Chop. "I worry about others."

"Pork Chop!" Hank yelled. He rushed to help with the box. "What the hell are you doing? This is too heavy to carry up here by yourself."

"Sorry, boss," Pork Chop said. "Just trying to play catch-up now that I know what I'm doing."

As Pork Chop and Hank made their way back to the section of the wall where they had been working, Hank, ever mindful of his surroundings, looked back to see the tools in his path. He stepped over them. "You need to make sure you pick up your tools," he told Pork Chop.

"Will do," he replied. But then he tripped. He stumbled forward, shifting the weight of the box into Hank's grip, unsettling his balance. Hank and the box fell over the railing.

The man I loved hit the ground with a thud, and my world turned upside down.

CHAPTER
Four

FOUR HOURS later I paced the emergency room. I had memorized every crack in the floor and every stain on the tile. I had practically worn a trail from the front door to the double doors that led to where the paramedics had rushed Hank.

Shortly after Hank arrived, the attending physician came out to tell me that Hank had suffered a serious head injury, and they needed to do surgery to release some of the pressure on his brain. Someone would be out to get me when it was over.

Every time the doors opened, my breath caught in my throat, and I clasped my hands together, praying for good news. But so far I had none.

So I waited and I paced. I couldn't just sit down while my fiancé underwent major surgery. I couldn't relax on a plastic chair while some doctor was drilling a hole in his skull. I had to keep moving and keep fighting, because that was what I expected Hank to do. He had to pull through this and come back to me.

Anything else was not an option.

Hank's parents evidently agreed. I had called them en route to the hospital, and they made it there from Lufkin in record time. After I explained the situation, Sharon burst into tears and Henry turned coolly distant. Hank's brother, Joe, who'd just moved to Texas, and I did our best to soothe her while Henry launched into a tirade against the hospital personnel for not keeping him better informed of Hank's progress. He screamed at anyone in scrubs and even snapped at his wife for crying.

He caused such a scene that hospital security had a talk with him. Afterward, he went back to silence, but the fear, masquerading as anger, still brewed underneath. Sharon managed to calm down some as well. Instead of crying, she incessantly wrung her hands and fidgeted in her chair.

"Okay, Mitch," Joe said from the other side of the room. He was talking on his cell to Hank's former roommates. After telling the Burtons, I lacked the energy to repeat the story. Fortunately Joe had offered to do it for me. As I watched Joe, I couldn't help but notice how different he was from his brother. He was tall just like the rest of his family, but his dark hair and eyes were more reminiscent of his mother. Hank, however, was almost the spitting image of his father, with fairer hair and steel blue eyes. If I didn't know Hank and Joe were related, I never would have guessed.

When Joe ended the call, I crossed over to him. "Are they coming?"

He nodded. "Darren was booking their flight. They'll hopefully be here by tomorrow morning."

"And your sisters?" Joe had called Cally and Taylor before phoning the boys.

"I'm keeping them posted."

That translated into they weren't coming. The Burton girls were more interested in their own screwed-up lives than anyone else's. "Okay." I turned around and went back to pacing.

"You should sit," Joe said from behind me. "You need to rest."

I shook my head. I wouldn't rest until I knew Hank was going to be okay. Until then, I'd be strong.

"Santi!"

I turned to see Jill rushing through the exterior doors and barreling toward me with her smock still tied around her waist. From the looks of her stained apron, she'd been in the middle of a color job when I finally managed to get her on the phone about thirty minutes ago.

"Any word?"

I opened my mouth to respond, but the sight of my best friend, the one person other than Hank I'd been able to let my guard down around since my parents died, caused my internal retaining wall to crumble. I broke into sobs. She wrapped her arms around my shoulders and stroked my head. "I know," she cooed. "I know." She led me over to the row of plastic chairs next to Sharon. While I let loose the fear I'd been unable to express, she lowered us both into a seated position before she took my head out of the crook of her neck and wiped the tears from my cheeks. "He's going to be fine. Hank's a strong and stubborn man. If anyone's going to come through this with flying colors, it's him."

"That's right," Sharon said at my side. She rested her hand reassuringly on my shoulder.

I nodded. Hank was the strongest, most stubborn man I knew, but right now I didn't see that man. I could only see the Hank who'd landed after the fall. The one with blood pooling around his head and out of his mouth. The one who lay perfectly still despite my cries for him to wake up. The one who looked helpless and hurt, and the one I couldn't do anything for to make it all better.

"Remember that," Jill said. "And remember he loves you."

"I know he does," I managed to say between sniffles. The river of pain had slowed. While the occasional sob still racked my body, at least I was able to speak coherently. "And I love him too. So very much. I don't know what I'd do—"

Jill punched my arm. "Stop that!"

I absently rubbed where she hit me, more out of habit than an actual sensation of pain. I couldn't feel anything, really. Sometime over the past four hours, I'd gone numb. The world, which had once been so bright and vivid, now appeared drab and lifeless, as if someone had sucked the color out of reality.

"Be positive." Though Jill's voice was confident, the fear in her wide eyes was obvious. She was attempting to be strong for me.

"I will be."

"That's right. After all, you've got a wedding to plan."

My wedding. It was going to be the most glorious and momentous day of my life. And I had enough hope to believe that it was still going to happen.

"MR. HERRERA?"

I stopped pacing and turned in the direction of the voice. A woman wearing blue scrubs and a hospital mask dangling around her neck stood behind me.

"That's me," I replied as the Burtons and Jill gathered around.

"I'm Beth Anglin, the neurosurgeon who's been operating on Mr. Burton."

"How's my son?" Henry asked. His previous anger had been displaced by Dr. Anglin's presence. Now only fear played across his face.

"He's in recovery, and he's stable."

Sharon praised God, and Henry exhaled in obvious relief. Joe gathered his parents into a big hug while Jill patted my shoulder as if to tell me that she told me so. What none of them noticed, however, was that Dr. Anglin was not wearing the smile everyone else was. Instead she brushed her blonde hair, which was matted with sweat, off her forehead. She was guardedly optimistic at best.

"What's wrong?" I asked. "What haven't you told us?"

My questions immediately put a stop to the rejoicing.

She took a deep breath before answering. "When Mr. Burton fell from the scaffold, he suffered a traumatic brain injury." A moan of despair escaped Sharon's throat, and she grabbed her husband and son for support. "While there was no penetrating injury, the fall did result in a skull fracture as well as an intracranial hemorrhage."

"What the hell does that mean?" Henry asked. "Speak English." His anger was back with a vengeance.

"It basically means that Mr. Burton suffered bleeding in his brain."

The world around me spun, and I stumbled backward. Fortunately Jill was there to hold me up.

"We performed a craniotomy to ease the pressure."

"That's good, right?" Jill asked.

Dr. Anglin nodded. "What we are worried about now is what is called a contrecoup effect. You see, since Mr. Burton fell from such a great height, we believe that not only did he injure the back of his head where the blow occurred, but that the impact caused the brain to move within the skull, colliding with the interior of the skull at the opposite point of impact."

"Let me get this straight," I said. "You think he may have suffered two traumatic brain injuries from this fall?"

"Basically, yes."

"What does all this mean, Dr. Anglin? Is my fiancé going to be okay?"

"I can't say anything for certain. What I can tell you is that CT scans show the bleeding has stopped, which means the procedure worked. Once Mr. Burton regains consciousness, we will be able to better gauge any further damage that might have been inflicted."

"When will he wake up?" Joe asked.

"That I'm not certain. As a result of the injuries, Mr. Burton has fallen into a coma."

"A what?" Henry asked. His face was beet red, and the vein in his forehead throbbed as if it had come to life. Sharon buried her face in Joe's shoulder and resumed sobbing while I held Jill's hand in a death grip.

This couldn't be happening. I had to be dreaming. God, please let me be dreaming.

"I know it sounds terrifying, but patients who suffer from these types of injuries typically enter a comatose state. It's the body's way of helping repair itself."

"And you have no idea when he'll come out of it?" I asked. My throat had gone dry, and I lost the ability to swallow.

"It could be six hours or six days," she answered. "But we will monitor him closely."

"I need to see him," I said.

She nodded. "I'll have one of the nurses escort you to his room."

When Dr. Anglin left, Henry started ranting and Joe worked to calm him down. I couldn't focus on anything around me. All I could concentrate on were the words no one else had seemed to catch.

What further damage *might* there be?

A WEEK later Hank still hadn't awoken, and I had yet to leave his side. Fortunately Wyatt didn't give me a hard time about the leave. We'd recently opened our own practice together after our old firm suffered under the strain of a new partner. It had been tough. I'd spent a decade at Canales, Crenshaw, and Emerson, trying to make partner, but the new managing attorney had been too big of a dick to work for, and I couldn't pass up the opportunity to be my own boss. I felt awful about leaving Wyatt to take care of our cases by himself, but he was more than capable. He even called me every couple of days to check on Hank and to get my opinion on a case he was working on.

Wyatt didn't need my help. He was a brilliant lawyer. He did that to take my mind off my troubles even if for just one phone conversation, and I appreciated the opportunity he gave me to flex my legal muscle. I owed him dinner and drinks for his thoughtfulness.

In fact, I owed everyone more than I could say since they took care of me, and the rest of my life outside these walls, while I took care of Hank.

It wasn't easy spending every minute of every day in the hospital or sleeping on the uncomfortable chair that seemed to be a prerequisite for all hospitals. I hadn't showered or shaved in days, and I obviously looked like hell. Whenever someone came into the room, they said I needed to get some rest.

As always, Jill was more honest in her assessment. She said I looked like shit. But what else could I expect from her?

Everyone tried to get me to go home and sleep or to take a break and eat something outside of hospital food, but how could I go? If Hank regained consciousness even for a minute, I intended to be the first person he saw.

He had to know that I was there, by his side, for whatever he might need.

So Hank's parents brought me breakfast every morning. Darren and Mitch handled lunch, and Jill brought me dinner. They became one big support network. Henry, who'd typically treated everyone as a nuisance, actually softened to us all. The love we showed his son broke through whatever barriers he usually erected. To me, his behavior had changed the most.

He hugged me every morning when he arrived and drew me close again before he left. Evidently I'd proven my love for his son. I was glad for the change, but I hated that it took Hank being in a coma to make it happen.

"We come with sustenance," Mitch exclaimed as he and Darren entered the room. He held aloft two big bags of food from Olive Garden. I hated that place, but Mitch loved it. I didn't have the heart to tell him that I mostly picked at the food and threw the majority of it away after they left.

"Great," I said, pretending excitement. "I'm famished."

"And you need a shower," Mitch said as he sniffed the air around me. "You reek."

"Tact," Darren said. "We've had this conversation already."

"Just being me," Mitch said with an unapologetic shrug. "I'm brutally honest to my friends, and I expect the same in return."

"Good," Darren said. "Now shut your hole."

Mitch harrumphed while Darren brought the spare roll-away table to the seating area we had established in Hank's room, and began taking out the Styrofoam containers. "I'm glad you're hungry," Darren said to me. "Because Mitch ordered way too much food as usual."

"Anything we don't finish, we eat for dinner," Mitch said as if that justified what appeared to be five different meals—lasagna, spaghetti and meatballs, chicken piccata, and at least two other pasta dishes, not to mention the salad and breadsticks.

How did someone as waifish as Mitch eat so damn much and still fit into skinny jeans?

"Before we eat, it's time for Hank's exercises."

Mitch and Darren nodded and assumed their positions. I grabbed Hank's shoulders while Darren took Hank's left foot and Mitch grabbed the right. We hoisted Hank onto his left side, as the nurses had taught us, and then repositioned him on the bed. I worked Hank's arms while Mitch stretched Hank's legs.

Hank had to be moved every two to three hours to avoid pneumonia and bed sores. Typically his nurses performed this task, but after a couple of days and X-rays that revealed no spinal injuries, I insisted on being a part of Hank's treatment. They'd denied my request, but I wasn't so easily put off.

The staff eventually realized it was easier to teach me than to argue with me.

"After we eat, I think I'm gonna go buy a razor and shave Bubble's legs," Mitch said with an upturned nose. "This is one hairy bitch."

"Don't you dare! I love my hairy man."

Mitch grimaced. "Why? Do you enjoy hacking up his blond pubes every time you go down on him?"

"Maybe I do," I said with a wink at Darren, who was giggling at our exchange. Darren and I were fans of manly bodies. Mitch preferred his men to be just like him—waxed, smooth, and a bit girly. "All right, next side."

We positioned Hank onto his right and repeated the movements.

"I don't know what you two see in hairy bodies," Mitch said. "It's gross. It gets everywhere and I think it holds in BO. I mean, who likes that?"

"Depends on the man," Darren said with a grin.

"Really, Grandma?" Mitch asked. "You like the stench of onion on your man."

"When it's my man," I said, "all I smell is my love. And Hank's manliness makes me hard every time."

We placed Hank on his back and then worked his limbs in that position. "You two are disgusting," Mitch declared with a judgmental glare at both of us.

"This from the man who frequents sex parties," Darren said with a snicker.

"All my sexual partners are freshly showered, thank you very much."

"I'd shower too if I had to have sex with you."

Mitch gasped at Darren's comment and clutched at his chest. I couldn't help but laugh.

"Grandma, did you forget to take your Metamucil this morning? You seem a bit constipated."

Darren shook his head at Mitch. "Nope. Took it right after we clipped in your extensions."

This time Mitch placed one hand on his slender hips and ran his fingers through his long blond hair with the other. "Every strand is mine, and you know it. You and your Brillo Pad hair are just jealous."

"And the Hag is out," Darren said with a shit-eating grin. Both Darren and Hank liked to rile Mitch up and turn him into the loving nickname they gave him—the Hag.

What a peculiar trio of friends they made—Bubble, Grandma, and the Hag.

I shook my head at Darren and returned his smile. Did he really have to get Mitch started on a bitch rampage? "Why?"

"I'll tell you why, my dear, sweet Santi," Mitch said as he placed Hank's muscular leg back onto the bed. "It's because Grandma here hates that I'm so much prettier than she is."

Darren rolled his eyes. "Yeah, that's it."

"It's true and you know it," Mitch continued. "I'm the veritable belle of whatever ball I attend. Men clamor for my attention and affection. I certainly don't see a line forming outside your bedroom door."

"There's no need for a line," Darren said. "I thought your motto was 'Two holes. No waiting.'"

I busted out laughing at that one. Mitch's love of orgies and double penetration was general knowledge among his friends.

"Don't you laugh at me!" Mitch said as he turned the Hag on me. "I've got a few choice words for you too."

Fuck! I knew better than to enjoy the show too much. Too much giggling made Mitch home in on you like a bitch-seeking missile. In times like that, only Hank could get Mitch to give it a rest.

Mitch opened his mouth to let me have it when a low, raspy voice spoke from the bed. "Hag."

We turned to find Hank staring at the ceiling. He blinked his big, beautiful eyes three times before closing them again. Mitch hit the nurse's call button while I sprinted out down the hall to the nurses' station.

BY THE time Dr. Anglin made it to Hank's bedside, he hadn't opened his eyes again.

"They were open," I told Dr. Anglin. I turned to Darren and Mitch, who nodded in agreement.

"I believe you," she said. She opened Hank's eyelids while shining her flashlight into his eyes. She then took a pin out of her coat and poked Hank on the bottom of his right foot. His eyes fluttered open.

73

"He's awake!" Darren yelled before Hank closed his eyes again.

"Not quite," she said. "He's just responding to pain stimuli, which is a good sign." She went back to work on Hank, testing his motor reflexes. "Mr. Burton, can you hear me?" When she got no response, she turned to me.

I crossed to the opposite side of the bed. I took Hank's big hand in mine and held it to my mouth. I brushed my lips against his flesh and said, "How's my love?"

Still no response.

"Come on, my sexy man, it's time for you to open your eyes. We have a wedding to get to soon, and we still need to get to our final fitting for our tuxes."

Hank's hand gripped mine.

"He moved his hand," I told the room. "He's responding."

Dr. Anglin smiled. She was always friendly, but she was mostly distant and scientific, which was typical of most medical professionals. Over the course of the last few days, though, she'd started showing affection and concern not just for Hank but for all of us. "He's definitely moving up on the Glasgow Coma Scale," she said before scribbling on Hank's chart. "This is great news."

Great? This was better than great. This was absofuckinglutely miraculous.

"When will he come out of it fully?" Darren asked.

"I'm not sure," she answered. "It could be a few hours or a few days."

"Can we move this along, Bubble?" Mitch asked, pretending to be annoyed. "I'm supposed to hook up with a hot twink this weekend, so if you'd kindly wake up so I can be back in San Diego in enough time to sample his creamy filling, I'd appreciate it."

"Hag," Hank replied in a low rasp.

Darren wrapped his arms around Mitch, who was tearing up.

"That's right, Hank," I said. I ran my fingers along the curve of his bearded chin. "He is a hag." Then I bent down and pressed my lips to his. For the first time in too many days, Hank's lips trembled under mine.

I collapsed on top of his chest, unable to stop the flood of tears that poured not only from my body but also from my soul.

My Hank was on his way back to me.

AS THE days progressed, Hank remained conscious for longer periods of time. He still wasn't back to himself, though. He wouldn't say more than a few words, and they usually didn't make a whole lot of sense. His usual response to any question I asked him was "hag."

I was getting a complex. Mitch and Darren had flown back to San Diego a couple of days ago to get back to work. Was I a hag because I kept talking to him and was always there when he was awake? Dr. Anglin assured me that it was just Hank's conscious mind resurfacing.

So whenever he called me a hag, I told him that I loved him too. He'd gaze at me out of the corners of his eyes and then fall back asleep.

While it was wonderful having limited interactions with him, I was nervous. It was like the man who'd woken up wasn't my Hank. He sure looked like him, but he didn't act like the man I'd fallen in love with.

I'd grown accustomed to the light in his eyes whenever his gaze fell upon me or the sensuous way his lips parted in a wickedly loving grin that told me Hank wanted me naked on top of him.

When Hank looked at me now, it was as if he wasn't really seeing me, as if he was stuck in a dream that had changed the landscape around him. Dr. Anglin said that confusion after an ordeal such as Hank's was common.

It made sense, but I didn't have to like it.

That was why I slipped out of Hank's room before he awoke that morning. I needed to go for a stroll to gird my loins for another day of being called a hag and having the man I loved stare at me with an expression devoid of emotion.

It wasn't easy dealing with this mostly by myself. Darren and Mitch had to get back to their jobs, and Hank's parents had headed home a few days ago. They had livestock to take care of, and their neighbor who'd been feeding the goats, horses, and chickens was going out of town for a few days. They had promised to return every weekend. Fortunately Jill stopped by for dinner every day. It was a welcome relief to have someone still look at me as they always had.

Even though I loved Jill for being such a good friend, she wasn't Hank. He was what I needed more than anyone else.

"Good morning, Santi."

I turned toward the voice to find Dr. Anglin walking toward me from the elevators. It was time for her morning rounds.

"Good morning," I replied.

"How's our patient?"

"Still asleep."

"He'll do that a lot," she reminded me. "His body's still recovering."

I nodded. What else could I say? That I wanted him to hurry up and return to the man he was before he fell from the scaffold? That was far too selfish. This wasn't about me. This was about Hank. Still, I was surprised when Dr. Anglin's rested her hand on my forearm. It was a warm, comforting gesture, which she evidently figured I needed.

"I know it's not easy," she said before withdrawing her hand. "He's made a great deal of progress, but he's not back to normal yet. I know that's extremely difficult, especially since you haven't left his side once."

"I love him. My place is by his side."

"I know," she said with a nod. "Still, you have to take care of yourself too. You won't do him any good if you don't. Most loved ones of my patients forget that. They get so wrapped up in being there for their loved ones that they completely neglect themselves and *their* needs. This isn't just about Hank because it isn't just happening to him. It's happening to you too. To all his loved ones. It's okay to be impatient or annoyed or even pissed off. That's normal too."

When she stopped talking, she smiled. How did she know what I needed to hear? "Thank you."

"You're welcome," she replied. "And just so you know, we have a gym here at the hospital. There's a punching bag. I think you might benefit from a visit."

I laughed. "I think you're right."

"Good," she said before nodding down the hall. "How about we go and see how Sleeping Beauty is doing today?"

"Sounds good," I said as we walked back toward Hank's room.

"His physical therapy seems to be moving along nicely. His therapist tells me that Hank's getting stronger and his motor impulses are improving."

"I've noticed. He's moving around more on the bed, and he's getting annoyed at having to be helped to use the bedpan."

"Who wouldn't be annoyed at that?" She placed her hand on the door leading to Hank's room.

"That's true," I said as she opened the door.

"Good morning."

Dr. Anglin and I stopped in our tracks. Hank sat up in bed with the television remote control in his hand. The blank, expressionless stare had vanished. His blue eyes danced with the usual affinity he had greeted people with every day since I'd known him.

He was here. My Hank was back.

Or so I thought.

CHAPTER
Five

I STOOD in the hall of the hospital with Dr. Anglin. Though her lips were moving, I didn't hear a word she said. Hank's last words still echoed in my ears. *I've never seen him before in my life.*

How was this possible? How could Hank have forgotten me, our love, and the future we'd been planning together? Next month we were flying to California to get married. We had planned an intimate wedding on the grounds of the Presidio. The invitations had gone out, the caterer had been hired, and our friends and family were planning on being there to celebrate our first moments as husbands.

How could any of that happen if Hank didn't even know who I was?

"Santi, did you hear me?"

My vision melted away as tears filled my eyes. "He doesn't remember me," I managed to choke out. After that, speech was impossible. My body had become overrun with sobs that quaked through my soul. I had to lean against the wall for support, and suddenly the bile in my stomach rose up my throat. If I didn't get myself under control, I was going to lose my breakfast along with the man I loved.

Dr. Anglin's voice, which had been cool and clinical a few moments ago, disappeared. The medical professional stepped back and the woman beneath the white coat stepped forward. "I won't lie and say I know how difficult this is for you. I've seen the way you've stayed by Mr. Burton's side since his accident. Your love for him is obvious to anyone who's had the fortune to witness it. Believe me when I say I've seen spouses who haven't shown a fraction of the dedication you have displayed since day one. What has happened is terribly unfair, and it really pisses me off."

Her words calmed the tempest of despair that swirled within me. It somehow comforted me to know that the love I felt, the one I still remembered vividly, shone just as brightly for others as it did for me.

It gave me hope. If Dr. Anglin could see it, then perhaps Hank would see it again too.

I took several deep breaths and willed my pain and fury from my guts into my fists, which I balled to keep contained. I'd definitely be hitting that punching bag later. "Will he gain his memory back?" I asked.

"I can't say he will or he won't," she admitted apprehensively. "Mr. Burton has suffered a traumatic brain injury. When he fell from the scaffold, the external force caused structural damage to the brain. The questions I just asked him are designed to initially assess the degree of amnesia we are dealing with."

"And?"

"Well, Mr. Burton...."

"Please, call him Hank. It's how he prefers to be addressed."

She nodded. "Of course. Hank obviously has lost some of his episodic memories, but he hasn't forgotten events from his distant past, such as his place of birth or his parents. That tells us he hasn't suffered complete memory loss."

"But he doesn't remember moving to Houston or me. Does that mean his more recent memories are gone? Just like that?"

"I won't lie to you. That may very well be the case. There is no biological reason for the amnesia. Brain scans show no brain abnormalities or diffuse axonal injury, which is a particularly devastating type of brain injury."

"If there's no lingering brain trauma, then I don't understand why he can't remember."

"Because Hank's fall injured the hippocampus region of his brain, which is responsible for storing more recent memories. This is a crude analogy, but think of it as a USB device to a computer. It stores information we aren't ready to commit to the hard drive because it's too new and we need to more readily access it in a form that we can carry around with us. But as newer files are stored on the USB, space is sometimes required. The files that have been on the USB or in the hippocampus are transferred onto our hard drives simply because our brain becomes accustomed to the memory and can recall it without the hippocampus."

"So you're saying I've been erased because I hadn't been uploaded to his hard drive yet?"

Dr. Anglin nodded.

Fear clutched at my heart, and my fists shook. The anger I'd managed to keep contained was on the verge of exploding. "Am I just gone forever? Will Hank never love me again?" She opened her mouth to speak. "Be honest with me. I need the cold, hard facts. No matter how unpleasant they might be."

"I wish I could honestly give you comforting statistics, but each person's recovery is different. Some patients have a full retrieval of their memories. Others never regain a thing."

"Is there anything I can do to help him remember? Like show him pictures of us or take him on a tour of our life?"

"That's called 'reminder treatment,' and I have to tell you that there is no scientific evidence to support that it works. But I won't tell you not to give it a try. You never know what might respark a memory. It could be something as simple as a word or a smell. Olfactory triggers are sometimes the most powerful. But if a patient does regain memory, it's typically because of spontaneous recovery."

"What does that mean?"

"Basically it means that it will happen all on its own, if it's going to happen at all."

More than anything, I wanted to lash out with my fists, punch holes in walls or turn over the crash carts that lined the hallway. Anything was better than just standing there feeling as if the love I depended on was slipping through my fingers.

"I wish I had a more hopeful and definite prognosis for you, Santi."

I nodded. But hope wasn't something that anyone could give. I'd learned that over the years. It had to come from within, and I had enough love and hope for the future Hank and I had planned.

So I unclenched my fists and released a healthy portion of my anger into the universe. It would do me no good.

Besides, nothing in the world was going to keep me from walking down the aisle and marrying Hank Burton.

I'd proven that once during a rather difficult time in our lives just six months before, and I'd do it again.

"THIS IS fucking ridiculous," Hank yelled. He rose from the couch where I'd just given him some unpleasant news. His tanned face turned red, and he stared at the wall as if he could bring it crumbling down by the sheer force of his will.

I placed my hands on his cheeks, rubbing my fingers through his blond beard. Eventually his breathing returned to normal, and his gaze settled on mine. He blew out a quick puff of air, and his shoulders slumped before he rested his forehead against mine and sighed.

"God, I love you so much," he said. He slid his arms around my waist. As usual, he rested his hands on my butt. It was his safe place, and I was glad my body could bring him comfort.

"And I love you too, my sexy man."

He nodded. "I know. I wouldn't be marrying you if you didn't," he said before kissing the tip of my nose. "So what are we going to do?"

The answer was easy. "I'll quit."

Hank reared back, his mouth hanging open. "What? You can't do that."

Oh yes I could. Ever since Mr. Canales had retired and Mr. Crenshaw became the managing partner at the firm, my professional life had not been as smooth as it once was. It had been a difficult transition for everyone. Felix Canales had always been easygoing and extremely liberal. He was more of a benevolent grandfather than a boss, and he genuinely cared for every person who worked for him. He treated everyone with dignity and respect, and as long as we did our jobs, no matter what was going on in our lives, we were all good as gold in his eyes.

Patrick Crenshaw, on the other hand, had a stick so far up his butt, it was a wonder he could walk like a normal human being. He was the extreme opposite of Mr. Canales. He scowled as if he couldn't escape the smell of shit that followed him around. He reminded me of Meryl Streep's character in *The Devil Wears Prada*. The office would cower in fear before he exited the elevator and made his way to his oversized office. He never said good morning and looked perennially constipated.

Naturally he was a joy to be around.

But he went from bad to worse when he began micromanaging the firm and even attempting to control our personal lives. Mr. Crenshaw had to personally approve time off work if it wasn't medically necessary. He evidently believed the office had grown too slack in billable hours, and he intended to whip us into shape. That was why he rejected my request for leave to marry Hank.

According to my new boss, I had professional duties that could not be shirked.

His real reason for denying the time off had more to do with the fact that he was a staunch Southern Baptist who wasn't pleased to have one, much less two queers in his employ, and he wasn't about to make it easy for two men to break the laws of the shortsighted God he worshipped.

"I don't think I can work there much longer anyway," I finally said.

Hank grabbed my hands and led me to the couch, where we both sat. "You can't quit. This job means everything to you, and you've worked so hard at this firm. Being made partner has been your goal since I've known you."

"Yeah, when Felix was our managing partner. I don't think I would want to be a partner in a firm that Patrick Crenshaw runs. Besides, I doubt the homophobe would make me partner anyway."

"Does Wyatt feel the same way?"

I nodded. "He's looking into other firms and says I should do the same."

"I just hate for you to do this. This job means so much to you."
Hank's face contorted in misery. He understood the importance of our
jobs. It was more than the money that kept us comfortable. We loved
what we did, and it kept us happy.

"I do love my job," I said with a nod. "But I love you more. And
nothing and no one is going to stop me from marrying you. If Patrick
Crenshaw wants to be an asswipe, he can go fuck himself. I'll quit, and
my clients should follow me. I've built quite a list these last ten years.
Hell, maybe I'll even open up my own practice. Be my own boss."

Hank smiled. "And I can build it. Or restore whatever space
you rent."

"That's more like it," I said, brushing my lips against Hank's.
"And it'll be beautiful."

"Just not as beautiful as you."

"That goes without saying," I replied.

That was why I left Canales, Crenshaw, and Emerson and opened
my own law office with Wyatt.

No one was going to stop me from marrying the man I loved.

BUT THAT was then. I had to deal with the present, so I took a deep
breath before walking back into Hank's room. To do what I now had to
would require more will and fortitude than I'd mustered when I
marched into Patrick Crenshaw's office with my resignation letter in
hand. I either had to make Hank remember our life together or get him
to fall in love with me all over again.

Neither was likely to be easy, especially considering Hank's
stubbornness and my cluelessness on how to even begin.

"Hey," Hank said when he saw me.

"Hey yourself," I replied. It was our standard response whenever
someone greeted us that way. Even though the use of "hey" as a
greeting was commonplace in the South, I hated it with a passion. The
word was appropriate if you were calling to a stranger to get his attention,
but for someone you knew, it was too impersonal and a bit rude. At least

to me. Hank hated it for a far simpler reason. His ex-boyfriend Karl had used it excessively, along with "like" and "you know."

He studied me as I sat in the chair that I'd been sleeping in. His eyes were wide, and deep regret filled the baby blues I'd planned on waking up to every morning for the rest of my life. "Why the look?" I asked.

Hank ran his fingers through his short-cropped hair and glanced at me from the corners of his eyes. Though he was six foot three and two hundred pounds, he resembled a child who'd gotten separated from his parents and had stumbled across a kind stranger, who just so happened to be me. "I feel like I've done something wrong."

"What do you mean?"

"Well, why else would you have run out of here after the doctor asked me if I knew who you were?"

Yeah, I hadn't handled that revelation very well. "Sorry about that."

"No need to apologize," he said. "I just want to know who you are."

"My name's Santi Herrera." I offered no more, hoping that the mere mention of my name might be the key he needed to unlock our memories. But Hank just sat in the hospital bed, devoid of recognition or emotion.

"I'd normally introduce myself and say it was nice to meet you, but I suspect there's no need for that, huh?"

I shook my head as I tried to suck my welling tears back. My name meant nothing to him. It appeared as if subtlety wasn't going to work, not as if it had ever worked on Hank before. He preferred to be direct and expected it in kind. Perhaps that was what I needed to do. I just had to wait for the right moment to lay it all out for him. "No, I definitely know who you are," I finally managed.

"How long have we known each other?"

The question was like a stab to my heart. "Three years."

"Damn. That's a bigass gap in my memory."

I nodded and forced a smile. "I'm sure it'll all come back to you soon."

"Is that what the doc thinks?"

"Dr. Anglin's hopeful." Under normal circumstances, I'd be completely honest with Hank. It was one of the strongest foundations of our relationship. But telling the truth wasn't what Hank needed to hear right now. He required hope. Hell, we both did.

"Good," he said before resting his head against the bed.

"Do you need to close your eyes for a bit?"

He shook his head. "Nah. I'll just sit up and wait for Mitch and Darren."

Shit, I hadn't called them to let them know Hank was awake. I also needed to bring Hank's parents up to date. "They won't be here for quite some time."

He curled his lips in annoyance. "Did those bitches drive to Palm Springs for the weekend or something and abandon me here in the hospital? Fuckers! I hope they left Gracie and Picasso with Joe."

My knees unlocked, and I fell into the chair behind me. Not only did Hank think he was still living in San Diego, but according to his recollection, both Gracie and Picasso were still alive. It had taken him six months to get over Picasso's passing. He couldn't handle the memories of his pets that lingered in every square inch of the house he once shared with Mitch and Darren.

What would happen when he found out that both of his beloved pets were gone now?

"So is that where they went?" Hank asked. "To the fuck hotel in Palm Springs?"

"I doubt it. As far as I know, they're still back in San Diego."

Hank nodded before my words had time to sink in. When they did, his mouth hung open and he gazed at me as if he couldn't tell if I was pulling his leg. "Back in San Diego? Am I *not* in San Diego?"

I shook my head. "We're in Houston."

"Texas?"

"Unless you know another Houston," I replied, hoping to jog his memory through our mutual love of sarcasm.

The attempt failed miserably. Hank not only didn't catch my playfulness, but my answer upset him. "What the hell am I doing in Texas?"

"Well, you live here now."

"What?" On the pulse monitor, his heartbeat started a steady rise. "Why the fuck would I move to the red state of Texas? There's nothing for me there!"

I swallowed hard. I'd never been "nothing" to Hank, not from the moment we met. But because of his accident, that was what I'd been relegated to—nothing.

I didn't have time to deal with my emotions. I had to calm the storm brewing in Hank's eyes. I'd never seen Hank this upset. While we had our share of arguments, he'd always been more bluster than anything else. Right now his heaving shoulders and expanding chest marked him a bull ready to charge. "For starters, your parents live in Texas now. They bought some property in Lufkin, and you built their house for them. Your brother, Joe, moved in with them a few months ago."

He eyed me as if I was crazy. "Joe hates Texas. He's lived in California all his life. It's where his job is, and where Soon-yi is too." Soon-yi was Joe's longtime girlfriend. Their breakup had been Joe's catalyst for leaving the state.

"Joe and Soon-yi aren't together anymore."

"What the fuck? Why?"

It was a long and complicated story that involved another man. That much information Hank did not need. "Does it matter?"

Hank paused. He closed his eyes and took several deep breaths. It was Hank's way of trying to calm down. "No, it doesn't," he said at last. "I'm assuming my parents are still together and that their move to Lufkin had nothing to do with a breakup."

"You assume correctly."

"So why did I move to Houston? I didn't just come here to work for my parents and decide to uproot the life I've made in southern California for nothing. What was the reason?"

It was my turn to take several deep breaths. I had no clue how Hank was going to handle the news. "That would be me."

His eyebrows stitched together. "You?" Was that surprise or disgust I heard in his tone?

I nodded. "We're engaged."

Hank's mouth hung open. He resembled a man who'd gone several rounds in a boxing ring. "That's impossible," he said. "I couldn't be marrying you. I'm in love with Karl."

I inhaled sharply. Hank and Karl had broken up two years before we'd even met, and their relationship had been a disaster. How could Hank remember the alcoholic, druggie Karl McClure and not remember me?

"ARE YOU fucking serious?" Mitch squawked into the phone. Whenever Mitch became agitated, his voice rose about two octaves. "He doesn't remember the last few years?"

I shook my head in response even though Mitch couldn't see. I was too distraught to say much else. I'd already communicated the same story to Jill and Hank's parents, and the response had been pretty much the same.

"What's the prognosis?" Darren asked. Although I'd called Mitch's cell, he and Darren had been having lunch at the house, and Mitch had put me on speaker.

"Dr. Anglin isn't sure. She says he might regain his memories of the past few years or not. There's no real way to tell."

"That's bullshit!" Mitch railed. "What about the stuff I bought from Mr. Xiang?" Mitch wasn't a big fan of Western medicine. He preferred the holistic approach of the East. When he and Darren came to Texas after the accident, he'd annoyed the doctors with suggestions of fish oil supplements and antioxidants to help repair memory functions. He even went to a Chinese herbalist to secure some ligustrum, polygonum, ginseng, and other herbs I couldn't recall, but since Hank hadn't been taking anything orally, there was no way for him to ingest them. They still sat in the plastic bag in the hospital room closet.

"I still have them here."

"And have you given it to him yet?"

"He just woke up, Mitch. Besides, you know Hank. If it's not Red Bull or a latte, he's not going to drink it."

Mitch snorted. "Well, I'll shove it down his throat when I see him, and you'll see how quickly his memory improves."

"Hank will get better," Darren added. "I know it."

I smiled. It felt good to know that I had the support of Hank's oldest friends. "From your lips to God's ears."

"We'll make arrangements to fly out this weekend," Darren said. "I'd leave now, but I've been gone a whole week already. My boss has been riding my ass hard."

"So you finally asked your boss out on a date?" I couldn't help but make the joke. Darren had had the hots for his supervisor for a couple of years now. Making the comment made me feel as if perhaps some semblance of normalcy remained in my life.

Darren laughed. "Don't I wish."

"We'll be there soon," Mitch assured me. "You tell Bubble we love him, and that he loves you."

"I will," I said before hanging up the phone.

"Santi!"

I turned around to see Jill trotting down the hallway. When I saw her in her low-cut blouse and her much-too-short shorts, the tears I'd managed to keep at bay poured out my eyes and down my cheeks. In a matter of minutes, she scooped me into her arms and held me close as I let loose the sadness and frustration.

"I'm here," she whispered before delivering a peck to the top of my head. "And we'll get through this together. I promise."

I clutched her and her words, hoping against hope that she was right.

JILL AND I sat in the waiting area down the corridor from Hank's room, and I told her what I had yet to reveal to anyone else.

"So it's more than not remembering you or the past few years. He believes he's still in love with his ex?"

I nodded, gulping down the painful sob that stuck in my throat. "And I don't know what to do with that. How am I supposed to get him to remember our love when he only remembers being in love with

Karl? You know how Hank is. He's a one-man man. When he's committed himself, there *is* no one else."

Jill wiped a stray strand of her freshly dyed red hair from her eyes and nodded. She'd witnessed Hank's devotion over the years. We'd frequented countless clubs when some random guy came up to Hank or tried to catch his eye. Hank rarely noticed. He only ever saw me. Sure, he'd spot a hot guy and grin at a nice butt or fine set of legs. He might be in love with me, but he was still a man. But after the second glance, the guy disappeared from Hank's world as if he'd never existed.

And if someone tried to touch me at a club, well, they were immediately presented with a six-foot-three-inch wall of tattoo and muscle that sternly but kindly informed them about the "look but don't touch policy" he strictly enforced.

Hank was serious about commitment. I belonged to him, and he belonged to me. There was no in-between. That had always given me great comfort.

But the dedication that had previously kept me secure in his love might work against me now.

"Let's deal with things as they come," she finally said. "We could make ourselves sick with worry about what might happen. We can't work that way. We have to hope for the best."

"And prepare for the worst?"

Instead of agreeing, she gripped my hand tightly in hers.

"So I assume Hank doesn't remember why he and Karl broke up?"

I shrugged. "I don't know."

"You didn't tell him?"

I blew out a lungful of air. "I didn't know what to do or say, so I got up and left."

Jill stood and yanked me up next to her. "Well, it's time to fill in the gaps of Hank's memory as far as Karl is concerned. He can't go on thinking he's still in love with that loser."

She was right. It wasn't like we hadn't already had this conversation a couple of years before.

"SO TELL me about him," I said to Hank as we lounged in his bed in San Diego. Hank had yet to move to Houston with me, and I still worked under the kindhearted Felix Canales, who had no trouble with me taking long weekends to spend time with the man I loved.

Hank groaned as he pulled me to his chest. I rested my head upon his flesh, which was slick from our lovemaking. "Why?" he asked. "It's not a pleasant time in my life."

"I just like knowing everything about you," I replied with a kiss. "It makes me feel close to you."

"Closer than this?" He pulled me on top of him and opened his legs for me to rest between them. My hardening dick nuzzled into the crevice of his blond butt. "Since your cock's been up my ass for the last hour, I'd say we've been pretty fucking close already."

I shook my head in pretend frustration. "You know what I mean."

Hank kissed my lips and thrust his ass against my hardening cock. "How about we go for round three first?"

I leaned into his lips, forcing my tongue inside his mouth and drinking in his perpetual sweetness. "You want it?" I asked after breaking contact.

Hank's eyes were crazed with passion. "You know I do. Always."

"Then tell me." I grabbed his legs and unwrapped them from my waist.

Hank's even stare told me he didn't appreciate the detour I was taking. "Are you serious right now?"

I nodded.

"You're just a Meanie McMeanerson," he replied with a pout.

I chuckled. "Out with it already."

Hank sighed. "Fine. What do you want to know?"

"How'd you meet Karl in the first place?"

"Through Dan." Dan Samuelson, an ex-marine, was a good friend of Hank's. They'd known each other for about seven years and met when Hank had volunteered at the local PFLAG chapter. They chaired a pride event together and had become close as a result. He met Karl at some PFLAG event. "Karl had a rough time with his family. They were even less accepting of him being gay than my father was. Henry Burton might have kicked me out, but at least he didn't beat me or send me to an ex-gay conversion camp."

"Fuck! That's awful."

Hank agreed. "Karl was at a pretty low point in his life and was looking for friends. And you know how Dan is."

I did. Dan collected people with problems and dedicated his life to fixing them. That was most likely a holdover from his time in the service. Never leave a man behind and all that. I nodded for Hank to continue.

"Anyway, Dan thought that Karl and I might hit it off, so he gave Karl my number and told him to call me up. He did, and we met for coffee. After that, we started hanging out, and we eventually got together."

"What was he like?"

Hank stared up at me, curiosity narrowing his eyes. "Why are you so interested in Karl McClure? He and I are no longer together, and there's no way in hell that we'd ever get back together again. I have you now, and I couldn't be happier."

"I know that, sexy." I molded my lips to his to drive home the point. "But you've only been in love with two men in your life, me and Karl. I guess I'm just curious as to the kind of guy he was. I mean, you were so in love with him that after you broke up, you went from being a one-man man to, as Mitch would say, a slut flashing his shit all over town. Something had to cause such a change in you."

"I'm gonna kill Mitch," Hank announced. "He's such a fucking hag."

"I'm the one who brought it up, so don't blame him." I sat up and straddled Hank's waist. His cock suddenly came to life and knocked at my back door. "Not now," I said over my shoulder. "Come back later."

Hank twisted his face in exasperation. "That's it. Mitch will die."

I grabbed Hank's hands in mine and laced our fingers together. "You must've been hurt really badly."

He reluctantly nodded. "It made me never want to put my heart on the line again," he admitted. "When things were good, it felt great. I'd never had so much hope in my life. I guess that's why I turned a blind eye to the inner demons. The alcohol. The drugs. The screwing around. I let the potential I saw get in the way of reality. He wasn't the man I wanted him to be. If he could've been, he and I would have been great together. But he wasn't. So I had to choose. It was either him or me, so when I finally kicked him out of my life, I spun out of control. It hurt so bad I wanted to die, and afterward I told myself I could never go through that again." The sadness in Hank's expression vanished almost completely when he cupped my face in his hands. "But then I met you. The sexy fucker who walked right up to me and introduced himself, and I thought, oh hell no! This guy is a player. He's far too smooth to be good for me."

I laughed. "Are you kidding me? You thought *I* was a player?"

Hank nodded and grinned big. "Sure did. But hell if I cared. One look at your gorgeous lips and those brown eyes and I was hooked. It was like you were a vampire and I'd just been glamoured."

"Just call me Eric Northman," I said with a wink. *True Blood* was one of our favorite shows. We watched it religiously, and we both had a crush on Alexander Skarsgård.

"Never," Hank said with a vigorous shake of his head. "Santi Herrera is my one and only love."

I beamed down at him. "And Hank Burton is my one and only love too."

"Good," he said before turning over and pinning me underneath his weight. "Now can we *please* stop talking about Karl? I really want you to fuck me again."

I brought my lips to his. "What a strange coincidence? Because I really want to fuck you again too."

"It's about time!" Hank said into our kiss that led to Hank's body welcoming me back home.

THAT MEMORY played in my mind when we entered Hank's hospital room. Jill wasted no time getting right down to business. She was a no-holds-barred kind of woman who couldn't be reined in by anyone, so I didn't even try.

"Hey there, Butt Munch," she said, addressing Hank by the nickname she'd given him. His narrowed eyes revealed he wasn't sure how to take the greeting. "I'm Jill O'Neal." She charged over to the bed with her hand outstretched. He shook her hand and was about to speak when she interrupted him. "Yeah, yeah, you don't know who I am. Santi filled me in. That's tough. Luckily I'm here to tell you who you are."

Hank bristled. Like Jill, he shot from the hip but didn't take kindly to being told anything. "You're going to tell me who I am when I don't know you from Adam?"

"Not Adam. Jill. J-I-L-L."

He lowered his voice in warning. "Having amnesia doesn't make me an idiot."

Jill grinned. "That's good to know. Because that means your tumble didn't completely scramble your noggin, right?"

Hank glanced from Jill to me. He clearly didn't know how to take her.

"I'll take that as a yes," she continued. "Look, Santi here is my best friend, and the two of you have been together for three years. You have a love you only really see in the movies. I mean every time you look at him, your eyes light up as if you're seeing him for the first time. It's so sweet that it's sometimes sickening. I was there when you two first met when Santi walked up to you in front of Rich's."

"In San Diego?" he asked me instead of Jill.

"Yes," she answered for me. "I'd finally convinced him to take a vacation from work, and he saw you on our third night there. And from that moment, I didn't really see Santi again until it was time to go home. The two of you couldn't get enough of each other—in or out of bed. Then, after you got engaged and you moved here, I figured the two of you would give the mattress springs a break. Boy was I wrong! Slipping a ring on your finger caused the two of you to shame all the bunnies in the world. And you couldn't wait to walk down the aisle and become Santi's husband. You told me that over lunch a few weeks before your accident. You said that you'd never been happier in your life and that Santi made you feel like no other man had ever made you feel before." She paused, evidently to let the information sink in. "Do you not remember that?"

Hank sighed and his gaze drifted from Jill back to me. Even before he spoke, I knew the answer. It was as plain as the overgrown beard on his face. "Look, I'm not saying I think either of you is handing me a bucket full of crap. I have to believe that what you both have told me is true. I really don't know any different. But I don't remember any of what you're telling me. They're just words to me."

"Bullshit!" Jill said. "What you and Santi had wasn't just words. A love like that lives in your heart and in your soul. Anyone who ever saw the two of you together got that right off the bat."

"Jill, stop," I said, putting my hand on her shoulder.

"I will not," she replied. "Hank *needs* to remember."

"Yelling at me isn't going to make that happen," Hank said. "All you're doing is upsetting me. Nothing else."

Jill grumbled. "So you're telling me you can look at this man and his gorgeous face and you can gaze into those dark eyes and tell me you don't feel a thing for him?"

I didn't want to hear the answer. "Please, stop!"

Jill turned to stare at me, completely oblivious to what she almost made Hank say. Hank, however, appreciated the interruption. He'd never been the kind of man who liked hurting anyone, even if he didn't know them, and he undoubtedly knew that the truth as it was right now would likely have devastated me.

"We can't stop now," Jill said. "We can make him remember."

I took Jill's hands in mine. "I love you, and I appreciate what you're trying to do. It means the world to me. But you and I know that we can't *make* anyone do anything. Especially the two of you." I glanced between them. "You're both even more stubborn than me, if that's at all possible."

"I am pretty stubborn," Hank admitted with a nod. "I *do* remember that."

The impish grin that stretched across Hank's fuzzy face made me want to hop on that bed and press my lips to his. But more than just Hank's amnesia prevented me from doing that. When he noticed me looking at him, he averted his eyes, just the way he used to whenever he'd managed to snag another gay man's attention.

His love for me had been the rampart that kept others away. Now I found myself on the other end of the wall Karl's memory had reconstructed.

"I'M SORRY about that," I told Hank after I asked Jill to wait for me in the hall.

Hank shook his head. "No need. She just loves you and is trying to help her friend. I know that."

"Yeah. She can be a lioness sometimes when it comes to me."

Hank snorted. "I hadn't noticed."

After a forced laugh, we sat in uncomfortable silence. The last time that had happened between us, I was getting ready to leave San Diego, and both of us were wondering if we'd ever see each other again. "Look, I know you don't know who I am."

"I'm sorry about that," he said. His wide blue eyes told me he spoke the truth, but I didn't need Hank's body language to tell me that. If Hank said it, he meant it.

"I know, and I'm not going to lie to you. The fact that you don't remember tears me apart." Before Hank could speak, I continued. "But I don't say that to make you feel bad. It is what it is, I suppose. It doesn't make it hurt any less, though."

"I'd imagine not." Silence once again descended, but this time Hank didn't look away. He suspected I had something to say, and he was giving me time to collect both the words and the strength to give it voice.

"What's the last thing you remember?"

Hank leaned against the mattress and closed his eyes. "Mitch, Darren, and I just got back from Hawaii, and Karl—" He stopped and opened his eyes, uncertain if he should continue. I nodded for him to keep going. "Well, Karl and I had fought because he didn't want me to go. He wanted me to stay in town and be with him because he couldn't get time off work and go with us. But we'd already made the arrangements, so I went. When I got back, I planned a special weekend for just the two of us. We were going to drive up to San Francisco. I'd booked a nice hotel there, and the last thing I remember is going to bed excited about our romantic getaway."

"And what year was that?"

"2010."

"And it's 2014 now."

He nodded. "I'm aware of that."

"Here's something you might not be aware of. About a year and a half ago, you told me about this San Francisco trip you took with Karl."

His eyes widened in surprise. "I did?"

95

"Yup. Want me to tell you how it turned out?"

"I want to say yes, but something tells me I should say no."

"Do you mind if I tell you anyway?"

After a few seconds, Hank motioned for me to continue. "You did take Karl to San Francisco. You'd hoped the time alone would rekindle your relationship. The two of you had been having problems. Karl had been drinking excessively and even started taking crystal meth when he went out to the clubs."

"I told you that?"

I nodded. "You'd hoped that being away from the new friends he'd made would get his mind off the drugs and the partying and remind him of how much you two loved each other. Things didn't turn out the way you hoped they would. You went to a club, and while you ordered your Red Bull, which you drink more than water by the way, you came back to find Karl popping pills on the dance floor. You argued. He called you a nag, and you left."

Hank grimaced. "I'm not a nag."

"I know," I said before continuing. "He didn't go back to the hotel that night, so you drove around looking for him. You couldn't find him. You searched for him the whole day. The following evening you went back to the club where you argued, and you found Karl there in the back room, fucking someone while another guy ate out his ass."

Hank opened his mouth to speak, but no words came out. Tears pooled in the corners of his eyes.

"You drove back to San Diego by yourself. A week later Karl called you, pissed off about you leaving him in San Francisco. That was when you'd had enough. You told him it was over. That you couldn't be around him if he was going to continue drinking and doing drugs. He cried. Said that he'd enter rehab, which he did, for three days. He checked himself out and made a beeline for a sex party, where he got hammered and high and humped anything that presented itself to him."

Hank shook his head. "No. It can't have gotten that bad. That can't be true."

Tears welled in his eyes. The information I'd just shared with him tore his soul apart, but I had to do it. Hank didn't love Karl. He loved me. "But it is," I finally said. "Ask Mitch. He was at the sex party. He was the one who told you that Karl was there."

"Why the hell are you telling me all this?" Hank asked. His face was red. His anger had dried up his pooling tears. "Do you think breaking my heart will somehow make me magically remember you?"

"I wouldn't mind if it did, but no. That's not why." I rose from the chair beside his bed. "I know you better than anyone, Henry Gale Burton. You work better when you have all the facts. You must remember that about yourself, and if you think you're still in love with Karl, then you deserve to know everything about him that you forgot."

"I need to be alone right now." Hank turned to look out the hospital room window.

I wanted to touch his forearm and run my fingers through the golden fur that spread up his arm. Whenever I caressed him, I'd been able to calm him, to chase away the problems that threatened to overwhelm him.

I didn't. If he flinched at my touch or got angry, my already broken heart would shatter.

So I turned around and walked out the door.

CHAPTER

Six

A FEW days after regaining full consciousness, Hank was transferred to Memorial Hermann. There he would undergo the final steps of the rehabilitation process that would hopefully help restore him to the man he had been before the accident. Since Dr. Anglin had privileges at Memorial Hermann, she was able to continue to supervise Hank's care.

So far she was more than pleased with Hank's progress. After a few weeks, his motor skills had recovered almost 100 percent, and with the exception of his memory loss, Hank suffered no mental or speech impairments.

It was truly a miracle.

Now it was time for Hank to go home. Where that would be, however, was still undecided.

"He should come home with us," Sharon said from the chair across from me. She let her eyes linger on mine before surveying the expressions of everyone else in the room where Dr. Anglin had taken us to sort out the logistics. When her dark gaze finally returned to me, a tense smile extended across her lips. "I'm sorry, Santi. I really am. But I'm his mother, and he doesn't remember you."

I didn't respond. I could only stare at my hands. When was the last time I trimmed my fingernails?

"Santi's his fiancé," Jill replied, immediately coming to my rescue. "That's where Hank belongs."

"If Hank remembered him, I'd agree with you," Mitch said. He and Darren sat on the opposite side of Jill. "But the last thing he remembers before the accident is San Diego. He has to go back there. To the home he remembers."

The last time I trimmed them was a couple of nights before Hank's fall. We were lounging on the couch watching *Scary Movie 5*. Hank loved those awful spoof movies. I thought they were terrible, but since I made him sit through actual scary movies, I had to grin and bear the ones he liked to watch too. I just didn't always pay attention. That night, I'd trimmed my nails and taken care of my cuticles while Hank bellowed next to me.

Every time something stupid happened, such as Charlie Sheen getting racked or Lindsay Lohan being, well, Lindsay Lohan, he asked me if I had seen it. I smiled and nodded. He then called me a liar, told me he loved me anyway, and drew me close.

To me, that was home. With Hank and me in each other's arms.

"But going back isn't going to help him remember," Jill argued. She turned to Dr. Anglin. "It seems to me that Hank needs to return to the life he led before his accident. That's the only way he's going to remember the part of his life that he's forgotten. Would you agree?"

"I can't say what he will or won't remember," she answered. "Being surrounded by the people who love him will make the transition back to his life much easier. He's been through a lot, and he's going to need a lot of care and support."

"We've been there for him for most of his adult life," Darren said. "We'll always be there for him."

"I'm his mother," Sharon reiterated. "I've been there for him since the day he was born." She gazed up at her husband, who sat quietly next to her. "Right, Henry?"

Henry didn't reply. His gaze remained fixed on me.

"No," I mumbled. "He's going home with me."

A smile stretched across Henry Burton's face before he finally averted his gaze to the others sitting around the table.

"He doesn't know you or your home," Sharon objected. "That won't be good for him."

Mitch nodded. "I agree. I know you love him, Santi. I really do. And you two are great together, but I think going home with you is just going to stress him out more than anything else."

"And going back to a city that has changed isn't?" Jill asked. "No matter where he goes, Hank's going to be uncomfortable. That's why he should be with the man he'd decided to spend the rest of his life with."

"I disagree," Darren said.

"Me too." Sharon gripped the edge of the table tightly. "He's *my* son, and he's coming home with me."

I stood up, and the gaze of every person around the table settled on me. "I know everyone in this room loves Hank. He's truly a lucky man to have so many people willing to disrupt their lives to help him get better. That's a testament to the kind of man he is and the kind of love we all have for him. But we need to straighten out some things here."

I turned to Darren and Mitch and smiled at them. They were two of the sweetest men I'd ever met. There was no doubt in my mind how much they loved Hank. They'd seen him through some of the most difficult times of Hank's life. They'd been his rock and his lifeline. It was only natural they'd want to take care of him now. "You two have been such an integral part of Hank's life. You were there for him when things between him and his family weren't great. The three of you became brothers, a bond that is just as strong as any that blood can make. You want to be there like you've done for so long, and I love you both for that."

Mitch smiled through his tears. "We love you too."

I moved to Sharon and Henry. I took Sharon's hand in mine and placed my free hand on Henry's shoulder.

"Don't try your lawyer tactics on me," his mother said. She crossed her arms and turned away. "I'm his mother, and I'm not leaving here without my son." Her eyes briefly flitted to mine. "He needs me."

"Of course he does. You're his parents. Who could possibly love him more than the two people who created him? I'm not a parent, so I don't know a thing about the strength of such a bond, but I know that as parents, you want more than anything to take your boy home and nurse him back to health like you did when he got the chicken pox in third grade. I get that. I really do."

Sharon nodded as if I'd made my point for her.

I walked over to the head of the table and placed my hands on the surface. "But despite all those wonderful relationships, Hank is still going home with me."

Sharon started to speak, but Henry silenced her. "Let Santi talk," he said.

She reluctantly sat back and said nothing while I smiled at Henry in appreciation. "I know you all don't think it's the right decision because he doesn't remember me. But he will. I have faith in that. And even if Hank doesn't remember, I do. And I can remember it for the both of us, use that love to make him whole again."

"That's too much pressure for him," Darren argued.

I couldn't disagree with that. "Maybe, but until he's ready to walk with me down the road we started traveling down together, I'll carry him. I'll be his strength, his rock, his lifeline. Whatever he needs to make a full recovery."

Mitch's smile told me he'd no longer protest, and even though Darren still didn't like it, my words made him feel better. Sharon, however, still seemed hell-bent on taking her son home with her.

"You may have forgotten this because of everything that we've been going through, but today was supposed to be our wedding day. Today I was going to walk down the aisle with Hank and pledge my love and fidelity to him and promise to be there for him no matter what. I might not have had the chance to make that vow before a member of the clergy, but I make it now in front of all of you. Hank will be my husband, and until he tells me differently, his home will forever be with me."

That did it. Tears streamed down Sharon's face, and Jill practically beamed up at me. Darren and Mitch opened their mouths to speak, but their lips didn't seem capable of forming words. Surprisingly, it was Henry who spoke. "That settles that," he said before standing. "Let's go get Hank packed so he can go home."

Everyone nodded. As they filed out of the room, Henry stopped beside me. He placed his hand on my shoulder, gave it a big squeeze, and then followed the others.

FROM HIS hospital bed, Hank observed everyone as they set to task gathering his things. His parents took care of the flowers and balloons that had arrived this past week from his friends and his coworkers. Pork Chop, who was still guilt ridden for his part in Hank's accident, kept tabs on Hank's progress through Vaughn Templeton, Hank's foreman, and sent a different floral arrangement each week. On Monday Hank received a bouquet of petunias. Last week it was sunflowers.

What Pork Chop lacked in skill, he more than made up in contriteness and consideration.

Mitch and Darren assembled the pictures I'd brought from the condo. There were photos of us with Darren, Mitch, and Picasso in San Diego and Palm Springs. There was another when we went on an Atlantis cruise. I grinned at the camera while Hank glanced mischievously at me. Hank resembled a child eyeing a piece of cake, and I just happened to be that cake. His expression told everyone who saw the photo that Hank only had eyes for me. I'd hoped the photos might spark a memory, but Hank never reacted to any of the images. He said it was like gazing at a life he knew nothing about.

That had been a tough day. One of many, actually. But right now that didn't matter. My only concern was getting Hank back to our home.

So I packed his clothes in his suitcase while Jill crawled up on the bed and sat beside Hank, who watched us like a man about to be sentenced by a jury of his peers.

"I don't know about this," he said.

"What don't you know about?" she asked.

"Going home with Santi," Hank answered. "I don't know him."

"Of course you do," Jill said. "He's been here like every day since the accident. You've seen him more than any of us while you've been recuperating."

"Still. It just doesn't feel right."

I didn't respond, and I sure didn't dare gaze in Hank's direction. His words shredded through me like a power saw.

"He's not exactly a stranger," Mitch said. "Besides the fact that you've been a couple for three years, you've spent time together since you've woken up. It's not like we're asking you to go home with some anonymous trick. Which you used to do quite regularly."

Henry shot Mitch a glance that made him stop talking immediately. While Hank's dad had made huge leaps in accepting his son as a gay man, he still didn't want to hear about his son's sexual escapades with other men. "Son, can I give you some advice?"

Hank shrugged. His normally friendly eyes lost all their warmth. "I suppose."

Henry caught on to the mood right away. He visibly bristled. "You suppose?"

"That's what I said," Hank repeated. He crossed his arms over his chest and locked eyes with his father. That wasn't good at all. Hank was assuming his combative pose.

"Where's all this coming from?" his father asked. "I haven't seen this defiant attitude since you were a teenager."

"You mean when you kicked me out of the house for being a fag?"

Hank's question exploded in the room like a pistol shot, and an eerie silence filled the air. No one moved or said a word. We could only watch as Henry's face turned redder with each passing moment while a snarl curled Hank's upper lip. What was going on? Hank had never behaved like this before things between him and his parents improved. He'd always made a concerted effort to play nice, despite all the anger he'd suppressed toward his parents.

"Honey, please," his mother said.

"Honey?" Hank asked. "You haven't spoken to me in years. Now you're calling me honey all of a sudden?"

Sharon recoiled from her son as if he'd turned a gun on her.

"What the fuck is going on with you?" Darren asked from across the room. "That's all water under the bridge. You're not in that place anymore."

Hank rose from the bed. He no longer wore the hospital gown that made him appear vulnerable and fragile. Dressed in his usual attire of shorts and a bejeweled muscle shirt, his body housed an excessive amount of confidence and aggression. "You know what, Darren? I'm getting pretty fucking tired of people telling me where I am. That's all anybody does. This is how you are now, Hank. You love Santi, Hank. Karl was an asswipe, Hank. You live in Texas now, and you get along with the parents who treated you like shit. Do you know how frustrating it is to be told by others what I am, what I should do, and where I should go? Why don't I get to make any decisions? It's my fucking life. Or did I lose that right when I lost my memory?"

No one replied. Jill rose from the bed and went to Sharon, who was sobbing into her hands. Darren turned to stare out the window while Mitch patted him on the back and gazed at Hank in wide-eyed shock. Henry took a step toward his son. In response, Hank closed the distance between him and his father.

The two of them were peas in a pod, not that either of them would ever admit it.

"Hank, you're right." My words halted Hank and Henry's progress toward each other and gained the attention of everyone in the room.

"What?" Hank and his father asked in unison.

"You're a grown man, and you should have the right to make decisions that affect you. I guess we all owe you an apology. We've just been so wrapped up in taking care of you that we've obviously overlooked the fact that you're not in that coma anymore."

"No. I'm not."

I nodded and moved between him and his father. "But no one's done any of those things because we're trying to hurt you. It's just the opposite, actually. We all love you very much. And we want to see you get better. To return to the man you were before your accident. That's what you want, right? To remember what you've forgotten?"

Hank studied the ceiling in deep thought. "Yeah, I guess it is."

"And that's why we—I want you to come home with me. That was where you were living before the accident. I know you don't feel as if you know me from Adam. From your perspective, you know Mitch and Darren the best in this room. I'm just a stranger, and Jill is just my annoying fag hag that you've resigned yourself to putting up with for the time being."

"Fuck you too," Jill said. She flipped me the bird and blew me a kiss at the same time. She knew exactly what I was doing because she'd seen me in action before. I was going all lawyery on Hank, treating him as if he was a witness I was leading down a path I wanted him to go.

"As for your parents," I said, turning to pat Henry on the shoulder, "you're still angry about your shared past. What you're feeling isn't wrong." Henry snuffed and gazed askance at me. "It *isn't* wrong when you look at it from Hank's perspective. For us, time has passed. It hasn't for Hank."

"Where are you going with this?" Hank asked. His arms still rested across his chest.

Mitch stood beside Hank. "I think I know where Santi's going with this."

"And that would be?" he asked, now eyeing Mitch instead of me.

"Look at it like this, Bubble. You want us to accept you are where you are, right?" When Hank nodded, he continued. "Well, don't you think you have to also be willing to accept that things have changed? I've known you longer than most people in this room, and I know you've wanted a better relationship with your parents. Before your accident, you had it. You might not remember it, but it's true. Wouldn't you like to remember all that instead of being as pissed off as you are right now?"

Hank shifted his focus to his father and then his mother. His yearning for a better relationship was apparent. It was as if he wanted to see past the resentment, but the haze of bitterness kept clouding his vision.

When Hank rested his gaze back on me, I took a few steps closer. "Whether you know it or not, I really believe I'm the key to all that. Our relationship changed me as much as it did you. I didn't seek friendships or really live my life. I worked all the time. Focused more on my career than on the people."

"I know that's right," Jill added with a playful snuff.

I rolled my eyes at her and continued. "And dating? Who had time for that? I might have had a good paycheck and a comfortable life, but I had no one to share it with. Then I met you, and you were like a gift from the heavens. This big, hairy miracle that God had handed to me that made me realize my career wasn't the most important factor for success. It was how we loved others and how others loved us." I closed the physical distance between us even more. Hank lowered his hands from his chest, and I took them in mine. I longed for the days when he caressed my body before resting his rough, warm hands at the swell of my ass, but no desire burned in Hank's eyes. With any luck, I'd find the right kindling that would once again set it ablaze.

"I just don't know," he said.

I nodded. "And that's why I want to try to share that gift with you again. Because if I can, then you will remember not only what you've forgotten, but you will regain everything you've accomplished."

Hank sighed before withdrawing his hands from mine. "All right," he said with a nod at me. "Take me to your home."

And while there was still no emotion tied to the word "home," it didn't lessen the exhilaration that sped through my body.

Hank was *finally* coming home, and with any luck, being back in our condo might be just what we both needed. That had certainly been the case a few years ago.

"WE'RE HERE," I told Hank, who stood on the front porch of the condo. He was freshly off the plane from San Diego, wearing his purple "Yay Gay" shirt from the Human Rights Campaign store. In California, people rarely took notice of it, or any of the other flashy outfits he sometimes wore, but every time he wore such clothing in south Texas, people gawked. I imagined most couldn't believe that a man as straight-looking as Hank was gay. I'd lost count of the many disappointed women who realized they'd been barking up the wrong tree. And if the shirt didn't tell them Hank was a lover of men, his big pink Hello Kitty suitcase sure did the trick.

It was refreshing being in love with a man who loved who he was and didn't give one shit what anyone else thought.

"Are we just gonna stand here?" Hank asked. He moved into me, leaning the length of his body against mine. "Because I'm dying to get you inside, strip you naked, and eat your ass."

My cock immediately stood at attention. Hank's rim jobs were pretty damn spectacular. I fumbled the keys out of the pocket of my shorts. "We're going in."

Hank grinned. "Oh yes we are."

Fuck! After two years Hank and I were still like horny teenage boys around each other. I hoped that would never change. I unlocked the door and swung it open. Hank was about to step through the doorway when I put my hand on his chest and stopped him cold.

"What?"

I took the suitcase from his hand and placed it to the side. I grabbed the backpack from Hank's shoulder and set it on top of Hello Kitty.

"What are you doing?" he asked, clearly suspicious.

I turned him around so that Hank's back faced the open door. I wrapped my arms around his waist and cupped his ass in my hands.

He leered down at me. "Can't wait 'til we get inside, huh? I like that."

Before Hank could crane his neck to plant a kiss, I bent my knees, grabbed the backs of his upper thighs, and lifted him off the ground. He immediately wrapped his arms around my shoulders. "What the hell are you doing?" he asked. "I weigh two hundred pounds! You're gonna hurt yourself."

"I'm not a weakling," I said. The strain in my voice was apparent, and my legs had begun to shake.

"I never said you were, but I'm heavy."

No shit. Carrying a man so much taller than me wasn't easy. "I'm taking you across the threshold," I said, taking my first tentative steps forward.

Hank laughed. "Silly man. You're going to hurt yourself."

I shook my head. I couldn't talk, walk, *and* carry Hank at the same time. Once I had officially crossed the boundary, I slowly lowered Hank to the wooden floor. "There," I said, embarrassed by my heavy breathing. I obviously needed to make more room in my schedule for the gym. "Now you're officially home."

Hank held my face in his hands. Whenever he did that, I'd let him do just about anything he wanted. That gesture always made me feel special and safe. "That was very sweet," he said before kissing me tenderly on the lips. His beard scraped across my cheek, and he slid his tongue inside my mouth. My breathing became even more labored.

"I'm so glad you're here," I managed to say when I broke free of our kiss for a few seconds.

"Oh me too," Hank gasped. "Now I can kiss you every day." He clutched at my back before resting his hands on my ass. "And feel you." He leaned in and inhaled deeply at the crook of my neck. "And smell you."

"I'm all yours."

He nodded. "I know. And I'm all yours too."

"I'm glad."

Hank rested his forehead against mine. "Now about the wedding."

We hadn't discussed the wedding since Picasso's passing. Hank hadn't been ready to discuss such a celebratory event in the wake of losing his handsome boy. All plans had been placed on temporary hold. Although I was champing at the bit to get married, I had faith it would happen. "What do you want to discuss?"

"It's time to set a date. If that's okay with you."

I squealed in delight. "Are you fucking kidding me? Of course it's okay with me." I wrapped my arms around Hank and lifted him off the ground again. This time my arms didn't strain and my legs didn't wobble. Love and excitement gave me all the strength I needed.

"I'm not used to being lifted," Hank said. His face twisted in equal parts amusement and unease. "I don't know how I feel about this."

"What? Are you worried this makes you less butch?"

Hank snorted. "Please. Taking it up the ass pretty much answers that."

"So does Hello Kitty," I told him with a big grin.

He slid his legs around my waist, and as I walked him over to the leather couch, he turned toward the open front door. "Shit! My stuff's still outside."

"We'll get it. Don't worry." I dropped him back onto the couch. When I fell on top of him, Hank grunted from the weight of my body.

A sly smile slid across his lips before he growled from the back of his throat. "I kinda like you taking charge. Putting me where you want me and taking what you want."

"Oh, believe me, I plan on taking you over and over again."

Someone giggled from behind the couch.

"What the fuck?"

Hank immediately scrambled out from underneath me and went into defensive mode. He squared his shoulders and he clenched his hands as he rounded the couch. When he spotted who was hiding on the other side, his hard expression softened. "Jildo?"

Jill sprang up from behind the couch. "Surprise!"

The lights suddenly went on inside the condo, and a chorus of voices yelled, "Surprise!" Our friends Jesse and Mario, whom I'd shanghaied into putting together a party for Hank that weekend, popped out of the kitchen, along with a few other friendly faces.

Everyone wore huge grins.

"We were hoping for a show," Jesse said with a wink. He was wearing a T-shirt with the word *pitcher* across the front.

His boyfriend Mario, who wore a matching shirt with *catcher* stitched across it, nodded. "And we would have gotten one too, had *someone* been able to keep her trap shut."

All eyes settled on Jill, who flipped them off. "Suck it."

"What's going on?" I asked.

Jill eyed me as if I'd just asked her how many eggs were in a dozen. "What do you think is going on, Nostradamus?"

I glared at her in mock hatred. "You know what I mean."

"For a lawyer, you don't ask very good questions sometimes."

"For a hairstylist, you're not very mindful of your roots," I replied with an arch to my eyebrow.

"Bitch!" she said with a grin.

"Cocksucker."

"I am," she said with a nod. "And I'm damn good at it too."

Hank wrapped his arms around me. "Not as good as my Santi."

"Is that a challenge?" she asked.

Oh shit. "No, Jill. It's not," I answered. The last thing anyone needed was Jill attempting to throw down in a cock-swallowing contest.

"Because I'll do it. Right here. Right now," she said.

"Maybe some other time," Hank replied. He retrieved his luggage from the porch and closed the door. "How about we get the party started instead?"

"Wouldn't a suck-off contest do that?" Mario asked.

I groaned. "No one is getting sucked off in this condo."

Hank glowered at me. "Um, excuse me, but I have a problem with that."

I shook my head. "You know what I mean!"

He glanced over at Jill, who nodded. "You're right, Jildo. For a lawyer, he's not very clear sometimes."

"You're impossible, you know that?" I asked Hank.

Hank took me in his arms and brushed his lips across mine. "I do. And you're gonna have to put up with that for the rest of your life."

I grinned up at him. "Do I have to?"

He nipped at my nose and nodded.

"Then I guess we should set that date."

"How about July 7?" he asked.

That was the day we met at Rich's. "It's perfect."

"Not as perfect as you," he said before he once again pressed his lips against mine.

"All right, that's enough!" Jill complained. "The two of you are going to give me diabetes."

Hank released me and smiled at the room. "Now we've definitely got a reason to celebrate. Next summer I'll officially be Mr. Hank Herrera."

"What? You're going to take my name?"

"Why not?" he asked with a shrug. "I love everything about you, including your name."

"Diabetic coma in three, two…."

I ignored Jill's mocking. "How about we take each other's names instead?"

"You mean hyphenate?"

I nodded, and Hank studied the ceiling. "Hank Burton-Herrera does have a nice ring to it," he said after a few seconds.

I couldn't agree more. "Then hyphenate it is."

Jill was suddenly at our side, poking us both on our shoulders. "Are you done?"

We both nodded.

"Good," she said. She handed me a beer and Hank a Red Bull. She held her glass in the air and turned to the other guests. "To the future Misters Burton-Herrera."

Everyone raised their drinks in congratulations, and I didn't even try to wipe the cheesy-ass grin from my lips. This had been one of the most momentous days of my life, and I couldn't have been happier if I tried.

As Hank and I once again stood outside our condo, sadness forced my shoulders to slump. This homecoming would not be as memorable as the first. At least not in a good way. I didn't let that stop me from hoping for the best. I took a deep breath and plastered on a smile. "Welcome home," I said after swinging the front door to the condo open.

This time Hank crossed the threshold under his own steam and carried his Hello Kitty suitcase and Pork Chop's flowers inside. He surveyed the interior, the cherrywood console on which sat the thirty-two-inch flat screen, the coffee table with wicker basket drawers, the big fluffy chair where Hank usually typed up contracts for his clients, and the chocolate brown leather couch where we snuggled and sometimes made love.

He glanced over at the sofa table. On it was the glass lamp with a beige cloth shade. It was the first item we had purchased together shortly after Hank moved in with me. Underneath it sat a picture of Hank with Picasso in his lap. To the left was one of Hank with his arms wrapped around me. Jill had snapped that photo at the surprise party where we'd finally set a date for our wedding.

All around us were remnants of our life together and our differing personalities.

Hank's red high-tops still sat where he'd left them, neatly placed by the front door, while one of my tennis shoes peeked out from under the couch. Its mate lay on its side a few feet away. The leis from our last trip to Hawaii hung over the mantel of the fireplace, next to Hank's collection of model antique cars and my superhero figurines. I'd been collecting those since I was a child. The DVDs visible through the front glass of the television console displayed Hank's love of comedies and

111

action and adventure. My movies were of the horror and tearjerker variety.

But none of the many happy reminders that proudly announced our love caused one flicker of recognition in Hank's eyes. Although his eyes briefly lit up at the model cars he'd always loved, he gazed past everything as if he'd entered a stranger's house, despite the fact that he now stood on the same spot where we'd decided to take each other's last names.

"Where do I put these?" he asked, holding out the flowers.

"The usual place," I responded, hoping that instinct might take over and lead Hank to where he needed to go.

He arched an eyebrow at me. Intuition clearly wasn't going to offer assistance. "And that would be?"

"Just put them on the kitchen counter," I said with a nod to my left. "I'll get a better vase."

He nodded. While he set the flowers down, I returned the photos I'd brought to the hospital to their place on top of the console.

"What about this?"

I turned around to see Hank with his suitcase once again in his hand. Hello Kitty waved at me from the casing, as if saying, *I remember you, Santi.*

I exhaled silently before answering. "Our bedroom's down the hall. Last door on the right. You can just leave the suitcase on the bed, and I'll put your stuff where it belongs."

I walked into the kitchen to grab the crystal vase under the sink. I turned on the faucet to rinse off the dust and fill the vessel with water. Perhaps talking would make things less awkward. "You know, there's a story behind this vase. We saw it at the Bellagio in Las Vegas. We went there for Darren's birthday last year. Remember?"

"You know I don't," Hank replied. His tone and demeanor had turned aloof.

I glanced up from drying the vase with a washcloth. The lack of familiarity in his blue eyes was like taking a jackhammer to my heart. "Right. Sorry."

"You were saying."

I swallowed hard. Hank was obviously growing tired of these one-way trips down memory lane. But how else was I going to get him to remember if I didn't at least try? "Never mind," I said after placing the petunias in the vase and moving them to the center of the kitchen table. "I can tell you some other time. You look tired."

Hank surveyed the room and sighed. "I am."

He was clearly talking about more than just physical exhaustion. I could read Hank like a book. The emotional wear and tear of this situation was taking a serious toll. His muscles were tense and his jaw was clenched. Whenever life hit him this hard, I'd cradle him in my arms. He'd take three big inhalations at the crook of my neck and then I'd kiss him until his troubles drifted away. Afterward, we'd usually end up naked and sweaty.

That wasn't going to happen today or in the foreseeable future. No matter how much I longed to be naked in his arms again.

"Well, go lie down, then," I said, grabbing Hank's suitcase. "I'll unpack your things after you wake up."

"Um."

I paused with my hand on the suitcase handle. "What's wrong?"

"I don't want to upset you."

I practically heard Hello Kitty whisper, *Uh oh*. Whatever was distressing him was also making him miserable. His lips drew into a flat line of despair.

"Don't worry about me. I'm a big boy." I faked a smile. Typically that wouldn't have worked, but on the new Hank, it did the trick. He nodded and smiled back. "What is it?"

"We need to talk about the sleeping arrangements."

It would have been easier if Hank had actually cut out my heart. "I see," I said, trying to maintain the grin on my face. Even though I expected this might happen, I'd managed to convince myself it wouldn't. That returning to where we lived together would somehow bring his memories back. I'd obviously been a fool.

"I know we're experimenting on getting my memories back, and I've agreed to that. It's just. Well, sharing a bed with a man I don't know isn't really what I should be doing right now."

"Why? Because you've never done that before?" I asked. My tone was snippier than I'd intended. But how was I supposed to process this? I'd finally gotten the man I loved home, and though I realized we wouldn't be having sex, I'd been content with the thought of once again lying next to him, of drifting off to sleep to his snore, of the warmth that emanated from him like a radiator. "We made out at Rich's and dry humped on the dance floor within the first few hours of meeting each other. We went back to your place and fucked like rabbits on Viagra."

He nodded. "That does sound like me."

His comment rattled me. Not because I had any delusion that Hank was virginal prior to meeting me. He had been single and was the most gorgeous man I'd ever met. He'd had dozens of men on standby, and once we got together, he had to make it known he was off the market.

But the Hank who loved me never discussed his sexual life before me. Hell, he used to hate even talking about Karl. What we did before each other just didn't matter. Plus, the thought of either of us with anyone else never really sat well with Hank or with me.

It seemed that consideration and those reservations were gone along with Hank's memory.

"You okay?" he asked. "You haven't said anything for a couple of minutes."

I slowly nodded. "I'll be fine," I answered. "I guess I'm disappointed. That's all. And I don't really see what the big deal is."

"What do you mean?"

I stood by the kitchen counter. I reached out to touch him, but I hesitated. My hand hovered in the air between us before I brought it back and shoved it in the pocket of my shorts. If he flinched at my touch, I'd likely run out the front door screaming. "I know we aren't going to be having sex. So you don't need to worry about me crossing the line or being inappropriate. I promise to be a gentleman and respect your boundaries."

"I appreciate that," he said with a pat to my shoulder. It was the first time Hank had consciously touched me since he'd awoken from the coma. I'd envisioned the first caress to be slow and loving, the kind of gesture reserved for the love of your life. What I got instead was how someone might greet a stranger who appeared down on his luck. "But it's just not right for us to be in the same bed together."

"And why is that? We are engaged. I know you don't remember, but we are."

He nodded at me as if he were tired of having to be reminded of something he'd rather forget. "I know. That's why I'm here. To see if the life everyone's told me about comes back to me. But you need to realize that I'm not where you are. I'm somewhere else. I can't just switch that off."

I was just about to ask what Hank was talking about when I figured it out on my own. When I snorted in a mixture of derision and laughter, he peered down at me with eyes half-closed. "This is about Karl, isn't it?"

Hank didn't answer. He stared at me, completely devoid of emotion.

"You won't sleep in the same bed with me because you still believe you're in love with Karl? After what everyone, including Mitch, has told you?"

"If you know me like you claim to do, then you should remember that I don't just do something because someone tells me I should or shouldn't. I do what I want and what feels right. And yeah, I've heard the stories about my past with Karl, but to me, those things never happened."

How was I supposed to argue with that? I sure as hell wanted to scream and throw things. I wanted to tell Hank he was being stubborn and that Karl wasn't worth any consideration whatsoever. I wanted to wrap my arms around Hank, press my lips to his, and force him to remember the love that still burned within me.

That would get me nowhere with Hank. He was always more stubborn than a barrel of mules when he was uncertain. He wasn't in the same place I was anymore, and I had to remember that.

"I'll stay in the guest room," I finally said.

He shook his head. "I should stay in there."

"No." My tone was firm. This was one concession I would not make. Whether he recalled them or not, our bed and our bedroom housed many memories of our life together. Sleeping on our mattress, under the sheets that twisted around our naked bodies, might help bring those memories to the surface. "I'll stay in the guest room."

"Okay." Hank picked up his suitcase. "I'm going to take a nap."

I didn't reply. I just stood there while Hank turned around and walked down the hall to the larger bedroom. My eyes filled with tears, but I didn't let them fall. I had to be strong. That was the only way I was going to make it through the day that should have been my wedding day.

HANK FINALLY emerged from the bedroom while I was in the process of making dinner. He'd gotten up at least an hour before. The opening and closing of the master closet door had been my first clue, but after he finished putting away his things, he hadn't come out. Instead he stayed in the bedroom, behind the closed door.

I had to fight the instinct to knock and make sure everything was all right. I even made it all the way down the hall. I just couldn't bring myself to intrude. He evidently wanted to be alone.

I didn't have to like it, but I had to respect Hank's wishes. So I started prep work for dinner.

I wasn't much of a cook. Hank usually handled meal preparations. He had a knack for making delicious meals that were healthy, while I tended to cook meals that were high in fat and carbs, and were either burned or undercooked. Hank once told me I was the only person he'd ever known who couldn't cook a protein to save his life.

"What are you making?" he asked as he leaned against the counter. Even though he was a few feet from me, I caught a whiff of Hank's musk and longed to lose myself in the comfort of his smell as I used to do after a long day.

"Chicken parm," I replied. I focused on butterflying the huge chicken breasts instead of the wonderfully soothing scent of the man I loved.

"Yum." Hank's response drew my attention. Whenever Hank was about to eat something delicious, such as a steak or my cock, he said "yum" with the exact intonation he just had. If I didn't know better, I would have said that the old Hank had magically reappeared. "What?" His blond eyebrows stitched together.

I smiled and gazed back at the cutting board. "Nothing."

"It was obviously something," he said with a sigh. "What did I do wrong now?"

"Why would you think you did something wrong?" I asked before placing the knife in the sink.

116

"You watch my every move, and every now and then, you get this funny look across your face. It's like a mixture of hope and disappointment."

"Sorry about that," I said. I took the chicken and the cutting board over to the counter by the shelf where I'd prepared the mixing bowls. One held the two eggs and the other a mixture of breadcrumbs and Parmesan cheese to dredge the chicken. "I'll try to watch my reactions from now on."

"Thanks," he said. He began washing the dishes I'd already gotten dirty, just like he had always done when I made dinner. "So what was that look for, then? When I said yum."

I placed the coated breasts into the heated oil in the sauté pan. "You used to always say 'yum' when you were about to eat something you liked. It was just nice to hear the old you, I guess."

Hank didn't reply. He washed the dishes while I continued to make dinner. An awkward silence swallowed up the space around us. That had happened to me many times in my life. As a social introvert, I often became self-conscious about what to say or do in social settings. If someone didn't carry the conversation, I was prone to just stand in silence before the other person politely excused him or herself and walked away.

It was an unusual trait for an attorney. In the courtroom, I came to life. Outside of it, I wilted.

But that had never been the case with Hank until right this moment.

With Hank, I'd acted on instinct, because it was as if we were meant to be. I still felt that way, but now that Hank didn't, I didn't know exactly what to do or say.

So I kept my mouth mostly shut. I only spoke when Hank asked me where to find the cutlery and the plates and what I wanted to drink. When dinner was ready, I put the food on plates and carried them over to the circular kitchen table.

"I hope you're hungry," I said as I placed Hank's meal before him.

"I am," he replied before picking up his knife and fork. "Especially for nonhospital food."

"Well, I'm not much of a chef, so consider yourself forewarned."

Hank cut into his chicken and placed his utensils back on the table. "Mine's not cooked through yet."

Fuck! After cutting into mine, I discovered the same pinkish center. "Sorry about that." I was mortified. It was my first chance outside of the hospital to make a good impression on Hank, and I blew it.

"Don't worry about it," he said after rising from his seat. He took his plate and mine back to the kitchen. "I'll just pop them in the microwave and finish these off."

While Hank operated the microwave, which had more buttons than the Starship *Enterprise*, I rested my face in my hands. After this meal, I wouldn't be surprised if Hank packed up and left.

"I take it I usually handled the meals."

I nodded with my face still buried in my hands.

"We all have our strengths."

I sat up in my chair. There was my old Hank again. He'd often said that whenever he was trying to make someone feel better. "Thanks," I said after turning around in my chair.

Hank studied the living room and kitchen again. "So this was yours before I moved in?"

"Yes."

"And I didn't have a problem with that?"

I laughed. "You had a big problem with it," I told him as he took his seat at the table. "You hated moving into a place that wasn't yours. It was one of the reasons you didn't want to move in the first place. You're a very proud man. You didn't want to be taken care of. You need to pull your own weight. Feel like an equal partner." Hank's nod told me this hadn't changed. "We split everything fifty-fifty. Rent. Utilities. Groceries. We even put some of my things in storage to make room for your stuff."

"Yeah, I noticed a few of my things here and there, like my grandfather's chest of drawers in the bedroom. And of course this," he said with a knock upon the tabletop.

"That's right. The table and chairs are yours. They used to be in the dining room of your house in San Diego."

"Yeah," he said. His tone was wistful and nostalgic. "I put a lot of work into that house. Redid the bedrooms, the bathrooms. I got the garden in perfect condition too."

"I know."

He grinned at me, and it wasn't forced or filled with regret. It was genuine, and it made my heart sing. "I guess you would. It's hard for me to imagine leaving that house and that life behind."

"I can see that from your perspective. You had a good life there."

"I did," he said with a firm nod. "But I can also see how losing Picasso would have sent me packing. I'm glad I don't remember that. Or Gracie's passing."

Without thinking, I reached across the table and covered his hand in mine. He tensed at the contact, but I didn't withdraw my hand. Not only did I need to feel the comforting warmth of Hank's touch, but I needed to offer the comfort I'd grown accustomed to giving the man I loved without hesitation. "It was tough. We all took it pretty hard."

"You were there?"

I nodded. "I was on the first plane to you after you called to tell me what was going on."

Tears pooled in the corners of Hank's eyes. Evidently just thinking about the passing of his handsome boy, without even remembering it, caused him to become emotional. "I hope I said thank you."

"Of course you did. But there was no need. I loved you." The dinging microwave told us the cooking cycle had ended. "I still do. That's why I'm here. By your side. Because there's no other place I'd want to be."

Hank rose to retrieve the plates, but on his way back to the kitchen, he gazed over his shoulder at me. A tiny spark flashed in his eyes before he turned back around.

AFTER DINNER Hank did the dishes and ordered me to sit. Since I had cooked, he intended to clean. I didn't argue with him, even though I spent most of my time getting up and showing him where things went before sitting back down.

It was nice to have Hank in the kitchen, banging pots and rattling pans in the sink. He was good at cleaning, but he was about as noisy as an elephant falling down a flight of stairs.

I wouldn't have changed a thing. His presence filled the house. He made it home instead of just the vacuum it had become in his absence. A lot had changed and there was no guarantee that life would ever be the same again, but right now, in that moment, with my eyes closed, it was as if the last few weeks had never happened.

My Hank was still with me, and he loved me as much as I loved him.

"You falling asleep?"

I opened my eyes to find Hank studying me. He scraped the breadcrumbs from the baking dish before placing it in the dishwasher. Instead of setting it in the bottom rack as he'd always done with his Pyrex bowls, he rolled open the top drawer and laid it next to the glasses.

It took me by surprise.

When I had done that during Hank's first week here in the condo, he said that the glass bowls should always go on the bottom. It kept them from breaking if they rattled around and smacked into a drinking glass. I thought it silly since the bottom rack should be saved for the larger items like the pots and pans, but Hank had been insistent.

Was this change a result of his amnesia?

"You okay?"

"What?" I asked, resting my gaze once again upon his.

Uncertainty hooded his eyes. "I asked if you were okay."

"I'm fine. How come?"

He squirted detergent in the dispenser before closing the dishwasher. "You're doing that slack-jawed stare again," he said, pressing the button that began the washing cycle.

"I am?"

Instead of laying flat the towel he'd used to wipe up the water in the sink, as he'd always done, he left it lying on the counter. It would never dry that way, something Hank had instructed me on as well.

"You're doing it again."

I apologized, but I couldn't help it. It seemed more than Hank's memories had been affected by the accident. What other changes could I expect? Was he now a slob instead of a neat freak? And if he was, so what? We'd just hire a cleaning lady or something. It wasn't like I was neat. But what if Hank was now a merciless top instead of a power bottom? I loved dominating such a big, strong man. It was hot, and the feel of his ass as it gripped my cock always made me whine. But I

120

could grow accustomed to Hank drilling me every night instead of it being the other way around.

Then Hank scratched at his overgrown beard and grimaced. Oh hell no! What the fuck would I do if he shaved off his facial hair and started waxing his chest? I loved his big, hairy body. The dark blond scruff of his cheeks and chin and the mat of hair that covered his expansive chest and taut tummy turned me on big-time, and the feathery brush of the light blond hair on his legs as he wrapped them around my waist always made me rock hard.

Would I be able to handle Hank the Hairless, Messy Top?

I just didn't know. So much had changed already.

But then my eyes settled on his once again. Whatever alterations to Hank's personality there might be couldn't edit the person he was or rewrite how I felt. My love for Hank had been tattooed onto my heart and soul. Hank could dress in drag and make everyone call him Bubbles. It simply wouldn't matter.

"You're being really strange," Hank said before exiting the kitchen.

"How so?"

"You mean besides the fact that you've been staring at me in silence for the last five minutes or so?" He sat on the leather couch and placed his hands behind his head. "Kinda made me feel like I had a stalker or something."

"Ah, that," I said, joining him on the couch. "Well, if staring means stalking, then I guess I'm guilty." I sat with my shoulders against the armrest so that I faced Hank, who stared straight ahead.

He gazed at me out of the corners of his eyes, an uncomfortable grin tugging up the corners of his mouth. "You're weird, you know that?"

I nodded and continued to stare.

Hank snatched the pillow to his left and tossed it at me. It hit me square in the face before landing in my lap, but I didn't let that stop me from staring at my man. "You'll have to do better than that."

His advancing grin suddenly halted and retreated. His lips became a thin line, and an uncomfortable expression froze his face. "Please," he said. His voice was low but stern. "Stop looking at me like that."

I averted my eyes and turned to stare at the wall that had so captivated Hank. My heart slowed in my chest, and an inescapable sense of dread and fear wrapped around me like a coiling python. "I'm sorry."

"Me too," he said with a sigh. "It's just too much pressure when you look at me like that. Like I'm the most special person in the world."

"But you are," I said, inching my way tentatively across the couch. I got close enough that the heat from our bodies warmed the space between us. "To me."

"Santi," Hank whispered. "Stop it." He rose from the couch.

"Where are you going?"

"To bed."

"Why? I thought we could talk. Reconnect."

"No," he said with a shake of his head. "What you're doing is pressuring me. And I don't like it."

"Pressuring you? To what? Talk to me?"

"No." His eyes rested on mine. A bitter resentment I'd never seen before reflected from his cold stare. "You're pressuring me to feel what you feel. To see you the way you see me. But I don't, Santi. And when you look at me like that, with those big brown puppy-dog eyes of yours, it makes me feel like an asshole. And I'm not an asshole. I've lived my life trying not to be a jerk like my dad. But after only a few hours with you, that's exactly what I feel like. And I don't like it."

Before I could respond, Hank was gone.

IT WAS two o'clock in the morning when I last glanced at my phone, and I was nowhere close to being able to fall asleep. My heart thrummed in my chest like a hummingbird's wings, and I had difficulty catching my breath. My legs itched as if dozens of bugs crawled over them. No matter how many times I scratched, they marched on, undeterred. To make matters worse, I was going back and forth from being unbearably hot to shivering.

Was I getting the flu or something? It sure would be just my luck.

Although fighting the flu would be much easier than fighting Hank. If I were ill, I could see the doctor and get some antibiotics. There was no miracle pill to bring Hank's memories back or to make him not be so angry and resentful.

Perhaps I shouldn't look at him the way I always had. It might be putting too much pressure on him. But I didn't know how to stop. I loved him. I didn't know any other way *to* look at him.

And feeling as if I had to change my actions was pissing me off. It wasn't Hank's fault that he had amnesia. It was Pork Chop's, that clumsy dumbass. If he were here right now, I'd toss him from the balcony for the crap heap he'd made of my life the past couple of months.

But it really wasn't Pork Chop I was angry at. It was Hank. As irrational as that was, I'd never been more furious with him in my life.

How could he not remember me or our life together? How could he look at me with cold, hard blue eyes? I'd only ever seen that look once before, when some guy came between us on the dance floor at South Beach. He practically shoved Hank aside, wrapped his arms around me, and grinded me on the dance floor. Since the guy was drunk and Hank tended to be overly good-natured, he initially let the error slide. He knew I'd take care of it.

But after my third attempt to get the guy off me, Hank's good nature wore out like a fan belt. He grabbed the guy's wrist and forced him off me, and his warm blue eyes turned arctic cold.

Once the guy stumbled off the dance floor, the chill in Hank's vision melted and he gazed down at me and held me in his arms.

But that frosty stare had returned, and it had been directed at me. After everything I'd done to nurse him back to health.

Goddammit, motherfucker!

I forced the pillow over my face and screamed into it before throwing it across the room.

It struck the small desk where I paid bills, and knocked over my favorite picture of Hank and me from Provincetown last summer. It fell onto the wood flooring with a crash. I scrambled out of bed and turned on the bedroom light.

The frame lay facedown with slivers of glass scattered across the floor. By the time I reached where it lay and turned it over, tears streamed down my cheeks. In the picture, we were at tea and Hank had his arm around me. His head was pressed against mine, and his eyes were closed. His expression was pure bliss, as if he'd never been happier than at that moment, and my big, toothy smile clearly showed I felt the same.

But that wasn't how things were anymore. That Hank was gone, and he might never come back.

I crumpled onto the floor, holding the photo to my chest, and let the sobs I'd been holding break free. They tore through me in spasming waves of grief.

I was lost, and I didn't know what to do. So much had changed. How was I supposed to put it all back together again? And why did all this have to happen? We were so happy. We were going to be married. For fuck's sake, we *should* be married right now. So why did this happen? Why was God so fucking pissed off at us?

I glared up at the ceiling and gave the heavens beyond the finger.

Then I waited for the inevitable lightning to strike me down.

Nothing happened. No righteous judgment. Not even the rumble of thunder in the distance. I was alone.

I stood up and brushed the remaining shards of glass on the picture into the wicker wastebasket to the left of the desk. I set the photo back where it belonged.

Dozens of questions floated through my mind as I stared at our images. Would my Hank ever return? What kind of person was he now? He certainly seemed far more bitter and distrustful than the man I remembered. Would he ever love me again? What would I do if Hank packed up and moved back to San Diego?

I had no answers, but the questions—and the emotional roller coaster I had just hopped off—made me sleepy.

I crawled back into bed, brought the blankets up to my chin, and closed my eyes. In my mind, Hank had his arm around me and draped his heavy leg over mine. It was how we slept, and the memory was enough to send me drifting off.

CHAPTER
Seven

THE SIZZLING of bacon and the smell of freshly toasted bread woke me the next morning. When I opened my eyes, blinding light filled my vision. I'd forgotten to close the blinds before bed last night, and the bright morning sun turned the interior of the guest room a glowing yellow.

I glanced over at my phone. It was ten thirty. I hadn't slept this late in for-fucking-ever, and I didn't want to get up now either. I'd been having such a wonderful dream. Hank and I had been walking along the beach in Hawaii with the sun dipping just below the water's edge. Our fingers were intertwined, and as the sun slipped below the water, Hank drew me into his arms and alighted on my lips.

That was the world I wanted to go back to, because right now the waking world sucked.

My phone started to ring. I checked the caller ID and groaned.

"Hello," I said, trying my best not to sound as if I'd just awoken.

"Good morning, sleepyhead," Jill said on the other end. "How are you today?"

"Still alive," I replied. "But just barely."

Jill snickered into the phone. "I guess you boys had a good night, then. I'm pleased to hear that even though Hank's big head isn't working right, it's not interfering with his little head."

I rolled my eyes.

"Don't you roll your eyes at me," she scolded into the phone.

125

How the fuck did she do that? "You don't know my business." That was a line from *Baby Mama*, one of our favorite movies.

"Oh, please. I know you better than you realize."

She thought Hank and I spent all night fucking—that showed how little she actually knew. "Yeah, right."

"Is that a challenge?" she asked. She practically chirped. Jill loved proving others wrong more than she loved hot, half-naked gay men.

"Not a challenge," I answered. Though Jill's friendly voice was exactly what I needed, I *didn't* need the smug superiority she held over me every time she proved me wrong.

"Too late," she said with glee. "Challenge accepted."

I groaned in reply.

"Let me see. You and Hank didn't screw each other's brains out last night, and you ended up sleeping in the guest room."

I swept my gaze around the room. Had she installed surveillance cameras in the condo or something? "How could you possibly know that?"

"I'm just that good." If we had been in the same room together, she would have been looking down her nose at me in arrogant delight. "Should I continue, or have I convinced you that I know all and see all?"

In the kitchen, a cabinet door opened and shut and glasses clanked together.

"Wait a minute. Where are you?"

I could practically see her eyes rolling. "Where do you think, Nostradamus?"

JILL WAS in the kitchen, scooping eggs onto two plates and munching on bacon. Her bright red hair had recently been cut into a chin-length shag with a fringe that grazed her perfectly manicured eyebrows. "Grab us some OJ," she said with her mouth full.

I nodded and set to complete my assigned task. As I poured the juice, I noticed that the door to the master bedroom was open and the bed had been made. Hank wasn't there. Anxiety quaked through me, causing my hands to shake so badly I spilled orange juice all over the counter.

126

"You're a mess," Jill said, wiping up the spill.

I couldn't look at her. I had to focus on getting the drinks to the table without dropping the glasses or losing my mind. There was only one reason Jill was here this early. Hank had told her he was leaving, and she came by to help soften the blow. I set the glasses at Hank's table and sat down without a word.

How much longer would this table be in the condo? If Hank was leaving, he'd be taking his belongings with him. I couldn't even imagine this place without Hank's stuff or without Hank. How was I going to survive this?

"I hope you're hungry." Jill placed my plate of food before me. The sight of the scrambled eggs and greasy bacon made me queasy. I'd likely only be able to eat the toast. "Aren't you going to say thank you?" she asked. "Or at the very least tell me how I'm the best best friend in the world and you'd be lost without me."

"Thank you," I said, not looking up from the food that turned my stomach. "You're the best best friend in the world and I'd be lost without you."

Her hand closed around mine. "Look at me."

I shook my head. I didn't want to cry. I'd done that enough already.

"Santi."

"Please just tell me," I croaked.

"Tell you what?"

"What you're here to tell me. Just say it." I still couldn't look her in the eyes. As it was, my vision turned fluid, and I gripped the edges of the table so hard my knuckles turned white.

"I don't know what you think I'm here to tell you," she said. The usual bitchiness in her tone disappeared. Her voice was the whisper softness I used to hear from my mother when she tried communicating with me in times of obvious distress.

Jill wasn't my mother, and she needed to rip the Band-Aid clear off. Then, after I cried for weeks and ate gallons of chocolate ice cream, I'd be able to try to deal with the Hank-sized hole in my life.

"Just. Say. It." I locked eyes with her, and as soon as I did, the tears streamed down my cheeks. "Tell me why you're here."

She gazed at me as if I were on the edge of a cliff contemplating one final jump. "I'm here because I love you, and I'm worried about you."

"And that's it?"

She sighed before shaking her head.

"I didn't think so." I inhaled deeply and tried to force the tears back from where they came.

"Hank called me this morning."

I nodded. So far I was right on the money.

"He said you two had a fight and that you had a rough night of things. He heard glass shattering in your room and you crying."

"So instead of checking to see how I was, he called you," I said with a sniff. That was definitely not the behavior of the Hank I loved.

"He wanted to," she said. "But he figured you needed your space. That you *both* needed space."

Here it comes. I steeled myself for the inevitable.

"I told him I'd drop by this morning and make you breakfast. Try and take your mind off things. You've been so focused on Hank and his recovery that you'd been neglecting yourself, and it's time for you to realize you're just as important and need just as much TLC as Hank does."

"And that's it?" I asked. "You're not here to tell me that Hank's packing up and moving back to San Diego?"

She snorted. "Is that what this has been about?" When I nodded, she scooted her chair closer to me and laughed. "God, you're such a drama queen. That's not what I'm here to tell you." She gave me a big hug before smacking me.

"Why did you do that?" I asked, rubbing the back of my head.

"Why not?" she asked with a shrug.

The laughter that flowed out of me surprised Jill. She sat back in her chair and stared at me as if I'd gone mad while I snorted and guffawed. I couldn't stop. No matter how strangely she looked at me, my hysterics grew exponentially. I clutched at my ribs and a sharp, stabbing pain stitched my sides.

I'd never been more relieved in my life.

"Are you done?" she asked when my hyena routine sputtered.

"I think so," I said in between giggles.

"Good. Now let's eat. And while we do that, you can fill me in on what's going on."

So we ate, and I brought her up to speed.

"And that's where you left it last night?" Jill asked after soaking up the bacon grease left on her plate with her overbuttered toast.

"Yes. He says I'm pressuring him, but I'm not trying to. I just want my Hank back."

"I know you do, and I want that for you too. But he's right, you know."

Her words validated my fears from last night. I wasn't making things easier, but I didn't know what to do. "I'm not trying to pressure him, but he wants me not to look at him the way I do. I don't know how I'm looking at him, and I sure as hell don't know how to control it." Jill opened her mouth to speak, but I wasn't finished. "It's like asking me not to breathe. It just comes naturally to me. Not that Hank knows anything about that anymore. He isn't the same man he used to be. The Hank I knew would've come into the guest room last night and checked on me, whether he felt I needed space or not. So this isn't exactly easy on me either."

"And it upsets you?"

Was she serious right now? "Upsets me? Oh, I'm so far beyond upset that it's just a small dot on the horizon. You can now find me at Fucking Pissed-Off Land. I know none of this is Hank's fault, but goddammit, it's not mine either. I didn't ask to have my life upset. To have the future I could see so clearly fade into a fog so deep and dense that I can't tell which fucking direction I'm going. This was *not* how I imagined my life, and it sure isn't how I pictured I would be spending the day after my wedding day. So maybe I'm pressuring Hank. Big *fucking* deal. He needs to deal with it. This isn't just about him. It's about me too, and that big hairy fucker is just going to have to put on his big boy undies and deal with it."

Jill smiled and nodded.

"What?" I asked. "Aren't you going to tell me I'm wrong? That I need to be more patient and loving and consider what Hank's going through?"

"Not on your life," she said.

I didn't know what to do with that response. I basically just threw a tantrum. Why did Jill seem so pleased with that? "Who are you and what have you done with Jill?"

"Hey, if you were wrong, I'd tell you. You know that."

I nodded. If Jill was known for anything, it was for her brutal honestly.

"But you're not wrong. This *is* about you too, and you have a right to feel as angry as you do. I'm just glad you're finally letting it out. You've been keeping your emotions bottled up, and it isn't healthy. It's really counterproductive. If you're going to make Hank fall in love with you again, you can't hold onto the bitterness and anger. You have to let it go. And if you do, then maybe Hank will too."

That certainly made sense.

"I've been worried about you for weeks now," she admitted. "You've been strong for Hank, for his parents, for everyone. You can't be strong all the time, and you don't have to be strong for me." She grabbed my hands and squeezed them. "Let me be strong for you. Think you can do that?"

I nodded and smiled at her. I couldn't talk because a rising sob strangled my voice.

"Good," she said before letting my hands go. "Now, can I give you some advice?"

"Please do."

"If you want to regain your normal life, you're going to have to go back to a normal life. You can't be hovering around Hank. That's just added pressure. You need to return to work. Be the person you've always been. That's who Hank fell in love with in the first place, right?"

I couldn't fault that logic, so I nodded once again.

"Remember, you can't make someone fall in love with you. It either happens or it doesn't. Just like Hank's memories. They'll either return or they won't. I know it's hard, but you're going to have to accept you have no control over that."

"I understand." I sniffled.

"But there's one more thing you're going to have to accept, and you're not going to like it."

I knew what she was going to say, and it was a possibility I was doing my best to ignore. But dismissing it wouldn't make it go away. I needed to hear the words, no matter how much I wasn't going to like them.

"You're going to have to come to grips with the possibility that the Hank you remember and the one who loved you might not be coming back."

We were both wrong. I didn't just not like those words, I *hated* them with every cell in my body. It made me sick to my stomach even contemplating the prospect, but I had to. It would do me no good to turn a blind eye to it. If I knew what was coming my way, I could prepare for it.

It was the only way I was going to survive.

"I know," I finally said. Admitting that risk made me shiver, but at the same time, I sat up straighter and my heartbeat slowed to a normal rhythm.

I wasn't giving up on Hank. I would never do that. I'd fight for him until my dying breath. After all, love couldn't be taken for granted. It had to be earned.

That was a lesson my father had taught me, when I asked him why he constantly took my mom on dates. They were married, and to me they were too old to be doing stuff like that. I didn't see why he still bought her roses or surprised her with nights on the town, and he'd told me something I'd forgotten until now.

"You can't ever take your love for granted. It's like a flower than needs sun, water, and food to survive. Without them, it cannot bloom. And besides, it's never too late to fall in love all over again, even for us old folks."

He was right. It wasn't too late.

Jill stood up. "I'll clean up the kitchen and you get ready for work."

"What about Hank?"

"Hank's a big boy. He might be a bit brain damaged right now, but he can figure things out for himself."

I was padding down the hall toward the guest room when Jill's voice stopped me.

"One more thing."

"What's that?"

"While it's important to prepare for the worst, don't overlook the small steps."

"I don't understand."

"Hank might not have gone into the guest room last night, but he cared enough to contact me. He's the one who said I should come over and talk to you, and he's the one who realized he couldn't be here while we did it. He's not the same Hank we both knew, but he's still looking out for you like he's always done."

She was right. It wasn't exactly the same, but it was a start.

We had to begin somewhere.

OVER THE course of the next month, I gave Hank the space he needed to find his own footing without my constant pressure or presence.

Although he had yet to be cleared to resume work, he started going out to lunch with Jill and performing odd jobs around the condo. His former workers also occupied his time. They'd drop by to see him or take him out for a latte. Even Pork Chop came by every now and then once he'd been made to feel that neither Hank nor I was going to kill him.

Hank didn't have any memories of these men, but he hung out with them almost daily. He'd promised to give remembering his life a try, and as always, Hank was a man of his word. I was glad to see that some things hadn't changed because of that damn accident.

Whether he knew it or not, Hank was once again developing his own life in Texas, and it seemed to make him less stressed out and irritable. He talked to his parents daily, and they promised to drive down to Houston to see him on the weekend. Even Mitch and Darren were already planning another trip to Texas.

While Hank did his thing, I did mine. I went back to work, and Wyatt couldn't have been happier. He'd been handling the workload on his own, and our new law office had been steadily growing. Even though it had become more than he could handle, he never complained.

He could have easily turned into a bastard, considering our past, but Wyatt accepted the fact that I loved Hank. It made working with him a whole lot easier.

"I think that's it," Wyatt said. He stretched in his office chair and let out a big yawn. "I'm done."

"Me too," I said with a nod. We'd spent the past few days getting me caught up on the accounts, and I was ready to take over my share. "Thanks for everything."

"Anything for you," he said. A smile dangled from his lips, and when he realized what he'd said, he quickly forced it from his expression. "We are partners, after all."

"That we are. But you've gone above and beyond recently, and I can't thank you enough for it."

Wyatt waved away my gratitude and rose from his chair. He opened the cabinet to the left of his desk and pulled out a bottle of scotch and two glasses. "How about a drink?"

"I really shouldn't," I replied. I stood up and gathered the files from the desk. "I should be getting home to Hank."

"Aw, come on," he said while pouring. "One drink."

I shook my head. "I really can't."

He held out the drink and grinned. "After *everything* I've done, you're going to deny me one little drink." His grin turned into a playful leer. The bastard was manipulating me and loving it.

"Fine." I took the offered drink and sat back down. "*One* drink."

"That's all I'm asking for," he said before sitting back down too. He took a long sip from the glass before asking, "So how goes things on the home front? Hank making progress?"

"He's almost back to himself," I said after swallowing a healthy portion of my glass's contents. Liquid fire burned my throat, but the spreading warmth eased the tension from the day.

"And the amnesia?"

I exhaled. "Still there."

"That's a bitch."

He had no idea. "Yeah, but what can you do?"

133

Wyatt shrugged. From the concern I detected in his eyes, he really wished he had a solution for me. "Keep moving forward, I guess. What else can you do?"

Not much else, that was for damn sure. "Yeah. I'm hopeful. I really want things to work out, you know?"

"I know. This is the man you wanted to marry. Hell, you would be married right now if life wouldn't have crapped all over your plans."

I held up my drink in a toast. "Amen, brother!"

He smiled and sat back. "I've missed you around here. Work hasn't been the same."

Typically that sort of comment from Wyatt would be dipped in seductive undertones, but there was nothing suggestive in his remark. Perhaps we'd finally arrived at a place where we could just be business partners and friends. "Probably because you haven't had me here to keep you on your toes."

He chuckled. "That's the God's honest truth! I'm ready to start butting heads with you again."

"Be careful what you wish for," I said. "Because I'm already thinking of a new strategy for the Henderson case."

Wyatt sat up. "What? Why?"

"What you've come up with is good, but I think we can do better."

He smirked. "I'd like to see you try."

"Oh you will!" I said before draining my glass and wincing. "And I think we can get an even bigger settlement too."

He shook his head and smiled. "I've missed you, Santi. I'm glad you're back."

"Me too," I replied, returning the smile.

"And I hope things work out for you. All I've ever wanted was for you to be happy."

"Thanks. I appreciate that."

My phone chimed. I fished it out of my pocket to see a text from Jill. *Meet us for drinks.*

I rolled my eyes and smiled.

"Hank?"

"No," I replied. "It's Jill."

Wyatt nodded. "I envy you. I wish I had a fag hag."

"You don't have one?" I asked while replying to Jill's text. I had no intention of going out and getting trashed.

"Never really made time for friends." He waved his hands around his office. "My work is my life."

Before I had a chance to hit Send on my text, I got a new one from Jill.

And I'm not asking. I'm telling you to meet us for drinks. We're at Meteor.

I deleted my previous text and typed a new one. *Who's we?* I returned my attention to my conversation with Wyatt. "I've been there. Before Hank and Jill. But life's so much more than just depositions and fact-finding expeditions."

The Pope and Lady Gaga. Who else, Nostradamus? Jesse and Mario, Jill replied.

I glanced down at my phone and then up at Wyatt. Profound regret hooded his eyes. "Tell you what," I said, grabbing my files from his desk. "Come with me to Meteor and hang out with me and my friends. After everything you've done for me, the least I can do is welcome you into my little circle."

Wyatt perked up in his seat. "Really? Because if you're serious, I'm so there."

"I *am* serious," I said with a smile. "But be warned: my friends are bizarre and a bit much."

He waved away my warning. "I think I can handle it, but what about Hank? I thought you wanted to get home to him."

I did. More than anyone else, his presence was all I really needed. But Jill was right. I couldn't hover, and I had to be the man I was, the man he fell in love with. And that man occasionally went out for drinks with his friends. So when I sent him a text letting him know I was going out for drinks, I didn't expect there to be a problem.

135

"He'll understand," I said. "He usually goes to bed early anyway. He's been getting bad headaches in the evening and only sleep seems to get them to stop."

Wyatt snatched his keys from beside his computer, and I sent Jill a text that we were on our way. Going out wasn't what I wanted, but it might just be what I needed.

Hank no doubt felt the same way. His text told me to have a good time.

BY THE time Wyatt and I stepped foot inside Meteor, the urban video lounge was packed. I hadn't expected it to be this crowded. It was Friday night, but it was still relatively early. Yet there were people everywhere. They sat on the many couches chatting each other up, or at the bars drinking and having a good time. The go-go boys had yet to make an appearance on the stage, but their fans were ready. All the couches facing the stage were jam-packed with horny gay boys ready to make it rain.

"Santi!"

I turned toward the screech to see Jill waving from the far side of the bar to the left. Jesse and Mario stood beside her. They held matching green martinis while Jill nursed her beer.

"Looking gorgeous as always," I told Jill once we made our way to her.

She kissed my cheek, grinned, and puffed out her predominantly displayed bosom. "Naturally."

"How are you girls doing?" I asked the boys, who were dressed in matching red polos.

"Doing great!" Jesse said, eyeing Wyatt. "I see you brought us a present."

I rolled my eyes. "This is my partner, Wyatt. Wyatt, these two troublemakers are Jesse and Mario."

"Partner?" Mario asked.

I smacked him upside the head. "Business partner."

"Oh," Mario replied, clearly disappointed. "And here I thought you and Hank had found an add-on."

I was too mortified to speak. I had half a mind to retrieve a pool cue from the pool table on the far side of the room and whack Mario across the forehead.

Fortunately Wyatt saved him from a bloody fate. "It's a pleasure to meet you two."

"There's more pleasure to come," Jesse said after grabbing Wyatt's hand and holding it much longer than was necessary. Jesse and Mario gave Wyatt the once over. Their eyes started at his full head of dark hair and traveled down the lean, muscular frame covered by his perfectly pressed aqua dress shirt and black slacks until they arrived at the bulge at his crotch.

"Put it back in your pants," Jill told them. "Jesus! You'd think you two had never seen another gay man before."

Jesse pouted and reluctantly released Wyatt's hand.

Wyatt grinned. "No worries. I enjoy being objectified."

Mario and Jesse tittered excitedly while Jill groaned.

"Why are you encouraging them?" I asked.

Before he answered, Wyatt positioned himself between Jesse and Mario and draped his arms around their necks. "Why not?"

"We like this guy," Jesse said with a nod.

Mario rested his head against Wyatt's shoulder. The grin on his face showed that he clearly agreed with his man.

"You guys suck," Jill commented before draining her bottle. "Wyatt's been here all of five seconds and he's already got these two sluts to go home with. What's wrong with me?"

I sidled up next to Jill and wrapped my arms around her waist. "Nothing. But you'd probably have more luck in a bar that doesn't cater to boys who like other boys."

Jill snuffed. "Just you wait. I'll find my perfect straight boy in a gay bar one day." She motioned for the bartender. "But first we drink and then drink some more."

"Just one drink for me," I said.

She locked eyes with me and chuckled. "That's what you think."

Three drinks later, I stretched out on one of the couches that sat in a more private part of the bar and rested my head on Jill's lap. The music from the main area, which was about fifty feet away, spilled over to our little hideaway. "Why do I let you talk me into these things?"

"Because I know what's good for you," she said with a proud jut of her chin.

"Um, excuse me," Jesse said from the other end of the couch. He stared down at my legs, which had almost forced him off the sofa.

"You're excused," I said, making myself even more comfortable by propping my feet on his lap.

Wyatt laughed from the love seat to our right. "Glad to see you relaxing," he said.

I wiggled my eyebrows at him. He had his arm around Mario, who practically beamed. "I could say the same to you."

He switched his gaze between Mario and Jesse. "It feels good to cut loose."

"Amen!" I said.

"See," Jill said as she ran her fingers through my hair. "Getting away from your troubles every now and then is a good thing."

I resented that comment. "Hank is no trouble!"

She swatted my forehead. Fortunately the three mojitos had made me almost numb. "That's not what I meant and you know it."

"I do." I grabbed her hand and held it against my chest. "I long for the old days, though. For the way our life used to be."

"I think you're overlooking the positives here," Jesse said. Instead of shoving my feet off his lap, he pulled them closer and massaged my leg. He evidently realized that what I needed above all else was the unconditional love, support, and comfort only good friends could provide.

"And what would those be?"

"You've got a once-in-a-lifetime opportunity here, and you're completely overlooking it."

I gazed up at Jill, who rolled her eyes and shook her head.

"Don't be hateful," he said with a fake sneer at Jill. He turned to me and said, "Despite how perfect you always claimed Hank was, there had to be some habits of his that drove you crazy."

"I have one!" Jill said before I could answer. "I hate that silly name bullshit."

"I find it endearing," I said before sticking my tongue out at her.

"So what, then?" Jesse asked.

I had to stop and think. There wasn't much about Hank that drove me crazy, at least in a bad way. There were a million things I could think of that worked me into a sexual frenzy. The way he smelled, the way his eyes sparkled whenever he looked at me, how he whimpered when I slid inside his body. I loved when he touched me. Whenever he kissed me, or cupped my cheek in his huge hand, or placed his hand on my ass, that always made me want to take him right then and there.

"Oh for God's sake," Mario complained. He adjusted his position on the love seat so that his back leaned against Wyatt's side and his right hand was laced in Wyatt's left. There would no doubt be a Wyatt sandwich in Jesse and Mario's future. "There *has* to be one."

"Okay, fine," I said. "Maybe I'd like it if Hank was a little less finicky in his cleanliness and need for organization. He's got a place for everything, and everything has its place. He's not quite as bad as Monica from *Friends*, but he comes pretty close."

"Now that's what I'm talking about," Jesse said. "This is the prime opportunity you have to change that."

"What do you mean?"

He shook his head as if I were denser than Tori Spelling. "Think about it. You can tell Hank that he was a slob and reinforce that every time he tries to put things in their proper place. You can say, 'Wow, you've never been this neat before.' After a while you'll condition that behavior right out of him. Then, you won't have to worry about making sure you put your shit away all the time. You can leave your nasty-ass undies on the floor and never have to hear one word of it."

"I wonder if that'll work with his need to make silly names?" Jill asked.

I glared up at her, and she bared her full set of teeth at me.

"You could do that with just about anything," Jesse continued. "Hate doing housework? Tell him he always did it. Tired of cooking? Say he's the chef and likes to eat only food he prepares himself."

"You can also let him know that you go out for drinks with your friends every Friday night," Jill said. "And that you and I have standing spa appointments every two weeks that he just insists on paying for."

I stared blankly at her. "I thought this was supposed to be about me, not you."

She shrugged. "Why should you be the only one who benefits from reprogramming Hank?"

"I've got one!" Wyatt announced with a smirk.

"*Et tu*, Wyatt?"

Wyatt snickered before saying, "You can tell Hank that he agreed to do a house remodel for me free of charge. As a thank-you for being so kind and considerate in regards to your continued absence at work."

Jesse laughed. "That's the spirit."

I couldn't have disagreed more, but I couldn't stop laughing. "That's *so* not the spirit. You guys are trying to take advantage of my man."

Suddenly a Cheshire grin stretched wide across Mario's face. "Not only that," he said, "you could totally reinvent yourself too."

"Why would I need to do that?"

Mario studied me up and down as if the answer was obvious.

"Bitch," I said before flipping him off.

"And that, my dear Santi, is one example of how you could reinvent yourself. You can tell Hank that you're not a spiteful prude who throws himself from one case to the next. You can create this badass adventurer who skydives on the weekends and swims with the sharks on vacations."

Naturally Jill just had to chime in. "You can also tell him that you weren't a dweeb in high school. That you were a jock who got cock and ass every weekend instead of the real you, who stayed at home reading comic books."

"Hey!" I complained. "This is getting personal now."

"You can also make the chubby years disappear," Jesse said with a nod. "If I remember from photos Jill has showed us, you put on some weight about four years ago, right?"

Mario agreed with a nod. His hooded eyes revealed he regretted me ever having to go through that.

"I was *not* chubby!"

Jill patted my head. "No, not chubby. Just hearty."

140

I surveyed the expressions of all my friends, who were doing their best to contain their spiteful laughter. They were trying to cheer me up, and it was working. "I hate all of you."

"All you'd have to do is destroy all those pictures of before you lost the weight," Jesse managed to say between giggles. "He'd never know that you were once a size thirty-six waist. Of course, you'd have to convince your best friends to destroy the evidence *they* have to the contrary, and that is gonna cost you." He glanced over at Mario, who purred like a cat with his head on Wyatt's shoulder. "What do you think we should ask for?"

Mario closed his eyes in thought. "I'm thinking an all-expense-paid vacation is a start."

Complete adoration filled Jesse's eyes. "I knew there was a reason I loved you."

"Is everyone done?" I asked.

"I don't know," Jill replied. "I'm sure there's other ways we could profit from Hank's amnesia."

"True," Jesse said. He was evidently in deep thought, trying to concoct further fake instances that would make me laugh. "Unless he never falls in love with you again. Then we'd all be screwed."

I immediately stiffened as Jesse took the playful ribbing one step too far. Jill cursed at him and threw her napkin at him. He complained loudly and evidently had no clue what he'd just said. Everyone glared at him before turning their pained expressions back to me.

I sat up and forced a chuckle from my constricted throat. "I'm fine."

I really wasn't, and everyone but Jesse knew better.

It wasn't as if I hadn't already considered the possibility that Hank might not ever feel the love for me he once felt. Jill and I had discussed it a while back. But to hear it again paralyzed me.

What if Hank never wanted me again? What if he decided to leave me for the memory of what he had with Karl? What was I going to do then?

BY THE time I got home, Jesse's words and my fretting spiral had all but cured me of the buzz I had worked on acquiring all night. The comforting numb the alcohol had briefly granted me had been replaced with a five-ton pachyderm of worry.

Popping a Xanax was definitely in my immediate future.

I swung the front door open and was surprised to find the living room lights on and Hank sitting on the couch, wearing only his pajama shorts. Before the accident, Hank usually wore nothing to bed, but ever since I'd brought him home from the hospital, he made sure he was properly covered.

"Have a good time?"

I forced the previous gloom away and nodded. "I did." I closed the door behind me and walked over to where he sat. "Headaches keeping you up?"

He rubbed the bridge of his nose with his thumb and forefinger. "Yeah. It's a real bitch tonight."

Even though I already knew Hank's stand on medication, I asked anyway. "Want me to get you some Advil?"

"No, thanks. I'll be fine."

I nodded and sat on the other end of the couch. I did my best these days not to invade Hank's space when it was all I really wanted to do. "Want me to call Dr. Anglin?"

He shook his head. "There's nothing she can do except advise me to take something for it. Besides, she told us that migraines were sometimes common after suffering from a brain injury. Something about my brain being hypersensitive for a while."

"Want me to massage your head?"

Hank sighed. "If you wouldn't mind."

"Not at all," I said before scooting next to him. He sat on the floor in front of the couch, and I moved in behind him. He leaned back against my open legs, and I immediately grew hard. His bare flesh felt like home. I tried to will my erection away, but I felt like a horny teenager all over again. My boner had a mind of its own. It knew exactly what it wanted, and it snaked a path toward what it desired most. If Hank rubbed against it, headache or not, he'd move away. I couldn't let that happen, not when I'd finally been able to get this close, so I shook the lustful thoughts from my head and set to massaging Hank's temples. He moaned in appreciation as I worked to rub the pain from his body.

That was when I noticed the open photo album lying on the coffee table to the left of the sofa. It was the one that held our pictures from our Labor Day Weekend in Key West.

"Looking at some old photos?"

He only nodded in reply.

"What did you think?"

"It appears we had fun."

Close, but not quite. It had been a difficult vacation for everyone. Mitch and Darren went with us, and we stayed at the Island House, which was considered to be the best gay resort in town. We'd hoped that would be the best place to drop our bomb on them, but Hank didn't need to know that. "That we did."

"Can I ask you something?"

"Anything you want."

He sat up and moved out from between my legs. He remained on the floor, but he positioned himself so that he could face me as we talked. "What was going on in Key West?"

"What do you mean?"

He motioned for me to give him the photo album, so I did. He flipped back to the beginning of the book and held up smiling pictures of the four of us in the taxi on the way to the resort. There were others of us in the pool together, trying to get all four of our faces in the shot, or at dinner, or in the middle of the dance floor at La Te Da.

"I don't understand," I finally said.

"The pictures at the start of the photo album are much different from the ones toward the end."

I gaped at Hank. While his memory might be impaired, he was still a master at putting things together on his own. He held up a page of photos as proof. In them, he and I lounged by the pool or at lunch at a small café. Others were of Mitch and Darren sitting in the hot tub or walking down Duval Street.

He flipped further through the book, and those pictures revealed the same thing. After the first day in Key West, the four of us didn't appear in another photo together. That was because we didn't speak to each other again until the taxi ride home.

143

"What happened?" he asked.

I had no choice but to tell him the truth. I couldn't blatantly lie to his face. "That was the weekend you told Mitch and Darren you were moving to Houston to be with me."

He slowly nodded, as if that explained everything. And in a way, it did. Hank knew Mitch and Darren better than anyone. "I assume they took it about as well as could be expected."

"Even worse than you thought they would."

He arched his eyebrows at me. It was his way of asking "really?" without actually saying the word.

"Yes. We'd talked about it before the trip, and you prepared me for Darren to get quiet and withdrawn and for Mitch to turn into a screaming hag. But neither of us were prepared for what actually happened."

"And what was that?"

"Well, I'll tell you, but it wasn't pretty."

WE HAD all just sat down at one of the garden tables at Michael's, which was a high-end restaurant in Key West. It had been Hank's idea to bring the boys here. He somehow hoped that a good meal might help soften the blow.

"What's everyone going to have?" Mitch asked while he surveyed the menu. Mitch liked to know what everyone was going to eat before he ordered. That way he could choose something no one else was getting but still be able to pick at our plates.

"I'm having the burger," Darren answered.

"Really, Grandma? A burger?" Mitch set his menu down and shook his head at Darren. "You should really try to broaden your horizons."

That was never going to happen. Darren was a creature of habit who just so happened to have a sensitive stomach. He only ate meals he knew he could handle when we went out for dinner. "You're just pissed because you never get to eat off my plate."

"Not true," Mitch replied before raising his menu again. "I always eat your fries."

"I'm not getting fries. I'm ordering onion rings."

Mitch practically gasped. "I hate onion rings."

Darren grinned. "I know."

"You're a spiteful little man," he said before turning his attention to Hank and me. "What about you two?"

"I'm going to have the cowboy steak," Hank answered.

"Wonderful!" Mitch said. "I just love cowboys."

"I'm ordering the mahimahi."

Mitch scrunched up his nose. "I'm not a fan of the fish, though."

I laughed. "So I've noticed. You've had a busy day sampling all the meat back at the Island House."

He brushed his long blond hair behind his ear and grinned. "I'm a hungry boy."

Hank chuckled. "At the rate you were going, I'd say you were famished."

"Is that how we're describing easy man whores these days?" Darren asked.

Mitch snapped his attention to Darren, and a snarl curled across his lips. "Don't forget to order some Boost, Grandma. You need to make sure you get your nutritional allotment for the day."

Fortunately the waiter arrived before Darren could launch a return salvo. We placed our orders, and after the waiter left, Hank's hand found mine under the table. It was apparently time to make the big reveal.

"I've got something I need to tell you," he said to Mitch and Darren.

"You've finally set a wedding date?" Darren asked.

Mitch clapped in delight. "Oh goodie! I've been wondering when you two were going to make it official."

"No wedding date yet," I replied. Hank had just lost Picasso, and planning a wedding was just not where he was at the moment.

Mitch and Darren looked confused. They focused their gazes simultaneously on Hank. "What is it, then?" Mitch asked.

Hank swallowed before letting out a lungful of air. "I'm moving in with Santi."

Darren immediately removed his hands from on top of the table where they had been resting and placed them on his lap. He was getting ready to withdraw just as Hank had warned. Mitch's demeanor hadn't changed. The words had obviously not yet sunk in.

"I don't understand. Are you moving to San Diego?" he asked me.

I shook my head.

"Then how—?"

That was when Darren lost it. "Goddammit, Mitch. They're trying to tell us that Hank is moving to Houston. That he's packing up and moving away from the home we've built together."

Mitch's gaze lingered on Darren's before he sought confirmation in ours. "Is that true?"

"Yes," Hank replied.

"When?"

"Once I finish up with my client," Hank replied.

"Could you be more specific?" Darren asked. His blue eyes, which had always been friendly, frosted over. "A few days? Weeks?"

"Two weeks at the most."

Darren didn't like the answer. His voice dropped just below a whisper. "And when exactly were you planning on telling us?"

"Well, right now," Hank said with a gesture of his hand. "That's kinda what we're doing here."

"Is that why you brought us here?" Darren asked, motioning to the restaurant. "You thought by bringing us to Key West and filling our bellies with good food that we'd not see this for what it is?"

Although Hank prided himself on being an easygoing guy, when someone pushed his buttons, they triggered his very short fuse. "What do you think this is?" he growled.

"It's a pathetic attempt to sweet-talk us into giving you our blessing."

A growl resonated in the back of Hank's throat. "I don't need your blessing for jack shit!"

"Hank, Darren, please," I said, trying my best to calm everyone down. "I know this must come as a bit of a shock, but Hank and I are engaged. Even if I was to move to San Diego, it wouldn't be like I'd be moving in with you three."

"Why not?" Mitch asked. Surprise no longer stole his voice. He was just as angry as Darren. "Is our house not good enough for you?"

"Watch it, Mitch," Hank warned.

"That's not it at all," I said. "You have a wonderful house, but there's not enough room for four people in it. Where would my stuff go? Besides, don't you think Hank and I deserve some privacy as we start our new life together?"

"So fuck Mitch and me, right?" Darren asked. "Who gives a fuck about the fact that we own a home together? What the hell are we supposed to do? We can't afford that house between the two of us. We purchased that house because we knew the *three* of us could pay for it together. When we signed that mortgage, it was a commitment we made to each other."

"And we're going to honor that," I said. "We can still pay on the mortgage and the bills until you find someone new to move in with you and take over Hank's share of the expenses."

"I don't want some fucking queen I don't know living in my house," Mitch replied.

"Well, you two could always sell it and move into something you both can afford."

My solution didn't go over well with Mitch or Darren. Darren snorted while Mitch crossed his arms over his thin chest.

"So we have to disrupt our lives because of you?" Darren asked. He eyed Hank with disgust. "We deserve better treatment than this, Hank. After everything we've been through."

That pushed Hank over the edge. One thing he hated above all else was being guilted into something by someone else. "And I deserve better treatment from the both of you. We've been friends longer than I can remember, and instead of being happy for me that I've found the man

147

I want to marry and that I want to move in with, you're too busy being selfish and self-righteous. That's pretty fucking fantastic of you both."

Without saying another word, Mitch and Darren left the table.

HANK STARED at me in stunned silence for a few moments. "What happened after that?"

"Well, we didn't speak to each other for the rest of the trip, which made for some uncomfortable moments. Their room was right next to ours. Every time we passed each other, they pretended as if we didn't exist."

"That sounds like Mitch but not Darren."

I nodded. "Darren took it the hardest because he'd come to rely on both you and Mitch far more than I think he ever let on. He's a pretty solitary creature, and he only lets a select few past his defenses. Hearing that you were leaving hurt him because it was like you were abandoning your family."

"I can see that," Hank said with a nod. "Besides the small group of people he talks to at work, Darren's life revolves around Mitch and me."

"Exactly." I grabbed the book from Hank's hand and flipped through the pages. It had been a difficult trip, one that most people wouldn't create a photo album for, but Key West solidified the four of us as a true family. I wasn't just Hank's Santi anymore. I was officially a part of the family. After all, who else but family and those we truly love do we get that angry at? "That was why it was so important for me to bring us all back together again. Everyone was hurt, and everyone had done or said something hurtful. But in the long run, that wasn't going to matter. All that was important was making everything better."

"I would agree." Hank rose from the floor and sat next to me on the couch. His hairy leg rested against my thigh as he looked over my shoulder at the pictures. "They mean a lot to me. They're like my brothers."

"I know."

After a few moments of silence, he asked, "How'd you do it?" His blue eyes locked on to mine. While they didn't glint as they used to before the accident, the distant gaze with which he regarded me since he woke up faltered a few hundred feet. "How'd you bring us all together again?"

"It wasn't easy," I admitted with a sigh. "Darren refused to talk to us, and Mitch wouldn't stop yelling. I was worried you were going to lose your temper and make things worse."

He chuckled. "I'm surprised I didn't if it was as awful as you are describing."

"It was. Believe me."

"Well? Tell me."

As much as I wanted to tell Hank the story, it was late, and we both needed to rest. Besides, the truth behind the reconciliation was most likely a story Hank wouldn't be too comfortable hearing right now. Whenever he was overwhelmed by information or emotion, he shut down. Right now I'd made peace with the baby steps we made. "Another night," I said before yawning. "We need to get to bed, especially since I can tell your migraine's gone."

Hank paused a moment before smiling. "Hey, it is gone. How'd you know?"

I shrugged and smiled in reply.

"I guess you do know me pretty well, huh?"

"I'd like to think so."

Hank rose from the floor and held out his hand to me. When he closed his hand over mine, my knees grew weak. He had to pull me to a standing position, and when he did, he forgot how strong he was. Hank yanked me right into him. He wrapped his hands around my waist and took a step back with his right foot to keep us from falling over.

But the almost fall wasn't what caused my breath to catch in my throat. For the first time in weeks, my entire body pressed firmly against his. I was once again back in the arms of the man I loved, and my body practically screamed in joy.

It had been too long since Hank's warm, sweat-slick body made contact with mine. It seemed like forever since the musk that clung to the air around him had invaded my nostrils and made me hard. Tonight

149

I'd go to bed with Hank's smell on my clothes and the memory of his body against mine.

"Sorry," I muttered once I realized how long I'd been leaning on him.

Hank's blue eyes gazed down at me. The bitter cold blue I'd grown accustomed to staring into in moments like these wasn't there. The ice had started to melt. "It was my fault," he said. "I forget my own strength sometimes."

I nodded. I really couldn't say much more. Perhaps Jesse had been wrong before. Hank might be able to fall in love with me again.

"Good night," he said as I turned to head down the hall toward my bedroom.

I glanced over my shoulder. Hank still stood where I left him. He stared after me as if there was something he wanted to say but didn't know how to give it voice. Whatever it was, I hoped he found the words he'd eventually need to say it. "Good night," I said before entering my bedroom and closing the door behind me.

CHAPTER
Eight

I WOKE up early Saturday morning filled with hope about the possibility of Hank falling in love with me again. Last night had been a turning point. I had no clue what had prompted him to rifle through old photos, but whatever it was, I owed it a big, wet, open-mouthed kiss. I hadn't felt this close to getting my Hank back since he first uttered the word "hag" before coming out of his coma.

We were on a trajectory out of the hell we'd been living in, and I intended to strike while the iron was hot.

I fired up the stove and poured some oil in one of the pans. While the pan heated, I took the eggs out of the refrigerator and cracked open six into a bowl, where I whisked them. I grabbed the bread from the breadbox, dipped one slice into the egg mixture so that both sides were coated, and then placed it into the heated oil.

While I waited for the first side to cook, I retrieved the lactose-free cheese slices from the refrigerator, grabbed two plates from the cabinet, and then flipped the bread over to cook the other side.

I hadn't made my unusual french toast creation for Hank in a few months, and though it was a caloric bomb with all the eggs, cheese, and bread, it had always been one of Hank's favorites.

"What smells yummy?" Hank asked as he exited his bedroom in just his shorts. He obviously wasn't wearing underwear, as his cock was clearly visible beneath the fabric. His hair was in disarray, and he scratched his ass while he walked. This must be what heaven looked like.

"French toast." I took the first slice of bread out of the pan and replaced it with the next egg-coated slice.

"I love french toast." He grinned like a child about to be presented with food he liked. He ambled into the kitchen and gazed over my shoulder at what I was doing. His face twisted in confusion. "What kind of french toast is this? Where's the powdered sugar and the syrup?" He pointed to the plate where I'd placed a slice of cheese on top of the bread I'd just fried. "And what's with the cheese?"

"This is *my* version of french toast," I told him while I continued to work.

"It looks strange," he said. There was no judgment in his tone. It was just Hank's honest assessment of what I was making, and it wasn't the first time he'd said it. When I first made my french toast, which he dubbed mexican french toast, he hadn't been too sure he'd like it. Hank had always been a health-conscious nut. While he enjoyed chocolate and ice cream, he rarely overindulged in food that was bad for him. Well, except for his Red Bull addiction. His goal was to remain forever healthy so he could be big and strong for me. So when I first made him my version of french toast, he ate it tentatively until the greasy, cheesy yumminess took over. Then he couldn't get enough.

"It is," I replied. "But it's the way my mom made it for me when I was a kid."

Hank leaned against the counter while I cooked. I glanced over at him and noticed a strange expression twisted his face. "What's wrong?"

"I just realized that I know nothing about you. The focus has been on me these past few months. My memory. What I've forgotten about my life and the details I've been trying to remember. I never once thought to ask about you."

He was right. I hadn't been the focus. That had to change for the both of us. "What do you want to know?"

"Well, since I haven't seen your parents this whole time, I assume they live too far away to visit or they have since passed away?"

I once again told Hank the story about my parents' fatal car accident.

"Holy shit!" He placed his hand on my back and gently massaged it. Then he moved his hand downward, and for the briefest of moments,

I held my breath. Was instinct leading his hand back to the place on my body he loved? But before he could reach the curve of my spine, Hank broke contact and rested his hand on the counter. "That must've been rough losing them at such a young age."

I nodded. "It was, but it also gave me focus." As I assembled more of the meal we'd soon be eating, I explained to Hank how my parents' deaths, while tragic, spurred me to accomplish what I'd achieved so far.

"I have no doubt they're proud of you." He took the plate I handed to him with four slices of bread, each fried in the egg mixture and each topped with a slice of cheese. At the top sat the last of the egg, which I had scrambled.

"I'd like to think so," I said as I followed him to the kitchen table.

"Orange juice?" he asked.

"Yes, please," I said before sitting down. "And your coffee should be ready."

"It is," he said, taking his cup out of the Keurig machine. He added his cream and sugar and then brought both drinks to the table. As Hank approached, I couldn't wipe the smile from my face. We both easily danced to our choreographed morning routine.

"What?" he asked.

"Nothing."

"Liar!" He set my drink in front of me and took a sip from his cup.

Things between us were definitely changing. Hank was starting to learn me all over again. He hadn't been able to detect my white lies of omission before, but they registered on his radar now.

"I was just thinking how nice this is," I finally admitted. "The two of us carrying on a breakfast conversation as if nothing between us has changed."

Instead of grimacing, he smiled. It wasn't the Hank smile that typically brightened up the room. It was far more cautious, but true joy backed up the expression. "Well, I don't remember how things were before," he said. "For all I know, we could've fought like cats and dogs before my accident, and you're just trying to get me to remember the good and forget the bad."

I was just about to correct him when I noted the playful grin on his lips. I waved my fork at him. "Don't make me hurt you."

"See," he said, quite proud of himself. "I knew it. I've been living in an abusive relationship."

"Yeah, because I'm so intimidating to someone who's six foot three and weighs two hundred pounds."

"And now you're saying I'm fat. We can add emotional abuse to the list."

I chuckled. What had brought about this change? "This is nice."

"It is," he said with a nod. "But it's important that we both accept that things *have* changed."

I'd rather not, but what choice did I have? "I know."

Hank stared dubiously down at his plate. "It's also important that you know I might not like this. It looks like a heart attack just waiting to happen."

"Gee, I haven't heard that one before."

He cut away a piece with his fork. "So what if I'm repeating myself? I don't ever remember saying it in the first place."

"Just eat." I pointed to his fork with mine.

Like a toddler being forced to choke down spinach, Hank closed his eyes and opened his mouth. He placed the food on his tongue, and as he started to chew, he opened his eyes wide and an even wider grin stretched across his face. "That's pretty damn good," he said with his mouth full of food.

I grinned. "I know."

After swallowing, he cut off another piece and promptly popped it in his mouth. "You can't call this french toast, though."

"Why not?" I asked before taking a bite.

"Because it's *not* french toast," he replied.

"And what exactly would you call it?"

He shrugged. "How about Mexican french toast?"

I smiled broadly and nodded. "Sounds perfect to me."

AFTER DEVOURING our breakfast and cleaning up the kitchen, I drove Hank down to Montrose. He'd always enjoyed walking up and down the gay district with its renovated mansions, bungalows with wide porches, and cottages located along tree-lined boulevards.

I parked in a lot that belonged to a local gay clothing store called M2M, a nail shop, several restaurants, and a Starbucks. Knowing Hank the way I did, we'd be stopping in there at least once during our outing.

"What are we doing here?" Hank asked as he surveyed his surroundings. "Trying to jog my memory?"

Actually, I wasn't. That was a first. "Not at all. I just thought you might like to walk around Montrose."

Hank inspected the area. Cars rumbled down the streets, horns blaring and tires screeching. People strolled up and down the sidewalks and crisscrossed the parking lots. Many were gay men holding hands or walking with their groups of friends. There were even straight people with their families, taking in the sights.

It was a beautiful day to be outside. The sun shone high overhead, and the clouds kept the sun's rays from immediately frying our skin. There was even a slight breeze that ruffled the leaves of the trees that spread their arms up and down the area.

Hank turned back to me. "Where do we start?"

I shrugged. "You tell me. What strikes your fancy?"

He pointed to M2M. "How about that store?"

The more things changed, the more they stayed the same. Hank loved M2M. They carried trendy clothes that often sparkled, and Hank loved his bling. He was definitely not a flamboyant homosexual, but when he wasn't working, he typically inserted at least one flashy accessory into his outfit. "Let's do it."

We crossed the lot and entered the building. Madonna's "Vogue" played through the store's speakers, and a young sales associate immediately greeted us. He wore seafoam green denim with a brown belt and a white tank top with multicolored stripes across the fabric. The light material made the young man's dark skin shimmer like ebony. "Welcome to M2M. I'm Andre," he said. "Anything particular you're looking for?"

"Just browsing," Hank said with a smile.

Andre practically peed himself under the full weight of Hank's smile. I certainly knew the feeling. He followed Hank around the store, explaining what the sale items were and pointing out the best deals. And naturally, if Hank needed *anything*, all he had to do was ask.

Hank greeted Andre's flirtations as he typically did—with kindness and a smile. "Thank you, Andre. We'll let you know if we need anything."

At the use of the first-person plural pronoun, Andre glanced over his shoulder at me and took notice of my presence for the first time. Fortunately I'd grown accustomed to becoming virtually invisible whenever I was with Hank. It wasn't because I was ugly or offensive. It was that Hank just had this aura about him that immediately drew people right to him.

Plus, he was smoking hot.

"How about you?" Andre asked. "Anything I can help you find?"

"No, thanks. I think we've got it."

Andre nodded and immediately retreated behind the cash register, where he continued to keep a close eye on Hank in case he needed assistance.

"I see you still haven't lost your touch," I said, joining Hank at one of the clothing racks.

"What are you talking about?"

"Andre," I whispered. "One look at you and he started ovulating."

Hank chuckled. "He's just being nice. I'm sure he works on commission."

His memories might be gone, but his clueless nature persisted. Hank had never been the type of man who realized when people were hitting on him. That was probably because people were *always* hitting on him. For him, that was just the way the world worked. Life wasn't the same for the rest of us.

"What do you think about this one?" he asked, holding up a bright green tank top. "Think it's too much?"

"For you? No."

"What's that supposed to mean?" he asked while draping the shirt over his forearm.

"Your motto has always been 'the flashier, the better.'"

Hank grinned. "I *do* like sparkly."

"If you like sparkly, follow me."

We both jumped at the voice suddenly behind us. It was Andre. Where the hell did he come from?

"Lead the way," Hank said, and we followed Andre toward the far back wall.

When we stopped, we stood before what could only be described as a disco paradise. There were sequined outfits, bedazzled tees and jeans, and more glitter than a fairy godmother.

"Good God," I said, unable to believe my eyes.

"I know, right?" Hank asked. His eyes had grown saucer wide. He was clearly in heaven. "But a lot of this stuff is even too gay for me."

Andre broke out laughing as if Hank had spoken the funniest words ever uttered on the planet. "Don't worry. Our bling ranges from subtle all the way to the most flamboyant drag queen you could imagine."

"How about something in the middle?" Hank asked.

"There's this," Andre said, pulling out a black T-shirt with a pride rainbow formed by sequins across the front.

Hank shook his head. "Nah. Too overdone."

Andre thought for a minute before walking over to another rack. He pulled out a white T-shirt with the phrase "So gay I sneeze glitter" printed on the front. Naturally the words were formed by rainbow-tinted glitter.

"I like," Hank said as he greedily snatched the shirt from Andre's hands.

Andre pulled more clothes from the store. There was a My Little Pony tank top, a red muscle shirt with the words "Keep Calm and Sparkle On," and various other shirts I'd never wear in a million years. On anyone else, those tops would look ridiculous. Hank had a way of making a glittering My Little Pony shirt look butch.

"Aren't you going to try anything on?" he asked as Andre led him to the dressing room.

"I think I'm good."

Hank stopped in his tracks. "If I'm trying on, so are you."

"Why's that?"

"It's more fun that way," he answered. He turned to Andre and said, "Get Santi here a dressing room and pick out some clothes for him."

"I really don't need new clothes," I told them.

They both looked me up and down at the same time. "Yes, you do," they said almost simultaneously.

What was wrong with my khaki shorts and collared white T-shirt?

"Let your hair down," Hank said after grabbing my hand and leading me to the changing area.

Once Hank's hand clutched mine, I didn't hear another word.

I STARED at myself in the dressing room mirror, unable to believe I'd actually tried on the clothes Andre had picked out. When had a pride parade thrown up all over me? I'd never worn powder blue shorts in my life, and despite what the T-shirt said, I was not as gay as glitter.

"How's it look?" Hank asked from the dressing room to my right.

I studied my reflection and sighed. "Unfortunate."

Hank chuckled. "I'm sure it's not that bad."

"You'd be wrong," I said, pushing back the curtain and emerging into the main dressing area.

Hank opened up his curtain and snickered. "Yeah. That's not you at all."

"No," I said emphatically. "It's not."

He did look great in his Sparkle On muscle shirt and white shorts. How the fuck did he do that? "You look good."

"You think so?" he asked, examining himself in the trifold mirror.

"I do."

Hank's cell phone chimed in his dressing room. "Okay, try on your next outfit, and I'll try on mine."

Before I could reply, he was back in his dressing room. I groaned and went back into mine. If I looked ridiculous in this outfit, I couldn't wait to see how awful I'd look in the next one. While I pulled the clothes that were definite "nos" from my body, the tap-tap-tap of Hank's texting drifted over to my dressing room. Who was he texting now?

For the past few days, he had been on the phone when I came home. He immediately got off every time he heard the front door open. The phone calls had turned into sporadic texts that had increased in frequency. Was it his mother, Darren, or Mitch?

"Everything okay in there?"

"Yeah," he said before the tap-tap-tap continued.

The new outfit I now wore wasn't as bad as the first, but there was no way I was going to buy it. The black shorts by themselves weren't bad. They were a little *too* short for my taste, but the pink button-down shirt just had to go.

"Okay, I'm ready," Hank said from outside his dressing room.

I stepped out of my changing area to find Hank wearing a black Hello Kitty shirt and gray shorts. He looked so fine I hated him. "How do you make this shit look so good?"

He shrugged. "Born that way, I guess." He gave me the once-over. "Love the shorts. The shirt not so much."

I nodded. "It probably would look better on you."

"Let's find out." He held out his hand.

I unbuttoned the shirt and gave it to him. It wasn't fair that clothes that fit me also fit Hank. Sure, they were really tight on him given our different heights, but I'd always found that aggravating. Hank's wardrobe had doubled when we had gotten together, but mine hadn't. His clothes were just too big for me to wear. "If you look stunning in it, I may have to kill you." The smile on his lips turned into an openmouthed stare. "What's the matter?"

Hank tried to speak, but he stumbled over his words. Did I have something on me? I turned to the mirror, but I didn't find a booger dangling from my nose or an embarrassing pimple sprouting from my bare chest. "Why are you looking at me like that?" I asked Hank's reflection.

He cleared his throat. "It's just.... Well, I wasn't expecting.... No, that doesn't sound right, does it?"

I turned around and faced him. "Nothing you're saying sounds right, much less makes any sense."

"You look good without a shirt on," he mumbled. "That's all." He disappeared behind the curtain and left me standing there, unable to move or think but with a bigass grin.

AFTER OUR little shopping spree, we headed over to the Starbucks, where Hank got a double skinny venti latte in a grande cup. As always, he ordered it at 140 degrees instead of the usual 160. Hank enjoyed his coffee ready to drink and didn't like waiting for it to cool down.

"Not getting anything?" he asked before surveying the pastry display. If he followed habit, he'd also get an apple fritter.

I shook my head. "Coffee's not my thing."

He froze and regarded me as if I were speaking gibberish. "How is that possible?"

I shrugged. "I never developed a taste for it, I guess. Plus I'm lactose intolerant."

He slowly nodded in understanding before turning to the server. "Can I have an apple fritter, please?"

I stifled my laughter.

"What about you?" he asked. "Chocolate-chip muffin?"

Did he remember that was my favorite, or had it been a lucky guess? "Sure."

"And one chocolate-chip muffin," he told the young girl, who placed his apple fritter in a bag.

I pulled out my wallet, but before I could take out my debit card, Hank rested his hand against my forearm. "I've got it," he said. "As thanks for taking me shopping."

I nodded and tried to swallow, but my mouth had gone dry. Hank's hand still lingered against my flesh, and I willed him to wrap his arm around me and claim me as his as he so often did whenever we were out and about together.

Instead he paid the cashier, and I was left with a rock-hard boner. I shoved my hands into the pockets of my shorts, hoping that would help conceal the tenting of the fabric. The place was packed—and there were women and children in there, for God's sake. I had to calm the fuck down, but that had always been difficult with Hank.

Maybe since he'd now seen me without a shirt on, he might start feeling the same way.

He handed me my chocolate-chip muffin. While he waited on his drink, I took Hank's bags from his hands and found a table between a middle-aged straight couple and two college boys who were obviously not gay. They wore baggy shorts that extended past their knees and their baseball caps in reverse. Every other word out of their mouth was "dude" or "bro." It was a bit annoying. The straight couple evidently thought so too. They occasionally stared askance at the two guys whenever they said something that clearly marked them as a couple of douche bags.

Dude, the taller and louder of the two, rambled on about the skank he'd banged the night before. As he told his tale, his friend, Bro, snickered and made off-color comments that annoyed the woman on the other side of me. She and her husband were small and mousy and obviously wanted to speak up, but Dude's and Bro's bigger athletic builds made them keep mum.

I did my best to ignore them. They were young and dumb and would hopefully outgrow being complete tools. I opened one of Hank's bags, making sure the receipt for the black shorts I'd purchased was in the bag. I still couldn't believe I'd actually bought a pair of short shorts. I could just hear Jesse and Mario now when they saw me wearing them. "Who wears short shorts? Santi wears short shorts." They'd be insufferable, but how could I not purchase them? I was wearing them when Hank saw me without a shirt and lost the ability to speak coherently.

I'd remember that forever.

As I dug around in the bag, Hank's "So Gay I Sneeze Glitter" shirt fell onto the floor. I snatched it off the ground, and when I sat up, Dude and Bro were staring at me and eyeing the shirt.

"That's so fucking gay," Dude said. Bro's scoff revealed he agreed.

I held the shirt up to my chest. "You think? I was worried it wasn't gay enough."

"What? You gonna wear a tiara too?" Bro asked. "Fucking queer."

"He is a fucking queer and so am I," Hank said from behind Bro.

When both guys turned to see Hank, their wagging tongues fell silent. Hank's eyes flashed an angry blue steel, and a low growl emanated from the back of his throat. He clearly was not happy, and from the uneasy glances Dude and Bro gave each other, they were regretting their words.

"Do you have a problem with that?"

Bro slowly shook his head.

Dude, however, got brave. He stood up. "And if I did?" he asked.

Hank placed his coffee on the table and took a step forward. "Then we'd have a problem."

I rose from my seat and stepped between Hank and Dude. "They're not worth it," I told Hank.

He turned his attention to me while still keeping one eye on Dude. "No one should talk to you that way."

Hank's protective nature hadn't been changed by his accident. I'd never felt safer or more loved than when he'd stood sentry around me in tense situations.

"You're right," I said, turning around. "What you two should know is that I'm a lawyer, and your words qualify as hate speech. As such, they are grounds for litigation."

"For what?" Dude asked, while glancing down at Bro, who shrugged.

"It's a grown-up word for lawsuit, dumbass." I was lying through my teeth. Dude's bile was covered by free speech, but I was banking on the fact that he was as clueless as most other douches in the world. "And all I need to do is make one little phone call to the district attorney and he'll have a patrol car over here in less than five. Hopefully you don't have any illegal substances on you once they cuff you and search your car."

That got Bro's attention. He rose and stood by his friend. "Dude, the cops can't search my car. They'll find my shit."

Dude nodded. "I got your back, Bro." He wiped the sneer from his lips and smiled, trying to use the charm that no doubt worked on gullible co-eds. "It's all cool, man. How about we just leave and call it even?"

"That would be smart," I said. "But first, I'd also like you to apologize to me and to this woman. Your derogatory remarks about women are misogynistic and would add at least a year to your sentence."

"My what?" Dude asked. "And who's Miss Ojanistick?"

"Dude, who fucking cares?" Bro asked. "Just fucking apologize."

"I'm sorry," Dude told the woman to my right. She shot Dude a disapproving glance but smiled up at me.

"And sorry to you too," Dude said to me.

"Apology accepted. Now go."

Dude and Bro scampered out of the building and sprinted toward their car.

"Well played," the lady from the next table said after Hank and I sat down. Her husband nodded and smiled at us.

"Thanks," I said, returning the smile.

"I'm impressed," Hank said after taking a sip of his coffee. A familiar sparkle danced in his eyes. It made me light-headed.

"Getting all lawyery on someone sometimes pays off. Especially when they don't know their rights from their lefts."

Hank laughed as the couple next to us got up to leave.

"The two of you make such a wonderful couple," the woman said before she and her husband walked away.

"See." I motioned to Hank. "Even people we don't know see it. What's the matter with you?"

Hank rolled his eyes before tapping his index finger against his temple. "Amnesia, remember?"

"Excuses, excuses."

I laughed at my own joke, but Hank didn't. Instead he studied me as if he were truly seeing me for the first time.

"I'M EXHAUSTED!" Hank said after we got back to the condo. He threw his bags on the overstuffed chair and plopped himself on the couch. "I think I need a nap."

I shook my head. "No nap. My plans for the day aren't done."

Hank groaned. "But I'm sleepy!"

"Oh hush, you big baby." I opened the cabinet in the television console and pulled out a movie that had been one of Hank's recent favorites. I popped it into the Blu-ray player, turned on the entertainment system, and sat down on the couch.

Hank stretched out next to me. "Well, we can watch whatever you want, but I'm likely going to fall asleep about five minutes into the movie."

"No, you won't."

"Yes, I will."

"Nuh-uh."

"Yeah-huh."

This argument could go on forever, so instead of continuing, I pushed Play. As soon as the word *Marvel* floated across the screen, Hank sat up. "What's this?"

"You'll see."

The villain began his monologue about the Tesseract and Hank was wide-awake. *The Avengers*, as always, had done the trick.

"I love Samuel L. Jackson," Hank said when the actor made his first appearance as Nick Fury.

I nodded in reply and watched as Hank got sucked into Joss Whedon's interpretation of Marvel's premiere superhero group. Whenever he became engrossed in a movie, he sat up straight, he spread his arms along the couch's back cushions, and he kicked his feet up on the coffee table. His eyes also glazed over and a smile took up permanent residence on his lips for the duration of the movie.

While Hank watched the movie I'd already seen with him at least ten times, I got up and made us some nachos. I even opened up a bag of peanut M&M's and poured them into a bowl. Whenever Hank watched a movie, he ignored his usual counting of calories and had to have snacks.

I placed the nachos on his lap and the bowl of candy on the coffee table in front of him.

"Food!" he squealed before digging his big hand into the M&M's. He popped a handful in his mouth and muttered, "Thanks."

"You're welcome." I sat next to him on the couch, and we made short work of the nachos. When we were done, I retrieved the candy bowl from the table and set it between us.

"Good idea," he said after retrieving more M&M's. "This way we don't have to move."

"I'm always thinking."

He chuckled and went back to the movie.

During the big battle scene between the Avengers and the Chitauri army in New York, Hank and I went for candy at the same time. Instead of coming away with a chocolate treat, we hooked each other's fingers instead.

The surprise contact tore our gazes from the fighting to our joined hands in the bowl. The surprise in his expression was more than likely as evident as the longing must have been in mine. The one thing we typically did whenever we watched any movie together was hold hands, and it had been what I'd missed the most.

All Hank had to do was caress my cheek and it would all be over. Everything would be back to normal. And while he didn't instantly withdraw his hand from mine, an unusual emotion stirred across his face. Confusion hooded his eyes, and guilt crept at the corners.

What was going on?

"Sorry about that," I said, pulling my hand from his. I gazed into the bowl. "I guess we're almost out of candy."

He nodded, but he didn't look away. He continued to stare into my eyes as the battle for Earth played out on our television. Why couldn't I shake the feeling that Hank had something to say?

"What is it?" I asked.

He opened his mouth to speak, and I steeled myself for the big revelation. "Thanks for such a great day."

I was thrown off guard. That wasn't what I was expecting at all. Though I breathed once again in relief, why did I have a strange feeling that wasn't exactly what was on his mind? "You're welcome."

"What's on the agenda for tomorrow?"

"What would you like to do?"

"More fun stuff," he said. "Like today."

"That can be arranged."

Hank nodded and turned back to the action on the screen. I was excited that Hank wanted to spend more time with me. That was definitely a step in the right direction. Yet I couldn't shake an uneasy feeling that caused me to tremble.

CHAPTER

Nine

A WEEK later Hank and I stood at baggage claim in the San Diego airport, waiting for our luggage to magically appear on the carousel. After our great weekend together, I had to strike while the iron was hot, and what better place to do that than where we first fell in love?

"I'm so glad to be here," Hank said. Instead of searching the conveyer belt for his Hello Kitty luggage, he gazed wistfully outside into the familiar southern California landscape. The strain of our problems in Texas seemed to fall off his shoulders. This was something Hank needed. Hell, it was what we both needed. "Thank you."

"You're welcome." I hadn't seen Hank smile so broadly in far too long. He practically beamed, and it quickly became contagious. My lips parted into a big grin that refused to be wiped from my lips.

"I see you're happy to be here too."

I nodded. "Why wouldn't I be? San Diego holds great memories for me." I winced as the words left my mouth. Hank wasn't a big fan of talking about the past. It made him uncomfortable because what others remembered no longer matched what he could recall. I gazed at him out of the corners of my eyes, waiting for his mood to inevitably darken.

"Me too," Hank replied before turning his gaze back to the sun-kissed land outside the airport walls.

To say I was shocked that his smile never faltered after my unintentional blunder was an understatement. Right then, a feather would most certainly have knocked me on my ass. When I had brought up the long weekend in San Diego to him, he'd been excited, but he'd also been worried. He hadn't wanted the trip to be about jostling memories from our past out of the damaged crevices of his brain. That was too much pressure. I agreed, and that had eased Hank's apprehension, turning him into a little boy waiting for his trip to Disneyland. He practically counted down the days and had had difficulty going to sleep the night before.

But my reassurance hadn't been entirely accurate. I did want us to have fun, but I had also planned the weekend to maximize the chance of setting free the past I knew waited to be found. All Hank needed was the right stimulus.

After all, that was the basis of reminder treatment. Though Dr. Anglin cautioned it was unproven, she'd been pleased with Hank's progress and had okayed him for travel. Hank had been so excited he'd left her office to call Mitch and Darren. I stayed behind and revealed what I planned.

She offered some advice but warned me to tread lightly. Reminder treatment might not lead to spontaneous recovery. She didn't want me to get my hopes up too high. Although I heard her, her words went in one ear and out the other.

All that played in the back of my mind were my father's words. *It's never too late to fall in love. All over again.*

Even though I accepted that Hank might not remember me, and loved him regardless, a part of me still wanted the memories of us I cherished to belong to both of us again.

That was what I banked on happening.

"WELCOME HOME," Darren said as he opened the front door to the house Hank had once lived in.

Hank gave Darren a big hug before rushing across the threshold. His gaze devoured the interior. I could tell by the way his eyes lit up that everything he saw triggered a memory. The bookcase to the far right of the front door still held pictures from his life before me. Hank, Mitch, and Darren had their arms around one another on the deck of an Atlantis cruise they'd taken years ago. Another had a picture of Hank with Gracie and Picasso. There were other photos of Mitch and Hank when they were in their teens, bare chested and sticking out their tongues for the camera, and a score of other images captured throughout the ages.

He brushed his fingertips across the glass-enclosed memories and a tear slid down his cheek.

"You okay?" I asked.

He turned around, an enormous smile on his lips. He nodded before wiping the tear away. "It just feels good to see things from my past that I remember." He picked up a photo of Darren. He stood on a pier with his arm across the wooden railing. "You remember this?"

"Of course I do," Darren said. "That was taken in Boston at Piers Park. We'd gone there after my family reunion in Maryland."

Hank nodded vigorously as if surprised that his memory matched someone else's. "That was a disaster," he told me. "Darren's sisters got into a fight. I can't remember about what. But it was awful. It pretty much shut down the reunion, and the three of us drove to Boston for a weekend away from family drama."

"Sure beat staying in the middle of that catfight," Darren said. "We had a great time there. We also took the ferry over to Provincetown for the day."

"That's right." Hank practically bubbled. "We'd never been before. That was when we met Harold."

Harold was a radiologist who owned a house in Provincetown. It was on the biggest piece of land in town, but it needed a ton of work. Hank had told him what he could do to fix it up, and their partnership had been born. Since that time, Hank visited Provincetown almost every year. He stayed in Harold's house for free, and he remodeled what needed work. That was why Harold's house was now worth over four million, and that was how we always had a nice place to stay on the Cape.

"His house is one of your masterpieces," I told Hank.

"Aww," he said before cupping my cheek.

I froze. I could count on one hand how many times he had touched me since his accident. To feel his warm, calloused hand on my face and to feel his thumb absently rub my jaw almost made me wrap my arms around his neck and bury my face in his chest.

But I didn't.

It was important for Hank and his emotions to take the lead. When Hank withdrew his hand, I had no doubt there would be even more such instances in the hours to come.

"Bubble, I'm so glad you're here."

We turned to see Mitch standing in the hallway. He was dripping wet and had a towel wrapped around his waist. "The water pressure in my shower is awful." He waved his hand to the basement. "Go fix it."

"Oh my God," Hank said with an eye roll. "I'm not here five minutes, and you're already trying to get me to do house repairs."

Mitch's eyes widened and he gaped in pretend surprise. "And you were expecting something different?"

Hank shook his head. "No. I really shouldn't, should I?"

Mitch snorted. "Of course not. And when you're done down there, I've made a list of other things for you to fix before dinner tonight."

"Why yes!" he exclaimed. "I live to serve you."

"Naturally," Mitch said with a nod as Hank headed for the front door. "When you know what you want to make for dinner, let me know. I'll make sure Grandma goes out to get whatever we don't have."

"And what's wrong with you?" Darren asked.

Mitch glared at Darren as if he were stupid. "I'm washing my hair."

"I can go get groceries," I offered.

"I won't hear of it," Mitch said. "We all have jobs in the house. Bubble fixes things, and Grandma gets things."

"And what do you do again?" Hank asked.

"I supervise," Mitch replied before turning around and walking back down the hall.

"Hag," Hank snorted before walking out the door. "I'll be back in a bit." He smiled at Darren and me before closing the front door.

"Well, you wanted us to act like we normally did," Darren said after they left us alone.

I nodded. This was going far better than even I suspected.

AFTER HANK fixed the water pressure in the house, replaced several broken window latches, and stopped the leak in the guest bathroom, he worked on dinner. He was preparing an old favorite of his, Hawaiian chicken with rice and broccoli.

"What can I do to help?" I asked. It was something I always asked whenever Hank made dinner. While my skills were certainly not a match for his, he'd always appreciated my help and company while he cooked.

"You can get the water for the broccoli and rice boiling," he said over his shoulder. "The teakettle is above the stove."

"I know," I said with a chuckle. "I remember this house too."

If Hank's smile broadened any more, he'd crack his face. "Sorry. It just feels nice being able to recall little things without having to think about them too hard."

I grabbed the teakettle from the cabinet and filled it. "I'd imagine so. I guess we should have done this a lot sooner. I apologize for that."

He placed the broccoli florets into a bowl filled with water. "We're here now. That's all that matters."

Hank couldn't have been more right. After turning on the stove to get the water boiling, I said, "What next?"

"Nothing until the water boils." He took his phone out of his pocket and set the timer before placing it on the counter between us. It was a habit of his whenever he boiled water. It gave him a countdown for how much time he had to get the prep work done before the actual cooking began. "When the alarm goes off, you can work on the rice and broccoli while I focus on the chicken."

"You got it," I said with a nod.

While Hank worked on seasoning the chicken before cutting it, he glanced up at me. I stood to his left sipping a glass of red wine Mitch had poured for me before sitting on the couch to watch television with Darren. As always, while Hank made dinner, his roommates sat on their butts watching their favorite shows. That had infuriated me at the beginning of our relationship. It seemed as if they were taking advantage of Hank, but they weren't. This was their routine, and as odd as it might be, that routine might just be what Hank and I needed to take us out of neutral and get us back into drive. "What are you thinking about?" he asked.

"Just how good it is to see you smile." It was a lie, but there was no point in scaring Hank with the truth.

170

"It feels good," he said, once again turning his attention back to his knife work. "Being here is like walking into a dance routine already in progress, but since I know the choreography, it's really no big deal. I just have to count to three and then step right on in."

His analogy suddenly made Hank's situation even clearer to me. "I'm sorry if I've made the transition difficult for you. That was never my intention."

"I know that, and I appreciate the sentiment," he said as he quartered the chicken. "This hasn't been easy on you either. For you, the dance hasn't changed. It's your partner who's forgotten the steps. That has its own set of challenges, huh?"

No shit. But instead of saying so, I nodded.

"I guess I never really appreciated that 'til right now."

"I don't understand."

"Well, I don't know if you know this, but I can be pretty bullheaded at times."

I gasped in pretend horror. "You? That's not possible!"

Hank picked up a piece of broccoli and threw it at me. I sidestepped his cruciferous projectile, which smacked against the cabinet behind me. "You need to work on that aim of yours along with your memory," I teased. "They both suck."

It was the first time I'd made a joke about our current situation, and I was surprised that we both laughed. Hank shook his head and continued, "As I was saying, I've been so focused on me and what I've been going through that I've overlooked how hard this must be on you. That really hasn't been very fair, especially after everything you've done for me." He stopped cutting and locked eyes with me. No sadness or regret hid in his big, smiling blue eyes. They sparkled like diamonds scattered across a pristine ocean. "I've never thanked you."

I swallowed the lump in my throat, but when I spoke, my voice quivered. "No need. It's what you do for the man you I—"

Our gazes lingered. His eyes, already bright and cheery, grew wider as if some unseen memory struggled to reach the surface, but then Hank's cell phone dinged. The intruding text tone sent whatever had escaped back into hiding and shut the door with a thud.

171

We both gazed down at the phone, which indicated he'd just received a message from someone named Weasel. The text asked, *You in town yet?*

Hank set the knife down and turned on the water and rinsed his hands.

"That's an interesting nickname," I said. "Who's Weasel?"

"An old friend," Hank answered. Was it the text or the moment we'd shared that rattled him? Based on past experience, I had to go with the emotions he must have been feeling. Whenever something sparked between us, like at M2M or when we watched *The Avengers*, Hank backpedaled. It made him nervous.

Although we hadn't discussed it in some time, he still believed he was in love with Karl, and I had to find a way around that.

After his hands were clean, the timer on his phone went off.

"Time to get cooking," he said.

"What about your text?"

He shrugged and placed the phone in his pocket. "I'll respond after dinner."

"How does one get a nickname like Weasel?" I asked.

"How else?" he asked with an eye roll.

I laughed. Mitch did love the nicknames he created, and they always seemed to catch on. "I'd like to meet your friend," I said after placing the broccoli in the boiling water. "I don't think I've met anyone named Weasel before."

"Probably not. We hadn't spoken in years. He contacted me after he found out about my accident."

I nodded. Crises suffered had a way of bridging the gap the years created. "Well, I'd like to meet him."

Hank motioned to the rice. "How about we focus on the food?" he asked. "Before the Hag starts asking about his dinner."

As if on cue, Mitch's voice drifted to us from the living room. "I'm hungry!"

"Shut up, you hag!" Hank yelled back.

"Grandma's hungry too," Mitch informed us. "She's about ready to gum my leg off."

Hank and I laughed while Darren had several choice words for Mitch.

"Chicken's going in now," I called out.

"About damn time," Mitch complained.

Hank blew raspberries in the direction of the living room, and I chuckled.

"I heard that!" Mitch yelled.

"That's because hags have bigass ears." I couldn't believe the words came out of my mouth. Judging from the surprise in Hank's eyes, neither could he. He burst out laughing as Mitch's telltale thudding footsteps told me he was on his way into the kitchen.

"You're in for it now," Hank whispered.

"I've never called him Hag before. What do I do?"

Hank grabbed me by my wrist and tugged me behind him. "Stay here. I'll take the brunt of the bitchiness."

When Mitch turned the corner, pretending to be outraged at me, I didn't hear a word he said. I could only bask in the fact that Hank had placed himself between Mitch and me, exactly how he used to do whenever his best friend went into full Hag mode.

AFTER DINNER, the four of us sat on the patio overlooking the San Diego skyline. A refreshing breeze whipped around us, causing the deck umbrellas to flutter. Down the hill, dozens of headlights zipped along the freeway that ran behind the house, and up above, stars winked at us from a semicloudy sky.

It had been a perfect night.

"I'm still trying to think of the perfect name for you, Santi."

"Give it a rest," Hank told Mitch.

"I will not," Mitch replied, still pretending to be annoyed. Only Hank and Darren had license to call Mitch Hag, mostly because he only ever addressed them by their nicknames. Anyone else who called him that was saddled with a moniker of Mitch's choosing, and according to him, the name would be etched upon my gravestone. "I have shown

Santi nothing but respect and restraint by not assigning him a pet name the past three years."

Darren nodded. "It's true. I'm surprised this hasn't happened sooner."

"That's because until tonight, Santi has walked on my good side." He tossed a fake sneer my way. "But now he stands with the rest of you on my bad side."

"You have a good side?" Darren asked before winking at me.

That turned Mitch's attention to Darren. "Grandma, isn't it past your bedtime?"

"I can't tell," he replied. "I usually know it's time for bed when you head out to the bathhouse. Is it not ten o'clock yet?"

I decided to come to Darren's rescue. "So is that why some of your friends have nicknames while others don't? Because they called you Hag first?"

Mitch eyed Darren carefully. The look clearly communicated that Mitch would deal with him later. "Precisely. I'd still call Bubble and Grandma by their first names if they hadn't started calling me Hag first."

"If the shoe fits," Hank added with a grin.

"Don't get me started, Bubble. I'm not the one who gets silicone injected into my ass."

I snapped my attention to Hank, who glowered at Mitch. "You do what? I didn't know that."

"You didn't know?" Mitch cackled. "How else do you think his butt has remained so perky all these years?"

I shrugged. "Exercise and manual labor."

Mitch stared at me as if I was too pretty to have a brain. "No one's butt is that perky without some medical help. Just ask Kim Kardashian."

"Why do you do it?"

"He's a bottom," Mitch answered for Hank. "I've never seen a boy love cock in his ass more than our dear Bubble. He feels he has to have the perkiest butt in all the land and does whatever he needs to make sure it is."

I couldn't have been more shocked if Hank had suddenly sprouted antennae. "Did you do that in Houston?"

Hank shrugged before knocking on his head. "How would I know?"

"Oh dear, clueless Santi, of course he did. I helped him research the doctors."

"Are no secrets safe with you?" Hank asked Mitch.

I turned the question on Hank. "Why would you keep it a secret in the first place?"

Hank's cheeks turned cherry red. "Mostly because I was embarrassed. That's why I've never told anyone."

"And who wouldn't be?" Mitch asked. "That's why I choose nicknames carefully. They are designed to be an endearing insult."

"Don't you just love a good oxymoron?" Darren asked. "In Mitch's case, he's just a moron."

As the boys bantered, I searched my memory for the nicknames I'd heard Mitch call people over the years. Hank's friend Dan was Poop Deck, which I hoped was a nod to his time in the Navy. Although with what I'd just learned, I had my doubts. He called Jill the Beav, which was a pretty obvious reference, but the only other nickname I'd heard was for Robert, Mitch's former boyfriend. "I have to ask. Why do you call Robert Lamisil? Is it because he has athlete's foot?"

Mitch snorted. "That Buddha belly motherfucker hasn't seen the inside of a gym in at least twenty years. Lamisil is his nickname because he's got a foot fetish, and I'm not talking about your standard shrimper. He gets off on guys sticking a foot up his ass."

"Are you shitting me?"

Mitch, Darren, and Hank shook their heads in unison.

"How bizarre."

"Try being the one who has to lube up his foot with Lamisil," Mitch said with a frown. "To avoid athlete's butt, I guess."

All of us burst into laughter, and the sound of our merriment caused my heart to soar. It had been too long since the four of us just kicked back and had a good time. It was good for my soul, and from the constant smile that lit up Hank's expression, it was good for his too.

"So you see, Santi," Mitch said once our laughter died down, "when I come up with a name for you, it will perfectly express my love and loathing for you in one fell swoop." He bared his full set of white teeth at me.

I rose from my seat and kissed him on the cheek. "And I couldn't be more honored, you old Hag."

Darren glanced at his watch. "On that note, it's time for bed. I've got an early day tomorrow, and it's time for Mitch to head over to the bathhouse."

Mitch nodded. "Past time, actually. I have fans I'd hate to disappoint."

When Darren and Mitch went back inside, Hank kicked his feet up on the table and gazed up into the heavens. "Not tired yet?" I asked.

"Exhausted, actually, but it feels so good to be here I'm not ready to abandon it for unconsciousness yet."

"Mind if I stay up with you?"

"Not at all," he answered. "When you're ready for bed, take my room. I'll stay in the guest room downstairs."

Although I'd hoped we'd share a bed, I'd also been realistic about my chances. "I can take the guest room."

He shook his head. "You've given up your room these past weeks, so it's only right I return the favor."

"It's not my room. It's ours," I reminded him.

"I know." Hank nodded. It was the first time the mere mention of our past didn't cause him to tense up. It was as if he was no longer fighting me. This wasn't him giving up or an unconditional surrender. It was simply a chink in the armor he'd worn ever since he woke up in the hospital room.

With any luck, it would be gone by the time we went back to Houston.

BY THE time Hank had awoken and showered the next morning, I had the car all packed up for our day out. He had been surprised to find me waiting at the kitchen table, his coffee already in a travel cup, once he climbed the staircase from the lower level. He wore his Sparkle On shirt from M2M, denim shorts, and blue high-tops.

"What's this?" he asked.

"Your coffee," I said, handing it to him before escorting him toward the front door. "You'll have to drink it on the go."

"Where are we going?"

Instead of answering him, I drove Hank over to the Presidio. Although he had no memory of our first time there, I could recall almost every moment. It was where we had truly began to connect on a far more intimate level, and it was where I hoped we would do so again.

"The Presidio?" he asked after we pulled into the parking lot.

I nodded in reply before getting out of the car and retrieving the picnic basket from the trunk of our rental.

"What are you up to?" He eyed the basket and then arched an eyebrow at me.

"Nothing," I said, pretending to be übercasual. "We only have two days here in SoCal, so why not live it up? Besides, who doesn't love a picnic?"

Hank clearly didn't believe me. How could he? It was obvious what I was doing. But after the progress from last night, it was time to throw caution to the wind.

Instead of becoming uncomfortable, Hank took the basket from my grip and led the way up the grassy hill. "The best spot is up here," he said, pointing to the shaded area where we'd sat the last time, also at his suggestion.

I pretended to scratch an insistent itch on my nose to hide my smile. "It's perfect."

When we reached our destination, Hank took the sheet out of the basket and spread it over the grass while I took out the sandwiches I'd made that morning. I placed the plates with our meals on the sheet while Hank took his seat. I popped open his Red Bull and handed it to him before taking out my can of Sprite.

"BLTs," Hank said as he snatched his sandwich from the plate. "My fave."

"I know."

For a few moments, we ate in silence, taking in the warm breeze as it wrapped around us and studying the tourists who roamed the grounds of the historic Spanish fort that had been turned into a state park. Between bites Hank filled me in on the history of the site and explained the building's architecture. As a contractor, he had a fascination with how things were made, and he relished in sharing that information.

Even though I'd heard all this before, I sat back and listened. It was almost as if we'd traveled back in time.

"I've told you all this before, haven't I?"

I smirked. "Maybe."

"Why didn't you say something?"

"It didn't bother me to hear it again," I answered. "I'd forgotten most of what you told me anyway. I'm not quite the history buff you are."

He nodded. "Most people aren't. But history is so important. It tells us where we came from and how we got to where we are today. Who doesn't find that fascinating?"

Hopefully Hank would apply that interest to us. In order for him to understand how he had moved from California to Texas and from Karl to me, he had to recall our shared past. The heart of our relationship resided in the small details we created every day. Those events were the needle and thread that created the tapestry of us. Without them, the gorgeous work of art we crafted together would fray and fall apart.

"Can I ask you a question?"

"Sure," I said, resting back on my hands and giving him my full attention.

"Since we're on the general subject of history, you've never told me how you managed to smooth things over with Darren and Mitch after our fight in Key West. Will you tell me now?"

I smiled. I'd begun to wonder if Hank was going to bring that up again.

HANK AND I stood outside the Island House, waiting for the taxi we'd called to take us back to the airport. His hand rested on the small of my back, and he was holding me close. While that was nothing out of the ordinary, since the fight with Darren and Mitch, he'd been even more affectionate than usual. It was as if he feared this argument might find a way to come between us, and considering the troubles he had had keeping peace between Karl and Mitch and Darren, it was easy to understand why.

That was when I realized the true problem we were dealing with. Even though Karl had tried to sever the family Hank, Mitch, and Darren had created, he'd never been able to. That was exactly what I was unintentionally doing. I hadn't set out to break up their life, but that was in essence what was happening. This wasn't just about Hank abandoning his obligations to his friends in favor of me. This was like a divorce. While no sexual relationship existed between them, Hank, Darren, and Mitch functioned as a married entity.

They shared household expenses, they made life decisions together, and they were an integral part of one another's lives. They didn't even really date anymore. They went out to clubs and fucked a whole lot, but when it came to their emotional well-being, the three of them took care of each other. The only aspect of their lives they didn't fulfill was sexual, and any random guy could fix that.

That made me, for all intents and purposes, the other woman. I was the person who came into their lives and destroyed their little happy family. That was why they couldn't be happy for Hank. How could they be when they'd obviously imagined I'd just be an addition to their lives rather than subtract something from it?

It also explained Hank's almost clingy behavior. He was trying to reassure himself that he was doing the right thing. Venturing into the unknown with me was like jumping from a plane without a parachute.

I was breaking up their family, and it was up to me to fix it.

I got out my cell phone.

"Who are you calling?" Hank asked.

I held up my index finger for him to wait while the line rang. After a few rings, I worried that Mitch was going to send me to voice mail, but he picked up. His voice strained a greeting. "Yes."

"The cab's on its way," I said. "Meet us out front."

I hung up before Mitch had time to respond. If given time to argue, Mitch would. I had to rely on his inherently frugal nature to ultimately win. After all, why would he split a taxi with Darren if he could pay only a quarter of the cost instead?

"What do you think you're doing?"

I gazed up at Hank.

He crossed his arms over his chest and glowered down at me. "Did you call who I think you did?"

I nodded.

"Why the hell would you want to share a cab with that hag after the way he's treated us? I'm not speaking to them until they apologize."

"That's fine," I said. "It'll be a quiet ride to the airport, then."

A few minutes later, Mitch and Darren exited the building with their suitcases in tow. They didn't speak, and neither did Hank. They eyed each other in silence before staring up and down the street as if they could magically summon the cab.

"I want to say something before the taxi gets here."

All three of them turned to me, unable to believe I was actually breaking the silence.

"I'm sorry for breaking up your family," I told Mitch and Darren. "We shouldn't have made this decision without talking to you both first. You should have been kept in the loop because this wasn't just about Hank and me. It's about you too. That was wrong, and I couldn't regret that more if I tried."

The distant glare in Mitch's eyes faltered as his eyes welled up with tears. Darren remained unchanged. He was a brick wall.

"I'm not going to come between you three, and I'm not going to even try. You've been family for too long, and I know Hank enough to know that he won't be happy if he doesn't have you two in his life." I turned to Hank and took his hands in mine. "That's why I think we should postpone your move."

"What?" Hank asked. He gripped my hands and pulled me closer. "Have you changed your mind?"

"Of course not. Now who's being Silly McSillyson?" I asked.

"Then I don't understand."

"We need to plan this better, let everyone's emotions settle, and then we can sit down and see how we can work this all out. There might be a simple solution we haven't even considered, but the four of us working together can fix just about anything." I gazed over my shoulder at Darren and Mitch. "At least that's my hope."

Mitch took a step toward me, a hopeful glimmer in his eye. "You'd do that for us?"

I nodded. "I love Hank, but I also love you two. His family is my family now."

"You're being ridiculous," Darren said from behind Mitch.

Hank was about to come to my defense, and even Mitch opened his mouth to tell Darren to hush, when I shushed them both. "Let him say his piece."

"You can't put your lives on hold for us," he said. "That's stupid. Almost as stupid as Mitch and I have been. We all fucked this up royally. Should you have included us in the process? Yes. Should we have not been selfish assholes? Most definitely. But you're right, Santi. We are a family of four now, and we'll figure it out. That's what family does."

"AND THAT'S what we did," I said to Hank as I finished the story.

Hank sat in silence. He scanned the sheet upon which we sat as if it held the answers to some difficult question he'd been searching for.

"Are you okay?"

"I'm fine," he said. "Just stunned."

"About what?"

"You were willing to put our happiness on hold for the sake of Darren and Mitch?"

That was why I'd worried about telling him the full story when he'd asked a few weeks ago: I feared learning what I'd been willing to sacrifice might put too much pressure on him. But it was time for Hank to know exactly what I was willing to do to be with him. "Well, yes. I meant what I said. I love them too. They're your brothers, which sort of makes them my brothers-in-law."

He didn't respond. Instead he gazed off in the distance at the arched walkways of the Presidio. Perhaps within the architecture he'd find the words that so easily escaped him.

"No one's ever done that for me before," he finally uttered.

"Sure they have," I said. "Mitch and Darren love you. The three of you built a life together."

He nodded. "I know, but I'm talking about a lover. The men I've been involved with have always been concerned with either changing me into what they wanted or showing me off like I was some trophy."

"Well, you are one hot man," I said with a devilish smile.

He rolled his eyes and swatted my thigh. That was the closest Hank had gotten to my crotch in weeks, and my cock sprung to life. I had to sit forward to hide the bulge in my shorts. "I'm being serious," he said, feigning a sneer.

I motioned for him to continue and held up my fingers in the Boy Scout salute as a promise I'd be good. Hank suspiciously eyed my fingers—he evidently didn't believe I was ever a Boy Scout—but he let the matter drop.

"What I meant was that most of the guys I've dated never really put me first. At least I never felt as if I was a priority. I'm not saying I have to be numero uno all the time, but I don't think I ever was." He gazed over my shoulder as his train of thought deposited him at a familiar station. "Not even Karl."

It was the first time he had ever associated his ex with anything negative. Should I board this train and steer Hank onto the track I wanted him to go? If I did, I could help my own case and take a sledgehammer to the wall Hank's love for Karl had erected between Hank and me.

As I was about to do just that, the sadness in Hank's eyes stopped me cold. No matter how much I wanted to paint Karl in a negative light, doing so would say more about me than about the man who had hurt my Hank, and I couldn't add to the heartache that slumped his shoulders and cast his eyes downward.

"It wasn't all Karl's fault," I admitted begrudgingly.

Only pulling a rabbit out of thin air could have surprised him more. "What do you mean?"

"He was an addict. The alcohol and drugs turned him into the man who hurt you. I'm sure the man he was before that would have done anything for you."

The last thing I needed was to have him see Karl as anything other than the asshole ex-boyfriend he'd always made him out to be. "Maybe," he replied. Why did I get the feeling that Hank wasn't quite sure?

The chirp of an incoming text stopped me from asking Hank what he meant. He fished his phone out of his pocket, glanced at the screen, and then promptly put it back.

"Not gonna respond?" I asked.

He shook his head. "So where to next?"

I grinned. "You'll just have to wait and see."

Hank stood up and held out his hand for mine, beaming down at me. "Then let's get moving."

THIRTY MINUTES later we walked through the turnstiles of the San Diego Zoo.

"I love this place!"

I chuckled. "Tell me something I don't know."

The smirk on his face told me he accepted my challenge. "Did you know that because of the preservation efforts of the San Diego Zoo, the California condor has bounced back from a population of only about twenty to over four hundred?"

"Oh my God!" I exclaimed. "That's new information that I've never heard before in my life."

Hank sulked. He evidently caught my playful sarcasm.

"Buck up," I said. "You forgot you told me that on the several occasions we've visited the zoo before your accident. Your memory has always been pretty shitty."

A smile teased across his lips. "I remember what's important. That's all."

That comment hit so hard I tripped over my own two feet.

"Fuck!" he said. "That came out wrong. Mitch has always teased me about my memory, and that's what I used to tell him."

That was true. I'd heard Hank say that before, especially when Mitch went on and on about how piss-poor Hank's memory was. He'd said that to rile Mitch up, and it had always worked. Mitch was a firm believer that he and everything he said were too important ever to be forgotten.

"No worries," I said once I recovered.

Hank stood in front of me and rubbed my shoulders. "Still, that was a pretty asshole thing to say, considering everything. I'm sorry." His blue eyes locked on to mine. "I really am."

"Apology accepted," I replied before grabbing his hand and tugging him forward. "Now let's go or we'll miss the tour."

Hank grasped my hand. "That's my favorite—" He stopped, no doubt realizing he was about to repeat himself again. "But you already know that, right?"

I smiled. Going on the guided bus tour was how Hank preferred to experience the zoo. He claimed he always learned something new from the tour guides that way. After a ten-minute walk, we boarded the bus.

We sat in the back row on the second level of the double-decker bus, another favorite of Hank's. Since he was so tall, I took the inside seat, as I always did. Even though I prepared myself for Hank to sit in front of me or across the aisle, he slid into the seat next to me. The seating was extremely cozy. His hairy blond legs brushed against mine, and he draped his arm around the back of my seat. Out of habit, I almost rested my head on his shoulder, but I stopped myself. Instead I closed my eyes, inhaling Hank's comforting scent, which clung to the air around him.

"Here we go," he said as the bus started and the tour guide's voice blared through the speakers.

For the next fifteen minutes, we enjoyed watching the big cats lazing in the sun, the red panda playing with its ball, and the monkeys grooming each other. We even got to see the California condor fly from one tree to another inside the enclosure. The brand-new baby giraffe peeped at us from behind his mother. He studied us with dubious curiosity in his big eyes while she munched on some leaves. The black rhinos rolled around in the mud, and the elephants swayed back and forth as they stuffed themselves. When we reached the koala enclosure, the tour bus came to a full stop. One of the koalas happened to be awake.

"I haven't seen one awake in years," Hank said as he pointed to the little fellow, who was crunching on some eucalyptus. He smacked his lips and gazed at us in a sleepy haze. "That doesn't happen often."

Koalas slept about eighteen hours a day, and seeing one awake was a rarity for most people. For me, not so much. "One is always awake every time I'm here." I smiled into Hank's astonished face.

"Really?"

I nodded.

"How many times have we come here together?"

"This would be visit number four."

"Wow! I can't believe that."

"I guess the koalas just love me," I said with a proud jut of my chin.

Hank ran his fingers through the back of my hair. "Evidently so."

The gentle and loving gesture combined with the glint in his eyes stole the breath from my lungs and stopped time. The world around me disappeared. Only Hank and I populated the world. It was one of the most special moments I'd experienced since he woke from his coma.

For the first time in weeks, the Hank I remembered stared back at me before the man Hank now was blinked him back.

"Sorry," he whispered. He withdrew his hand from my head and turned to sit forward in his seat.

"No need to apologize," I said. I leaned against him. "It was nice."

"I just don't want to give you the wrong idea."

What the hell did that mean? "I don't understand."

"I know what it's like to feel pressured," he said with a sigh. "Pretty much everyone wants me to remember what I've forgotten. I can see it when Mitch acts like the drama queen he is. He's hoping by being even more of a hag that he'll force my memories to the surface. When I talk to my parents, they bring up things from the past I can't recall to see if it jogs anything, and you hope that by bringing me to the places that used to be special to us that it will somehow trigger an avalanche of memories." He gazed at me askance. It was his way of seeing if his words had upset me.

"I guess I wasn't hiding my intentions very well, was I?"

He chuckled and shook his head. "But I don't blame you, and I'm not angry at all. I just don't want to hurt you, especially when you look at me the way you sometimes do. It feels like I have all this power and your happiness rests in my hands. That's a lot for any one person to handle."

"I can't argue with that," I said. "But there's something you should know. You do make me happy. In fact, I've never been happier than when I met you. My life was no more exciting than a bran muffin until I saw you outside of Rich's. And I'm sorry if that puts a lot of pressure on you, I really am, but you don't have any power over me that I haven't willingly given to you. That's what happens when you fall in love. You give your heart to someone and hope they are gentle and loving with it, and that is something you have always been."

"But I'm not that Hank anymore," he said. He averted his gaze to the metal floor of the bus.

I hooked my fingers under his chin and brought his attention back to me. "But you are still Hank Burton, and that's the man I fell in love with and the person I gave my heart to."

"How can you say that?" he asked. "I'm so screwed up right now I don't know what I feel, but I do know I don't want to hurt you. Or anybody."

He didn't have to tell me that. I knew Hank better than anyone else. He went out of his way *not* to hurt people. "And I love you even more for it. But you should know, I'm willing to be hurt because that's what love is."

Hank stared at me out of the corners of his eyes. Clearly he was questioning my sanity.

"It's true," I said with a firm nod. "It's not always hot sex and romantic candlelit dinners. Or picnics in the park or fun days at the zoo. True love exists in the gaps between those moments. It's in the arguments, where you're so angry at each other that you may want to throw a tantrum and walk out the door, but you don't. It lives in the hard times when one of you is sick or exhausted, and you have to carry each other for miles with no rest, and even though your body aches and you want to let go, you don't."

"I don't think I've ever known that kind of love." He glanced at his hands in his lap. "My relationships have always been the bad kind. Where one of us gives up or gives in."

"Well, love that is worth anything isn't like that. It blooms in the dead of winter because we have fed its soul in the spring and summer. *That* is what I fight for. You may not feel what I do because you lack the memories I have, but you feel something. I can see it in the way you look at me or touch me, and I can see you fighting it. Maybe because you're afraid of hurting me or because you don't understand what these emotions are. I don't really know, but you should know this: Fighting it won't make it go away, and it won't change how our story will end. We *will* get married. We *will* grow old together. And before we breathe our last, the final words we will utter will be each other's names."

Hank rested his forehead against mine and sighed. I loved when he did that. It was as comforting and intimate as a kiss. "And I thought I was stubborn."

"I can be just as bullheaded as you."

"So what now?"

"Now we get out of here."

Hank pulled away. I had evidently surprised him. "What? Why?"

"No more trips down memory lane," I said. "We're going to forge new memories. Ones we both remember."

He smiled. "I'd like that."

When the bus came to a stop, I once again grabbed Hank's hand and led him down the steps and out of our past. Now we walked toward what I hoped would be our future.

CHAPTER
Ten

"OH, GIRL! I'm so gonna get fucked tonight," Mitch squealed as we walked toward Numbers, which was a popular club in Hillcrest. It was Daddy Night, and Mitch was dressed to be pummeled. A shoulder harness fit snugly around his small chest, and he wore a leather strap on his right bicep, proudly announcing to all his potential suitors that he was a bottom. But Mitch's sashay and the fact that he now said "girl" in almost every sentence revealed his sexual position far more clearly than the leather band.

"And what makes tonight any different?" Darren asked. A sly grin cut across his lips. He loved egging Mitch on. What he didn't love was going out to clubs, but Mitch had managed to nag him into coming out with us. He refused, however, to put on leather. Instead he wore jeans and a polo shirt that he'd left untucked. Darren didn't give a shit about impressing others. People either liked him for who he was or not.

"Oh, Grandma. Don't waste your time trying to be clever," Mitch replied. "Not when you need to be watching where you walk. It's dark out, and you don't want to break a hip."

"Will the two of you give it a rest?" Hank asked from my side, dressed in his seven-strap full-body harness. The top two straps looped around his shoulders and through the metal ring on his chest and at his back. The next two ran horizontally across his blond, furry chest. The other three were the far more interesting ones. Two of the straps wrapped around the front ring before looping around his back and disappearing beneath the waistband of his tight denim. Those two straps lifted his already perky ass while the seventh band connected to the cock ring that held Hank's junk in place.

The leather, the muscle, the piercings, the ink, and the body hair turned Hank from a hunky stud into one hot badass motherfucker. Every gay boy we passed turned around to gawk at him or said, "Well, hello there, Daddy."

Hank only smiled in reply. He didn't return their obvious come-ons or give them the time of day. Even without his memories, he still respected that he was there with me.

Mitch's complaining brought me out of my thoughts. "I hate going out with you, Bubble."

"Why's that?" he asked.

"No one's looking at me. All they can see is your big hairy ass, and all these girls are already lubing up their tired holes for you. Little do they know you're a bigger bottom than they are."

"Sounds like jealousy to me," Darren said as we drew closer to the front door. I was surprised that there wasn't a line to get into the club and that no one was outside collecting the cover charge.

"Oh please," Mitch replied. "What Bubble's doing is false advertising, and it's annoying."

"What do you expect me to do?" Hank asked. "Shave my beard and wax my chest?"

"Oh hell no!" I replied so quickly that everyone looked at me before laughing.

Hank dangled his arm around my shoulders. "See, Santi likes it."

Mitch stopped in front of the door. No one seemed to notice that the inside of the club appeared practically empty. They were all focused on the hag storm Mitch was about to unleash. "Santi isn't a reliable source. He's far too biased. Not only that, he's another false-advertising bitch."

What was he talking about? There was nothing fake about the way I looked. I had on a skintight leather vest that made it extremely difficult to breathe. It was zipped a quarter of the way up my chest, and I sported a leather band on my left bicep, which was the universal sign that I was a top. "Are you trying to say I look like a bottom?"

Mitch eyed me up and down. "Girl, you not only scream bottom, but bossy bottom at that, especially with that fancy leather vest. Who made it? Prada?"

"Hank and I actually got this at FK Leather."

"In Provincetown?" Hank asked from my side.

I nodded to Hank before returning my focus to Mitch. "And who cares if people think I'm a bottom? If they approach me, I'll just send them over to you."

Mitch chuffed. "I don't take sloppy seconds."

"That's not what I've heard," Darren said with a snicker.

Hank grabbed Mitch and Darren by the backs of their necks and walked them forward. "Enough," he said. "Let's get inside."

Once they crossed the threshold and made their way into the club's interior, Hank gasped, Mitch cursed, and Darren broke into hysterics. I was behind them and still in the small narrow hallway, so I had no clue what had caused such different reactions. When I rounded the corner, words completely failed me.

Only three people occupied the dance floor, and they were *not* dressed in leather. They wore brightly colored outfits. One guy had on only fuzzy pink leg warmers and a jockstrap. His hair had been dyed into a rainbow mohawk. The girl he danced with wore a yellow tube top and a yellow miniskirt. Ripped fishnet stockings that had been draped over yellow stretch pants covered her legs, and she carried around a red-and-white sphere with a black stripe separating the two colors. On her cheeks, two bright red dots had been painted, and a pair of yellow-and-black cat ears sprouted from her head. Their friend was dressed more strangely. For some reason he was wearing a full costume that resembled a dragon, and every time he danced, his red-and-yellow tail swept across the floor.

"What in the name of all that is holy is going on?" Mitch asked.

None of us had an answer, especially when we turned our attention to the bar. A few more people congregated there, and they all had Hello Kitty backpacks on.

"I think I'm having a stroke," Mitch said. "Because I can't be seeing what I'm seeing."

Darren, who couldn't stop laughing, leaned against Hank for support. "And I was worried I'd stick out like a sore thumb."

I gazed up at Hank, who looked down at me. He narrowed his eyes. It was his way of telling me he wanted to get the fuck out of there. I couldn't have agreed more.

"Maybe we should go elsewhere," I said.

"Oh hell no," Mitch replied. "I'm getting to the bottom of this shit." He cut through the dance floor to get to the bar on the other side. He did his best to avoid the dancing dragon, but the guy was hopping all over the place. His tail happened to cross paths with Mitch, who stumbled and collided with one of the Hello Kitty crew.

That did Darren in. He laughed so hard he collapsed on the floor.

"I'll pick up Grandma," I told Hank. "He's fallen and can't get up. You go with Mitch."

Hank nodded and left, and I helped Darren off the floor.

"Did you see that?" he gasped, clutching at me. His powder blue eyes could outshine the sun. "Did you see Mitch?"

"Everyone saw him," I replied, leading Darren across the dance floor.

My answer made Darren laugh even more. It was difficult trying to get him to move past the dragon, who was grinding against the guy with the fuzzy pink leg warmers, without him practically bending in half in hysterics. "Let's get you something to drink," I said. "That will help calm you down."

"Maybe," Darren snickered. Then he glanced over my shoulder. Whatever he saw made him lose it completely. He howled in laughter, which caused the dancing threesome to stop and stare.

I turned around and I couldn't contain my own laughter. A Japanese cartoon called *Pokémon* was being displayed across the stage wall, and all around the stage were Pokémon balls of various shapes and sizes. Even the disco balls had been painted to resemble the red-and-white containers used to catch the animals in the cartoons.

"It's a Pokémon party," Mitch said from behind us.

Darren, who'd completely surrendered to hysterics, once again collapsed onto the floor.

"No shit," I said, nodding to the cartoon. "What happened to Daddy Night?"

"It was canceled," Mitch said as he waved his hands around. "For *this*." This made Darren laugh even louder, and Mitch glared down at him. "I think Grandma is going senile."

I had to agree. "So what now?"

"We get the fuck out of here," Mitch replied.

"No," Darren said as he struggled to get up. "I want to stay."

"Are you serious?" Hank asked. Mitch evidently was too shocked to speak. He stared at Darren as if he truly had gone insane. "Why?"

"Look at this place," he said. "I've never seen anything like it, and I want to stay. You were the ones who made me come out. Well, guess what? I'm here, and I'm not leaving yet." He surveyed our expressions, clearly realizing he was outnumbered. "One drink. That's all I ask."

Hank and I reluctantly nodded while Mitch groaned. "Fine," he said. "One drink, and then we leave."

A smile stretched across Darren's face. As we headed to the bar, a guy dressed as Pikachu, which was one of the cartoon characters, ran past us while another dressed like a little Japanese boy chased after him. He stopped in front of us and said, "Gotta catch 'em all" before continuing on his way.

Mitch turned on his heel and headed for the door before Hank grabbed his arm. "One drink," he said. "We promised."

Mitch glowered at Darren. "If any of these freaks hit on me, Grandma won't make it through the night."

HANK AND I leaned against the bar. I sipped on my Cape Cod while he knocked back his Red Bull. Darren had struck up a conversation with the girl in the yellow outfit while Mitch sat at the bar, practically crying in his martini.

"So you're really into this cosplay?" Darren asked the girl. From what I'd overheard from their conversation, cosplay was short for costume play, which was what these Pokémon lovers did as a hobby.

They dressed up in costumes inspired by the cartoon and partied the night away as they pretended to be their favorite characters.

She nodded. "It's awesome. It's kinda like your friends and leather," she said with a nod to us. "Except our fetish is Pokémon."

"You have sex dressed this way?" I asked.

"Fuck yeah!" she said. "If you've never been boned by Pikachu, you don't know what you're missing."

"I think I'll pass," Mitch muttered.

"That's too bad," she said. She flipped her blonde hair over her shoulder. "My guy's got a dildo shaped like Pikachu's lightning-bolt tail. It fucking rocks my world, and when he comes, he shouts out his name like they do in the cartoon." She started mimicking her boyfriend's moans and grunts before screaming, "Piiiiiiiiiiii-kaaaaaaaa-chuuuuuuuuuu!"

"I think you need professional help," Mitch told her.

Her slanted eyes revealed she didn't appreciate the comment. "You know that's pretty sucky. Do you like being hated on because you're gay? What makes you think we're any different? We are who we are, so I don't give a flying fuck what you think."

"Pardon my friend," Darren said. "He's grumpy because he was expecting tonight to be Daddy Night."

She tossed one final sneer at Mitch before replying to Darren, "They moved it to next week."

While Darren continued his questions into the bizarre world of Pokémon play, I turned my attention to Hank. "Well, when I said I wanted us to create new memories, this wasn't quite what I had in mind."

Hank chuckled. "I'd think not." He surveyed the dance floor while he ran his hand up and down my back. To have Hank once again touch me as he used to and to do it without even thinking about it made hope swell inside me. "I've got to give these guys credit, though. They are committed."

I motioned to the two of us and our leather. "Are we any different?"

He leaned in closer. His hot breath plumed across my ear and my neck. I held my breath and bit my tongue. It was the only way to stop myself from diving into the crook of Hank's neck and devouring him whole. I hadn't had him that close to me in a long time. "Yes," he finally replied. "We're the normal kind of kinky. This is much more bizarre."

I nodded in reply, and before I could think, I moved my body against his. He pulled back, gazing down at me. A mixture of desire and fear clashed in his gaze, and the hand that had caressed my back clutched at my leather vest. By the way his grip trembled, I could tell he was once again wrestling with himself. He didn't know if he should fight instinct or give in to it, so I helped move him along.

I wrapped my arm around his neck and brought us closer together, bridging the gap between us. When our trembling lips met, I moaned into the kiss. I clutched Hank, practically clawing at his skin. I moved my hands from his broad shoulders to his harness, and I pulled hard. He growled in response as the strap attached to his cock and balls jerked forward, delivering the mixture of pain and pleasure that had always turned Hank on.

Reluctantly, Hank moved his hand down my back to rest on my hips. He clutched them tightly, as if years of pent-up sexual frustration yearned to be free, but while he held me and his tongue invaded my mouth, I willed his hand to return to his spot on my body. For some reason I believed that if Hank held me in the special way he always did, he would remember everything.

And then it happened.

Hank put his hand on the small of my back and dipped his fingers beneath my waistband. He sighed into our kiss as if he'd found home.

And just like that, I no longer cared whether he remembered. I leaned harder into the kiss, wrapping my arms around his neck and standing on my tiptoes. I had waited for this moment for so long, I inhaled every second. My Hank was in my arms again. His lips touched mine, and the desire we'd always enjoyed rushed back to fill the void the accident had created.

Each kiss made the pain of uncertainty I'd suffered worth it. Every time he dove his tongue into my mouth, I tasted more than Hank's sweet kisses. The meager reserves of faith and hope I'd been living on had been restocked, especially when he drew me closer to him and ground the erection straining in his denim against my own throbbing wood.

Nothing was going to make Hank recall the events he'd forgotten or the emotions we once shared. I accepted that now. But so what? I had him here with me now, and living in the present was always better than pining for the past.

"What's wrong?" he asked.

I suddenly realized that I'd been staring at Hank while we'd been kissing. I'd been so lost in his expressions of ecstasy and the way he held and kissed me that I hadn't noticed he'd opened his eyes. Confusion now replaced the want in his gaze.

"Absolutely nothing," I replied, leaning my forehead against his chin. "I guess I just couldn't believe that we were finally kissing."

"And it wasn't good?" he asked. "I'm not kissing like I used to?"

I laughed. "Are you kidding me? It was great." I gazed up at his bearded face and smiled. "Your kisses have always been awesome, but this one was fucking fantastic."

"Really? Why?"

I scratched my fingers through his beard, followed the hair across his jawline before tracing the edges of his lips. "Because you finally let me in."

Hank grinned down at me and rested his forehead against mine. He cupped my cheeks in his big hands. God, how I had missed that!

"So have your memories finally returned?" Mitch suddenly stood beside us. He arched an eyebrow at the way we held each other.

"No," I answered for Hank. "And I don't give a good damn whether they do or not." I wrapped my arms around Hank's waist and leaned against his chest.

Mitch studied Hank for a few seconds. He was about to say something when the dancing dragon passed behind him. Mitch hopped up, and his mouth turned into a big O.

"What?" I asked.

"That dragon just grabbed my ass. It's time to go."

"Fine," Darren replied. He'd obviously seen us kissing as well. He grinned at us before saying, "Let's go home. I'm sure these two would like to be alone."

"Oh, hell no! These bitches have the rest of their lives to fuck each other's brains out," Mitch said. He grabbed Darren by the wrist and tugged him backward. "We're going to Pecs."

Darren complained. Pecs was another bar where it wasn't unusual to find guys in leather. "What? Why?"

"Because I'm gonna find me a daddy tonight. Bubble's not going to be the only one getting some."

Hank grabbed my hand as we followed Mitch and Darren out the door. "No. That wouldn't be very fair, now would it?"

While Mitch hollered in agreement, my cock throbbed in response. Not only had Hank kissed me, but tonight we'd obviously be sharing the same bed again. This night couldn't get any fucking better.

TWENTY MINUTES later the four of us stood inside the packed bar that was Pecs. While not everyone was wearing leather, there were pockets of leather daddies in the crowd. Mitch tittered with excitement.

"Now that's what I'm talking about!" he said before cutting a path through the crowd.

"I hate it here," Darren griped. He eyed the throng of men and then the door behind us.

"We'll be with you, Grandma," I said as I held Hank's hand.

Darren locked eyes with me. "I'm so gonna help Mitch come up with a good nickname for you," he teased. "Something like Resting Dick Face, I'm thinking."

I bared my full set of teeth at him while Hank wrapped his arm around my shoulder. "Be nice," he told Darren.

"Why? He just called me Grandma."

"That's because you are a grandma, Grandma."

Darren flipped Hank off before we followed Mitch toward the bar. He'd ordered a drink and sidled up next to a smooth-looking leather daddy. Although Mitch did prefer younger, effeminate men, when he strapped on his harness, only a daddy could scratch his itch. But that daddy had to be just right. Not too fat, not too old, and not too hairy. He was the Goldilocks of the leather set. Fortunately, the dark-haired guy he was flirting shamelessly with filled that order.

"What did you get us?" I asked once we stood at his side.

He stared at me out of the corner of his eye as he sipped his martini. "What I always get you," he answered. "Nothing. Now go away." He rubbed his hand along his new friend's upper thigh while, Hank, Darren, and I ordered a round of drinks, which the kind-faced older bartender promptly filled.

"I haven't seen Mitch this forward in a long time," Hank said before taking a sip of his Red Bull.

"That's because you've forgotten how much of a slut he's become," Darren replied. He nursed his Diet Coke and rolled his eyes at Mitch, who now had his tongue down smooth daddy's throat.

"That's one part of my life I'm glad I can't recall." He sat on the barstool and pulled me between his legs. He rested his hands on my ass. I practically creamed my jeans. Things between us were progressing nicely. "I really wish I could remember other stuff, though."

I put my alcoholic beverage down on the bar. "Forget about all that. It doesn't matter now."

"But it does," he said. "I see the way you look at me, and I know there are tons of memories that have caused that. It pisses me off that I don't know what they are."

I pressed my lips to his, and he opened his mouth to allow my tongue entrance. When I pulled away, I smiled. "Remember what I said at the zoo. We'll create new ones. That's what we'll spend the rest of our lives doing."

"I've got to ask," Darren said. "When did all this happen?"

"I'm not really sure," Hank answered. He stared down at me instead of looking at Darren. "It's been gradual. I guess I've been hurt so many times in my life that I didn't want to hurt someone who obviously cared so much for me. What else but love makes someone take care of someone else the way Santi has taken care of me? It made me feel guilty. That I didn't deserve such wonderful treatment, especially when I couldn't return that love."

"So you love him now?" Darren asked skeptically.

Hank's smile retreated slightly. I already knew the answer. I might be at year three of our relationship, but for all intents and purposes, this was day one for Hank. I nuzzled his cheek. It was my way of letting him know that his honesty wouldn't devastate me.

"I don't know what it is right now," he finally replied. "I'm just not fighting it anymore."

"And that's all I can ask," I said before I kissed the tip of his nose.

After settling once again into Hank's arms, I turned to Darren, who had a huge grin plastered across his face. "Good. I'm glad. The two of you needed to get past that hump."

"What's this I hear about humping?" Mitch asked. He tore his attention away from his trick and settled his eyes on us. Even in the face of an obvious score, he just had to be included in any sexual conversation that occurred around him.

"I didn't say 'humping.' I said 'hump.'" Darren blew out his frustration. "Why don't you go back to kissing your friend? I like you much better when you can't talk."

Mitch sniffed in derision before once again gobbling up tongue.

Hank grimaced. "God, that's disgusting."

"You think you two are any better?" Darren asked with a snort. "The two of you have been going at it since you met. The only reason you stopped for a while there was because you fell on your head, Hank. But not even a landing headfirst on pavement can keep you two apart for long." He pretended to be exasperated, but he was clearly pleased to see us happy.

Hank blushed a deep red, which was quite an accomplishment for someone so tan.

"Nothing can stop us," I said, quite confident in my appraisal.

"Definitely nothing can stop you," Hank added. "That's for sure."

I nodded. "I'm quite tenacious."

"Like a bulldog."

I leaned my forehead against his. "Yes. Like a bulldog."

I was pleased that my tenacity was obviously paying off.

THREE DRINKS later I had to pee so badly I was about to burst, but I didn't want to leave Hank alone. Mitch had already left with his trick, and surprisingly enough, a random guy had started a conversation with Darren. He was short like Darren, about five foot two, and had a weird fashion sense. He sported a striped button-down long-sleeve shirt, a polka-dot bow tie, and red shorts. He was a cornucopia of patterns and colors, but he seemed quite taken with Darren the moment he saw him. He introduced himself as Carmichael and then bought Darren a drink. Now they hunched together at a corner table, as far away from the crowds as they could get, which wasn't easy. Pecs had become seriously packed. But for once the throngs of men didn't bother Darren. He had probably the biggest grin I'd ever seen on his face.

"I'm glad someone's talking to him," Hank said. "Darren's such a great guy, and he's so down on himself all the time. He pretends not to care about what people think about him, but he really does. I can tell. That bullshit he spouts about not wanting to dress up is just that. Bullshit. He does it so he can avoid rejection."

I had recent experience with that. With any luck, that was all behind me now. "No one likes rejection."

"Of course not," he added with a nod. "But Darren's terrified of it, and he's such a good guy. He just has to give people a chance."

I switched my gaze over to Darren, who'd just been on the receiving end of a kiss. "I think Carmichael might get more than a chance. He might actually get some ass."

Hank laughed. "Darren's a top."

My jaw about hit the bar. Since Darren's personality was typically docile, I always imagined him to be a bottom. "Really?"

"Really." He fluttered his fingers across my cheek.

I leaned into it and practically started purring.

"Is there a reason you're hopping from one foot to the next?"

"I have to pee."

He rolled his eyes and pointed to the men's room at the back of the bar. "Well, go."

"I don't want to leave you alone."

Hank grabbed my shoulders and turned me around. "I'm a big boy. I can take care of myself." He then swatted my ass and gently prodded me forward.

I cut my way through the crowd, but not before staring back over my shoulder. Hank watched me walk away, a twinkle in his eye and a smile on his lips. I'd never been happier. I also never had to piss so badly in my life.

I walked up to the door and was about to reach for the handle when a voice stopped me. "There's a line here."

I turned to my right to see two guys staring at me. "Sorry about that," I said as I filed behind them. "Didn't see you boys standing there."

"No worries," one of them uttered as the person who occupied the bathroom shoved open the door. He wore a white tank top cut low at the sides so that his chiseled body was clearly visible. The tight jeans he wore barely contained the massive bulge in the front. He also sported rainbow suspenders. The dichotomy of the color splash on such a brute of a man reminded me a bit of Hank, but the manly swagger and the way he peered out into the crowd as if they were all subjects there to serve him couldn't have made him more different than my man.

"Boys," he said to the two guys in front of me before he ran his hand through the full head of dark hair that he had styled into a two-inch pomp. His do probably made him about three inches taller than Hank. This guy was massive.

"Damn," one of the guys in front of me muttered. The guy with the rainbow suspenders walked back into the crowd, barely acknowledging anyone's existence.

The two guys in front of me evidently liked what they saw, because they abandoned their need to potty and went chasing after him. That left the way free and clear for me, and my bladder couldn't have been more pleased.

After I'd completed my urgent business, I exited the bathroom and made my way back to where I'd left Hank. He wasn't there. I surveyed the crowded area around the bar, but I couldn't find him anywhere. Not even Darren and Carmichael were where I'd last seen them.

Where the fuck did they go?

I was cutting back through the front of the bar when I noticed a side door to the outside patio. Perhaps Darren needed some air and Hank had come out with him. I headed outside.

Smokers crowded the patio, but there was no Hank or Darren to be found in the smoke cloud. I noticed that the patio extended around the corner, so I headed in that direction. I was about to turn the corner when Hank's voice drifted from the other side.

"What are you doing here?" he asked.

"I'm here with friends" came the gruff reply. That wasn't Darren or Carmichael. Who the hell was he talking to? "I thought you were going to text me when you came to town. I've been texting you."

This guy had to be Weasel—whoever the fuck that was.

"I haven't had the time," Hank replied.

"But you've had the time to come here? What's going on, Hank? I thought we'd gotten past the shit from our past."

Past? There was only one person who Hank had a past with: Karl.

"We did," Hank said. "I'm glad you've gotten your head on straight. Sobriety looks good on you."

How the hell did he know Karl had gone to rehab? Had they been communicating before this?

"It feels good too," the man I figured was Karl said. "Like I've told you, I wanted to meet with you. Apologize in person for all the shit I did to you. I was real messed up. I know that's not an excuse, and I'm not trying to make it out to be. But I was in a dark place, and the drugs and the alcohol seemed to make it bearable."

"And the cheating?" Hank asked.

"I thought you'd lost your memory in your accident?"

"I have, but people have filled me in."

Karl snorted. "Of course they did. I bet your two roomies couldn't wait to say shit about me. Those needle dicks never did like me."

"So it's their fault, then?"

"No. I own what I did," Karl said. By the tone of his voice, I could picture him standing tall, puffing out his chest in confidence. "But you must remember how hard they made it for us to be together. They never liked me from day one. They resented me in your life. As if they were jealous or some shit. They hated the fact that I refused to live my life by committee the way you three do."

"You've never understood our relationship," Hank replied. He most likely had crossed his arms over his chest. It was what Hank did when he got defensive.

"No, I didn't, but I understood you." Karl's voice softened. The pissiness brought on by the mention of Darren and Mitch floated away. "Why do you think I've been giving you the advice I have?"

Advice? What advice?

"I can't thank you enough for that." Hank had no doubt let his arms fall to his side. The combative timbre to his voice had faded.

"And did it work? Have you been able to patch things up with Santi? Because I gotta tell you, life must suck from his perspective. Remembering everything and you remembering nothing. That's why I wanted you to go easy on him. To give him a chance. Only someone who loved you would do everything he's done."

Was that why Hank's attitude had suddenly changed all those months ago? I had never figured out why he went from distant to trying as hard as he was to remember. It was as if someone had flipped a switch. I'd chalked it up to lingering feelings for me that he just couldn't explain or fight, but that hadn't been it at all. He'd done what his ex had asked of him. That left a bitter taste in my mouth.

"You don't think I know that?" Hank asked. "Why do you think I've been trying so hard to make things work between us?"

His words hit me like a sucker punch to the gut. I leaned against the wall for support. Had it all been pretend? Everything we'd been through in Houston and here? Was Hank merely doing all this because he had a debt to repay? That couldn't be it, could it?

"But you can't force those kinds of feelings," Karl said. "They either happen or they don't. Remember what I told you. You owe it to both you and Santi to discover your feelings. To see if you can fall in love again. You're not doing him or you any favors by staying out of guilt. You'll only end up resenting each other."

"I know," Hank said with a sigh. "I don't want that either."

I had enough. I could no longer just stand there eavesdropping. "Is that what's been going on?" I asked as I stepped around the corner. Hank's eyes grew wide in surprise, and so did mine. Naturally Karl just happened to be the muscle man in the rainbow suspenders who'd left the men's room before I went in. He couldn't have been smaller than me like Darren's Carmichael. He had to be even bigger than Hank.

I might not win in a fight, but I'd yank out all his short and curlies by the roots before he beat me down.

"Who the fuck?" Karl asked. His dark eyes grew stormy.

"I'm Santi," I replied as I stood between them. "The one you've been giving my fiancé advice about."

Karl eyed me up and down before arching an eyebrow at Hank. "This is Santi?" His question clearly communicated his disbelief.

Even though I might regret it later, I closed the space between us. "Yeah, you've got a problem with that?"

"Whoa, there, little man," Karl said. "Why don't you calm down?"

"And why don't you stay the fuck away from Hank?"

Karl took a step forward before Hank suddenly stood between us. He placed his hands on Karl's chest. "This isn't getting us anywhere," he said.

"You're right," Karl said with a nod. He peered down at me and extended his hand as an olive branch. "I apologize for being an ass. It's just that I—" He turned his gaze to Hank. His eyes lit up like a candle burning in the night, trying to lead a lost loved one home. When he returned his gaze to me, the flickering light immediately snuffed out. "Well, it doesn't matter. I'm just sorry."

I didn't take his hand. I shoved my hands in the back pocket of my jeans. "Yeah, me too."

"I'm gonna get back to my friends," he told Hank. "Text me or call me if you want. I would really love to catch up."

Hank nodded as Karl walked away. As I gazed into his expression, I could see the internal war play across his face. He was truly a man in conflict. He obviously still had feelings for Karl. The emotions and memories he'd awoken with hadn't been cast aside as I'd hoped. Despite whatever he might now feel for me, his past with Karl still clung to him like ivy crawling up a brick wall.

"Are you okay?" Hank asked.

No. I wasn't okay at all. So much had been revealed to me in the last few minutes that I didn't know how to take it all in. I couldn't even look at Hank. All I could do was stare at the spot where Karl had once stood.

"Santi?"

"I have to go," I said before turning around.

"Santi, wait!"

I didn't stop. I dodged through the crowd and headed out the front door. I needed to be alone. I needed to think.

SHORTLY AFTER leaving the club, I hailed a taxi, which took me back to Hank's house. I used the spare key Hank, Darren, and Mitch hid under a decorative fire hydrant to unlock the front door. I headed onto the patio, where the refreshing night breeze wrapped me in its cool embrace.

I leaned against the rail and closed my eyes, trying to focus on the sound of the city instead of the waves of turmoil that churned within my soul.

No matter what I did or tried, Karl somehow seemed to stand between us. Hank's persistent emotions for his ex refused to go away. The way they interacted with each other made that abundantly clear, but so did the fact that they'd obviously been communicating for some time now. Even though Mitch and I had told Hank what Karl had put him through, Hank still reached out to him.

Karl's words had brought him comfort, and it was his advice that Hank had listened to.

I inhaled deeply, and when I exhaled, I tried to blow away all the problems I had with that bit of knowledge. Ultimately it didn't matter. I knew that. All I should really be concerned with was what Hank wanted to do. Who he wanted to be with. I had about as much control over that as I had over Hank's accident.

I'd finally accepted that while his amnesia sucked, in the end the fact that he couldn't remember didn't matter, because I did. All the wonderful times of our past remained locked in the treasure chest of my memory, and I'd house them until the end of time.

What we needed to focus on was our present and our future. That was what truly mattered. So what if Hank didn't remember our first night at Rich's or our first time in our condo? Those events, while special, didn't define who we were or who we were going to be. Only the two of us did that, and like any couple, we had to evolve and grow and accept the obstacles life placed before us.

Nothing was insurmountable as long as we faced it together, and that was what was going to happen as far as I was concerned.

I'd stopped relying on the return of the past. It would hold no more power over the present or shape the future. Whatever pressure I'd inadvertently heaped upon Hank's shoulders would cease. What I'd cling to now were the memories we'd created since the accident, the ones that started to form a bond between us.

My feet were now firmly planted in the present, and my eyes looked solely to the future.

But were Hank's? He was straddling the fence between what he remembered and what he was struggling to find. I existed in the ethereal void of uncertainty while where Karl resided was far more concrete.

I hadn't seen that more plainly than tonight, when Hank's eyes darted between Karl and me. He was once again stuck in neutral, when I'd believed we had been moving forward.

I'd even begun to believe we'd taken five giant leaps forward, but now I wasn't as positive of the progress we'd made. I had to find out what Hank's motives were. That was going to require difficult answers to tough questions, but it was time. For the both of us.

"There you are." Hank sounded relieved as he shoved open the patio door. "By the time I got the car keys from Darren, you were gone. Why did you leave like that?" He stood by me. Only a few feet separated us, so why did it now seem like miles?

"I needed to be alone," I answered, still looking into the night sky instead of into the comforting blue hue of Hank's eyes.

"Why?"

Was Hank serious right now? He was sometimes so dense he had to be smacked upside the head with the obvious, but was he really that oblivious? "Are you serious?"

His stitched eyebrows of confusion answered my question.

"Karl knew you were coming to San Diego. That means you've been talking to him. How long has that been going on?"

He hesitated before replying, "My first night in the condo."

I winced. That hurt. "Why?"

"When I woke up, the life I remembered was the one I had with Karl. I didn't know who you or Jill were. And my parents? They were practically strangers to me too. Mitch and Darren were the only familiar faces. I needed someone else, someone I actually remembered, like Karl, and I resisted the urge to call him. Hell, when I told Mitch that I wanted to talk to Karl while I was still in the hospital, he told me he'd shove my phone up my piss slit if I did, so I didn't. But coming back to your place, to the place where we had lived and that I couldn't remember, was too much for me. And the pain in your eyes broke my heart. So I called him that first night, and even though it made me feel like a complete ass, it was something I had to do."

I nodded. "And?"

"What do you mean?"

I fought the urge to bite off Hank's head. A tempest brewed inside. "And it's been going well?"

Hank leaned against the rail. Like me, he stared straight ahead at the San Diego skyline. "Honestly, it was good for me."

The rumbling in my chest grew stronger. "How so?"

"He was surprised to hear from me after the way things ended between us. When I told him what had happened to me, he was shocked and he said I was lucky to have you in my life."

I glanced sideways at Hank. Did he really expect me to believe that Karl had changed *that* much? That he didn't have some other agenda that involved getting Hank back?

Hank must have intuited my thoughts. He nodded and said, "It's true. He's changed from the person you and Mitch told me about. He told me about most of the awful things he did to me, and he apologized for it. He's been through rehab and has been living the clean and sober life for two years now. He said he wanted to contact me, but he's been too much of a coward. But since I had contacted him, he had the chance to make amends for all the shit he put me through, so he encouraged me to lighten up and give you a chance. I moved from California for you for a reason, and I owed it to myself to find out what that reason was."

I'd already overheard all that, and I didn't like it. Hank was supposed to have changed for me, not for Karl.

"So that's what I did," Hank continued. "And I got to know you, and I learned that you are a good man with probably the biggest heart and the most stubborn personality I'd met. Nothing stops you once you set your mind to something."

Unless I was banging my head against the wall. Had that been what I'd been doing all this time?

"And we've gotten close," he said. "Or at least I thought we were. I'm not so sure now."

I sighed. "Neither am I."

After a few minutes of silence, he asked, "What now? Where do we go from here?"

"That depends," I answered. "I haven't asked you this question for a while, but it's time to broach the subject again. What exactly do you feel for Karl? Do you still love him?"

Hank exhaled. He ran his fingers through his hair. I evidently wasn't going to like the answer. "I think I do," he finally said. "Seeing him today made me remember all those feelings I woke up with in the hospital."

I gripped the railing so tightly my knuckles popped.

He then turned to face me. He placed his hands on my shoulders and turned me sideways so we could look in each other's eyes. "But I feel something for you too. I'm not really sure what that is, but there's this pull toward you that I can't explain."

"You feel something, but it's not love, is it?" I gazed into his eyes with tears streaming down my face.

Hank didn't have to answer the question. It was obvious. I wiped the tears away and stepped out of his touch. "Never mind. Don't answer that."

"It's like what I told Darren at Pecs. I'm not sure what it is. I'm just not fighting it anymore, and you said that was all you were asking for."

"It was." I nodded.

"But it's not anymore?"

"I don't think so," I replied before switching my gaze to the cars zooming along the interstate. Why couldn't I be one of the people down there, ignorant to all the pain and suffering taking place up here? "It was okay when I thought we might be rebuilding something. Now that I know you're still in love with another man even after all these months, well, it hurts." My voice quavered. "I've tried so hard. I've fought for you so hard, and I could battle on knowing it was just your lack of memories that I was swinging my sword at. But how can I get past what you feel for Karl? I know the kind of man you are, Hank. You're extremely loyal, and having these feelings for Karl and me at the same time has got to be killing you. Is that what I've been seeing in your eyes these past few weeks? Is that where the guilt has been coming from?"

Hank swallowed hard and nodded. "I've tried to move past it. To do like Karl suggested and just give myself over to the moment. But when your heart's conflicted, it makes knowing where to go a real bitch."

"And that's not fair to you," I said. "Or to me."

"What does that mean?"

"It means it's time for me to go home." As much as it broke my heart to say the words, it was the only path to take right now. Hank and I could never be together as long as unresolved feelings remained between him and Karl.

"So that's it, then?" he asked. "You're giving up?"

I snorted. "I wish it was that easy." I turned and gazed up into his eyes. They were hooded in deep sadness. His internal misery had diluted their typical bright blue. "But I can't keep pretending that everything is going to be okay. That we're going to come out of this on the other side together. Don't get me wrong—that's precisely what I want. Imagining my life without you is unbearable, but if we are going to have any hope of a future, you're going to have to deal with your past. I want you to be happy, Hank, but I want me to be happy too. And neither of us will be happy if we continue going the way we have been. You say you love Karl. That's what you remember. I have to respect that. I have to let you see if that is what you truly want. It will hurt like a bitch if it is, but I love you enough to let you go, because I'd do anything to make you truly happy."

"I don't know what to say." Hank sniffled.

I held his face in my hands and scratched my fingers through his beard. I didn't know if I'd ever get the chance to do that again. "You don't have to say anything. I'm going to get my things and head to the airport."

"You're gonna leave tonight?"

"I have to. It's what's best for me right now. I hope you can understand that."

He nodded, but he clutched my arms as if he didn't want me to go.

"You're home now," I said, forcing a smile. "Where you remember things. Perhaps this is where you should have always been. Who knows? But what I do know is that this is where you need to be right now. But I want you to know something." A sob lodged in my throat and strangled my words. "You're in my heart. You've always been there. You are *my* home, and you'll *always* have a home with me."

"Santi—"

I pressed my lips against Hank's, and though I was crying, I kissed him through my tears. Saying good-bye to the man I loved was like cutting out my heart with a hacksaw. "It's time for me to go."

Hank held me close, kissing the top of my head. I pulled out of the embrace and gazed up into his red-rimmed eyes. I stepped away and headed for the patio door.

"I'll see you around." Hank's voice cracked, and he forced a smile.

I returned the fake smile. "Take care of yourself, my sexy man."

"You too, Santi."

I grabbed my things and called a cab. After the taxi driver arrived and I climbed into the vehicle, I completely fell apart.

CHAPTER
Eleven

THE FIRST week after I returned from San Diego almost destroyed me. I didn't leave the condo and spent most of my days crying on the bed where Hank had slept, inhaling his scent, which clung to the sheets and the pillowcases. Nights were practically cataclysmic. For some reason, when the daylight disappeared, my anxiety worsened. I'd pace around the condo, unable to get my breathing and heart rate under control.

After spending two nights wandering around in the dark, I took to popping Xanax and drinking vodka. While they helped me achieve a comatose state so I could sleep, Jill, Mario, and Jesse worried I would become addicted. They tried to keep my mind occupied by calling me every couple of hours or insisting on bringing me meals.

"You've got to eat," Mario said as he cut a piece of tuna casserole surprise out of the dish he and Jesse had brought over. "You're practically skinny enough to be a Victoria's Secret model."

The disgusting fish aroma, combined with the half a bottle of Svedka I'd just drunk, didn't sit well with my stomach. "I'm not hungry." I was extremely nauseous, though.

"Nonsense," Jesse said. He eyed my growing collection of empty liquor bottles and shook his head. "Your liquid diet isn't doing much for you, you know?"

"That's right." Mario handed me a plate piled high with foul-smelling food. "How do you expect to find another man looking the way you do?"

I eyed the meal and then Mario before heading back to the couch. "I don't want another man."

"Bitch, please," Jesse said. "The quickest way to get over one man is to get under a new one."

Their concern only made my depression worse.

I chased them out of the condo after promising them both I'd eat and call them tomorrow. After I shut the door behind them, I threw away the food, plate and all, and turned off my cell phone.

Food, friends, or another man weren't going to cure what ailed me. Only Hank would.

But when I thought about Hank, all I could picture was him and Karl together. Their bodies pressed against each other. Karl's hands running down flesh that belonged to me. I could envision Karl on top of Hank, forcing himself brutally in and out of my man's ass while Hank kissed him and told him he loved him.

For the next week after that unfortunate image, I had to double my Xanax and stiff drinks before I could drift off to sleep. I even stopped answering my phone or my door entirely whenever my friends called or came by. I didn't want to see anybody.

I wanted to be left the fuck alone.

Jill, however, refused to be shut out.

"If you don't open up," she screamed one night as she banged on the front door, "I'm going to kick this open and then bust open your skull." She pounded and then kicked the entrance twice for good measure.

When I'd finally had enough, I undid the latch and crawled back onto the couch, where my bottle of Smirnoff waited for me to return. I pressed my warm flesh against the chilled glass and sighed in pleasure before Jill finally entered.

"Took you long enough to realize it was open," I mumbled.

Jill closed the door behind her and stared at me with wide eyes. "You look awful," she said, sitting next to me on the couch. "And you smell even worse. When was the last time you showered?"

I shrugged. "Don't have anyone to impress, so who fucking cares?"

"I do." She snatched the bottle from my loving embrace.

I jumped off the couch and followed her to the kitchen, where she prepared to dump the contents down the sink.

"What are you doing?" I tried to take the bottle, but she shoved me back with little effort. I lost my footing and fell back into the wall. "Hey!"

As she poured the vodka down the drain, she eyed me. "You need coffee and a hot shower. I'm not leaving here until you get both." She pulled the coffeemaker out of the cabinet and searched for a cup.

"I don't drink coffee," I reminded her. "That was Hank."

She stopped with her hand on Hank's mug, the one with the words "I love my lawyer" stamped across it. "Some tea, then."

I placed my hand on her arm. "What I need is to be alone. You may not like it, but *that's* what I need."

She surveyed my unkempt surroundings. "It's not healthy, Santi. I'm scared for you."

"Don't be," I said, ushering her to the front door. "This is just something I have to do alone."

Like the best friend she was, she left even though it was not what she wanted to do. But everyone had to do things they didn't want to. That was part of life. With my personal life in so much turmoil, it was only a matter of time before my professional world started to crumble as well.

Wyatt hadn't been pleased with my absence at work. He'd spent all that time getting me up to speed only to have me bow out of working again. Things were falling apart at the office, and he couldn't handle everything on his own anymore. He was currently looking for a new partner, and if he found one, he was considering drafting up a buyout agreement that would sever our working relationship.

That would likely have started me on a downward spiral I might never recover from if Henry Burton hadn't stopped by to see me.

"What are you doing here?" I asked. When I'd heard his voice on the other side of the door, I couldn't quite believe Hank's dad was there. I had to stare at him through the peephole for a few minutes before I opened the door.

"I'm here to see you," he said before walking inside without being invited. He surveyed the condo, noticing the mess of vodka bottles and takeout containers that littered the floor. He nodded. "About as I expected."

"What is?"

He motioned to the floor. "You're taking this like any man would. With excessive drinking and eating shitty food. How's that working out?"

I thudded over to the couch, cleared a clean patch for both of us to sit, and sat down. "Just great."

"I can see that," he said before tentatively sitting down. "Might want to think about a shower sometime soon." He sniffed the air and grimaced. "You smell like Parmesan cheese and Whataburger onions."

I laughed. I hadn't done that since before San Diego. "That's the fragrance I've been going for."

"Well, mission accomplished, then."

We sat in silence for a few minutes. Henry scanned the bottles of vodka strewn across the floor while I tried to figure out why the man had driven all the way from Lufkin to see me. Now that his son was back in California, he had no reason to give one good damn what happened to me. "Why are you here?"

Henry sat back, his large frame taking up more than just once section of the couch. "I'm not certain," he said. "I told Sharon I was coming up to Houston to service the truck and buy some medicine for the heifers that we can get cheaper here than back home for some reason. But in the back of my mind, I knew this was where I'd end up."

"That still doesn't answer my question," I said.

"Do you remember back at that party you threw for Hank when he first moved to Texas? You told me that you loved my son, that you wanted to make him happy, and that you wanted to be a part of my family."

Of course I remembered. I wasn't the one with amnesia. "What about it?"

"What did I tell you?"

"You told me to prove it. Actions spoke louder than words."

213

He nodded. "And you've done that, Santi. I didn't think it was possible, and that's the God's honest truth, but you did. You stood by my boy the day of his accident and every day after that. No matter what happened, you were there. I'll never forget that, and I can never repay the debt we owe you."

What was it with the Burtons and debts? "You don't owe me anything. I love Hank. I would have walked through fire for him if it would have helped."

"And you did," he said with a smile. "I can't imagine anything more painful than what you endured over those months. And when you realized that my son was still battling himself—" He stopped, clearly upset. "You let him go."

Was that what this was about? Henry was pissed that I didn't put up more of a fight, and he was here to let me have it? "What did you want me to do?" I asked. My body and emotions, which I'd deadened with alcohol, suddenly sparked back to life. The anger I still hadn't dealt with and the grief I couldn't release swirled into a twister of resentment that spun around inside me. "Did you want me to put a gun to his head and make him love me? I can't force him, Henry. Leaving Hank was the last thing I fucking wanted. Hank should be here with me. In this condo. In our bed. In *my* arms. But he's not. Not because I don't want him to be, but because he doesn't know where he wants to be. I can't make him love me. Like he said, he loves Karl, and that guilt has been eating him alive. That's the relationship he *does* remember, no matter how shitty or wrong it was. Staying with him was hurting him, and I love him too much for that. I had to let him go." My voice broke. "I had to."

Henry sat forward on the cushion and patted my knee. "I know you did, and I'm sorry you think that decision upsets me. Because it doesn't."

I studied him carefully. "What?"

"Nothing has proven your love more than when you let him go."

When did Henry Burton start taking words from those sickening inspirational quotes people loved to bandy about? "I don't understand."

"I've learned some things over the course of my life, and I've made some pretty fucking big mistakes. The way I treated Hank as a child is just one of many. I loved my son, and I thought I knew what was best for him. That's why I kicked him out. I figured tough love would work. That Hank would see the error of his ways and come back home the boy I always pictured him to be. But that's not how people work, and that's not how love works either. You can't force people to be other than who they are, and you can't make them feel anything other than what they feel. I didn't realize that until it was too late. When I did, my son hated me and wanted nothing to do with me or his mother."

He swallowed before continuing. "Then came you, Santi. You're the reason we have rebuilt the burned-out bridge between us. You did that for his mother and me before his accident and again after he lost his memories. And not once did you try to make him other than what he was. You loved him for the bullheaded, forgetful bastard he was, and then you loved him in spite of the fact that he couldn't remember you. You didn't force-feed my son his previous life even though you could have. You let him venture out and find things out on his own. And when he was hurting, you didn't guilt him into staying or try to force your way into his life. You let him go not because you didn't care enough to fight. I know better than that. You'd have fought 'til the last breath was knocked out of your body. You let him go because you were more concerned with Hank and what he wanted and how he felt."

Henry wrapped his big arms around me and gave me one of the most powerful hugs of my life. "And that is the very definition of true love."

By the time he stopped talking, I was a blubbering mess. I clasped Henry, finally giving release to the pain I'd kept bound to my soul with alcohol and prescription medication. I expelled all the poison that had turned me into someone I couldn't recognize but someone I'd been unable to keep from becoming.

With each tear shed and each sob released, I slowly reversed my steps and walked back toward the man I'd always been.

"Thank you," I said after catching my breath. I withdrew from Henry's embrace and smiled. "I needed that."

He nodded. "I thought so. Sharon and I have been keeping tabs on you. Your friend Jill has been worried, especially since you stopped talking to everyone. She didn't know what else to do, and frankly neither did we. We've been wanting to call, but we were worried hearing from us might just upset you."

I shook my head. "I don't want to lose touch with you and Sharon. Or Hank, Darren, and Mitch. All of you have become my family. I feel lost without you in my life."

"And that's when I realized I had to come. I know you have your friends, but you asked to become a part of my family all those months ago, and you deserve to be treated like one. So that's why I came. I might not be your real father, but I'm here for you if you need anything."

I smiled and wiped the stray tear that dribbled down my cheek. "Thank you, Henry. I appreciate that."

Henry's face grew stern. He evidently had something unpleasant to say. "Now as a father figure, I think it's time for some fatherly advice. You ready to hear it?"

Even more tears streamed down my cheeks. I nodded since that was the only way I was capable of responding.

"You need to clean up your life, son." He once again surveyed the living room. He cast a disappointed grimace across every piece of trash. "This isn't you. It's not the man you've worked hard at becoming, is it?"

I shook my head.

"I didn't think so. It hurts. I know. You've been kicked in the balls and then had your face slammed into a brick wall. That'll bring down just about anybody. But you're better and stronger than what's trying to bring you down. We all know that. Now you need to know it too."

He was right. I'd taken control of my life from an early age. I set my path and chartered a route to a successful life. Not even my parents' deaths made me deviate from my course. That had been the worst pain imaginable. If I could survive that, I could weather anything. Even the loss of Hank. "I do," I finally said. "I just forgot that for a while."

His big bearded face broke into a smile. "We all forget sometimes. That's why we have family. To remind us of what we've forgotten and to see us back on the right path."

"I'll get my life back on track." How I would accomplish that, I didn't know, but that wasn't important. All that mattered was the renewed confidence that fortified me. It told me that I'd do it somehow.

"Good. Now there's just one more piece of business we have to discuss."

"What's that?"

"My son," he said. The grin that had tugged itself across his lips retreated. Something was wrong.

"What is it?" I asked. "Is Hank okay? Please don't tell me there's been another accident."

Henry shook his head. "Nothing like that," he answered. "But I have to ask: Do you still love my son?"

That was the most ridiculous question I'd ever been asked in my life. "Of course I do."

And just like that, he once again beamed. "Good." He got up and headed for the door.

"Why did you ask me that?"

He glanced at me over his shoulder, a smile dangling from his lips, before walking out my front door.

A FEW days after Henry's visit, I went back to work. I had two cases going to court in the next couple of weeks, and I still had a lot to get accomplished. Wyatt was thrilled I had returned to the office. He even abandoned his search for a new partner.

It turned out work was exactly what I needed. Sure, I was throwing myself into my work the way I had before I met Hank. That didn't amuse Jill, but taking my mind off my troubles and focusing on something else was what I needed.

Jesse and Mario thought differently. They still believed a nice fuck would cure everything that ailed me. It had been over six months since I'd been naked with another man, and while my pipes definitely needed a good cleaning, the thought of sharing a bed with someone other than Hank turned my stomach. Even though it wasn't, it felt too much like cheating.

And that was exactly what I was trying to get my friends to see.

"I'm not ready," I said. I had Jill, Mario, and Jesse on a conference call, and their collective sigh echoed through the speakerphone.

217

"It's time!" Mario whined.

"I think I'm a better judge of that."

"Oh please," Jesse said. "A good come will lighten your load. Pun intended."

I rolled my eyes even though they couldn't see it.

"Will you two stop it?" Jill asked. "If he's not ready, he's not ready."

"Thank you."

"You're welcome," she replied. "But I still think you should come out with us. We're heading to Meteor."

The three of them were there so often they should be paying rent. "I've got too much to get done."

"All work and no play," Jill began.

"I'm not falling for that shit again," I cut her off. "The last time you told me that, I wound up in San Diego."

"Well imagine where'd you end up this time?" Mario asked.

"I'm hanging up now," I said as my finger hovered over the disconnect button.

"Not until you agree to meet us at Meteor," Jesse pleaded.

"If you want me to lie to you like your tricks on Grindr, I will."

"Come on, Santi," Jill said. "It'll be fun."

"I love you all, but no."

"Yes," they said in unison.

"I'm hanging up now."

"Don't you dare!" Jill yelled before I ended the call. I'd pay for that when I saw her again, but I didn't have the strength to deal with them anymore tonight.

"Something wrong?"

I glanced up from the phone to find Wyatt leaning against my office door. "Just my friends being annoying."

He chuckled. "They're just worried about you." A friendly smile snaked across his lips, and grave concern reflected in his eyes. "I am too. Want to chat?"

"I don't really want to talk about it."

"Liar!" he said before entering my office and sitting down. "That's exactly what you want. I can tell."

Wyatt was right, and I hated him for it. Talking about my feelings might help. Visiting with Henry had gotten me started on the right path. Maybe that was just the type of forward momentum I needed, not the anonymous tricking Jesse and Mario seemed intent for me to have.

"Are you sure?" I asked. "Because once I start, I'll likely not shut up again for a few hours."

Wyatt laughed before settling back in the chair. "Go for it," he said. "We're the only ones here anyway. I told Lupe and Jamie to go home early. I figured you might need to talk."

I smiled at Wyatt.

"It's been tough these past few weeks without Hank. He's been such a part of my life for so long that I go through my day as if a part of me is missing. And when I wake up, I forget that he's not here. I reach out for him, but after a few moments, when I realize that he's in San Diego now, my stomach hollows out and the tears start."

"I'm so sorry," he said. He rose from the chair and rounded my desk. He sat on the desktop and rubbed my shoulder. "I can only imagine how difficult this has been for you. You loved him very much."

"I still do," I said.

We sat there for a few moments before he asked, "So what do you want?"

"I don't understand."

He stood and paced the room. It was as if we were in court and he was cross-examining me. "Out of your life now. What do you want?"

The answer was pretty fucking obvious. "I want Hank."

"I get that, but do you want the Hank who's here now or the one you remember?"

That was a silly question. "They're one and the same."

Wyatt shook his head. "Biologically, yes. Emotionally, they are two different people. The Hank you remember is the one who fell in love with you, the one who swept you off your feet before anyone else had a chance." He cleared his throat, evidently regretting his lapse. Maybe Wyatt wasn't the best person to discuss this with, especially if he still hoped for more between us. "This Hank is different. He didn't fall into immediate lust with you."

"It wasn't lust," I clarified. "It was love."

Wyatt rolled his eyes. "Oh please. It was lust. Most guys don't have instant love with another guy. Our dicks get hard when we see something we like. It's not about wanting to build a life with that person when we run across a new hottie at a club or at the gym. It's about getting into their pants. Love comes after that."

"I didn't know you were such a romantic." I couldn't help the disgust in my tone. Wyatt had just reduced my initial encounter with Hank to a trick, and I didn't like it one bit.

"You can hate me all you want," he said. "But it's the truth, and you know it. I'm not saying that you and Hank didn't fall in love quickly. What I'm saying is that it wasn't love that made you walk up to Hank and introduce yourself. That was your cock, pure and simple."

"Is there a point to this vulgarity, Counselor?"

He nodded. "That insta-lust you felt is still there for you, but it's not there for Hank, is it?"

I suddenly felt the need to defend my looks. "Hank finds me attractive. We were at M2M a few weeks ago and he practically turned stupid when he saw me without a shirt on. And in San Diego, we were getting closer."

"I have no doubt, but did anything come of it? Did he take you right there in the dressing room? Or did you fuck your brains out like you used to do before the accident?"

"No, but so what? He's been sick."

"Yes. He has been. But from what I've heard, when you two had the flu last Christmas, you quite literally fucked the snot out of each other the whole time you were bedridden."

I chuckled. That was true. We were both feverish and felt like death warmed over, but that didn't stop our craving for each other's bodies. "Those were the best sick days of my life."

"And you still want Hank even if he never feels that way for you again?"

What was sex if it wasn't with someone you loved? It was just a biological act. Being intimate with the one you loved was what made sex so special, and there was no one else I wanted in my bed. "But you're assuming he won't," I finally answered. "I'm assuming it's always a possibility."

"Maybe. But I think it's important for you to ask yourself these questions. Because there's no sense in stalling out your life on the slim chance that a miracle might just happen. There's so much more out there for you, Santi. Life's too short to be waiting for something that might never happen. You left Hank in San Diego because you realized it was the best move for him. And probably for you too. But you can't stop there. You can't just stop living. You have to learn to live again without Hank."

I stood up and turned to look out my office window. Wyatt was right. And so were Jill, Mario, Jesse, and Henry Burton. I had to get my life back together. I had to move forward in more ways than just at work. But could I really get involved with someone else?

"Are you okay?" Wyatt asked before standing behind me. He rested his arms on my shoulders and gave them a brief squeeze.

"Not really," I replied.

Wyatt turned me around, wrapped his arms around me, and drew me close. He patted my back and ran his fingers through my hair while he rocked me back and forth.

"I just miss him so much. I don't know if I'll ever find a love like I had with him again."

"You can," he said.

I wiped the tears from my face with my sleeve before looking up into his handsome face. "Do you think so?"

He nodded. "I'll likely hate myself later for this, but I'm not about to let this moment pass me by. I did that already, and look where that got me."

"What are you talking about?"

He stroked my cheek the way Hank once did, and I immediately tensed. "You can have it with me," he said. "I've been in love with you for years, and even though it killed me to see you with Hank, I loved you enough to be happy that you were happy."

I tried to step back, but my body betrayed me. I was too shocked to move or respond.

"But you haven't been happy for a while now, and it's been killing me. All I've wanted was to offer you comfort. To take you in my arms and tell you that it will get better. To give you the love and affection I could see you desperately needed. But I didn't. Out of respect for you and Hank."

This wasn't happening.

"But you and Hank aren't together anymore, and it's time to find happiness again with someone new. Maybe what you need is to embrace the man who's standing before you now." He hooked my chin between his thumb and index finger and closed the remaining distance between us. "The one who can give you everything you want right now."

Wyatt's lips pushed against mine, and he clasped my shoulders. He ground his hips against mine, rubbing his hard cock against my lifeless groin.

The slamming of a door in the outer office snapped me out of my paralysis. Didn't Wyatt say we were alone? Who had just entered our office complex?

The answer to that question didn't matter. I knew what I wanted, and this wasn't it. It never could be.

For better or for worse and in sickness and in health, the only man I wanted was Hank. I pulled myself out of Wyatt's kiss and gently shoved him away. "Stop."

Wyatt evidently realized his gamble wasn't going to pay off. "I'm sorry," he said. "I shouldn't have done that."

"No," I said, putting my desk between us, "you shouldn't have. We are friends and business partners. That is all we will ever be, because whether Hank loves me or not and whether he will ever feel the way I feel for him doesn't matter. I love Hank. Maybe it's stupid to carry a torch for him. Maybe it's illogical. I don't fucking care. Love isn't logical, but it's the way I feel. I don't want another man, because no other man will ever make me feel the way that Hank does."

"But he's not here. He's in San Diego with Karl. You realize that, right?"

"Actually, I'm right here."

I snapped my attention to my office door to find Hank filling the doorway. "Hank?"

A smile stretched across his face. "I may have forgotten many things, but I do know who I am."

"What are you doing here?"

"I'll tell you in just a bit," he said before stepping into my office. He turned his full attention to Wyatt. "I appreciate everything you've done for Santi and for me these past few months. You've been a good friend to him, and because of you, he hasn't had to worry about his job. I'll forever be grateful to you for that."

Wyatt struggled to speak, but words failed him. It was as if a ghost had just appeared in the room.

"But I want you to know that I overheard your little speech to Santi about him and me. And you know what? You're right."

"I am?" Wyatt asked. He switched his gaze to me before returning it to Hank.

Hank nodded. "Santi shouldn't stall his life for anyone. Not even me." He tore his eyes from Wyatt and focused them on me before strolling over to where I stood. "Santi deserves so much more than *any* man can give him because his heart is so big and his love is so strong that it can beat for the both of you when it needs to." He drew closer. His lips parted into a smile, and tears welled up in his eyes. "Santi's love is a gift that he gives freely. It's a miracle in itself, so no, he shouldn't wait for any bullheaded man to realize what an honor it is to be loved by someone like him." He stood in front of me. He cupped my face and caressed my cheeks with his thumbs. "There's just one problem. Do you know what that is?"

I swallowed hard before shaking my head.

"This bullheaded man doesn't want you to move on. He wants you to forgive him. He wants you to know that he hasn't stopped thinking about you since you left. He wants you to know that nothing with Karl ever happened because you were the only one he could ever think about, but he didn't want to make another mistake by rushing things. He had to be sure, and so he waited to see if things would change since so many things had changed in his life so far. But then something happened. Something did change. He realized what he felt for Karl McClure had *become* a memory because of what he felt for Santi. What I *feel* for Santi is what's in the present and hopefully my future. As you know, I'm not the sharpest knife in the drawer. Just the shiniest. It takes me longer to figure things out that others have worked out long before me. That's just who I am. But when I looked back at everything you did for me, how you stood by my side at the hospital, how you took care of me, how you wanted only what was best for me, I suddenly realized that what I felt for you wasn't some debt I had to repay. I knew that because being indebted to someone else doesn't make you feel sick when that person's not there. It doesn't make you unable to sleep or pissy all the time. It doesn't occupy every single fucking thought in your head every hour of every day. That's love. True love. And that's not the kind of love I had for Karl. I'll always love him. He was a big part of my life. But what I felt for you these past few weeks, I never felt for anyone else." He smiled down at me. Tears of happiness streamed down his face. "I love you, my sexy man, and if you'll still have me, I'm all yours."

I answered Hank the only way I could. I leaped into his arms and dove onto his lips.

I BROKE all kinds of traffic laws as I sped through Houston in my quest to get Hank back home and into our bed. After I pulled into the driveway, we dashed to the front door, where I fumbled with the keys.

"I can't get it in," I said.

Hank kissed the back of my neck. "You better not be saying that later."

I turned around in his arms. I grabbed his cheeks firmly and fell upon his lips. Our tongues darted back and forth. He groped at my ass before resting his hands at the small of my back. I moaned into the kiss before I hesitantly pulled away. "I definitely *won't* be saying that later."

"Good," he said before gently nipping at my nose. "Now get it in there so you can get *this* in me." He grabbed my hard cock through my pants and tugged.

I almost came right there. Hank hadn't grabbed my dick in months. What would happen when I finally entered his body again? I was going to have to calm the fuck down or all I'd be good for was two pumps and a squirt. That was not how I wanted this evening to play out.

Once I finally managed to get the door open, we sprinted inside and shut the door. Hank immediately set to work unfastening the buttons of my work shirt. When he was done, he spread open the fabric. He skimmed his fingers across my bare flesh, and my body trembled. "God, you feel good. Have you always felt this good?"

"I'd like to think so," I answered before lifting up his Hello Kitty T-shirt and pulling it from his body. I fanned my fingers through his blond fuzzy chest hair. Each tickle of his coarse hair sent shivers down my spine. Touching him was like sticking my tongue in an electrical socket. "But you've always felt better to me."

"Nuh-uh."

"Yeah-huh."

He wrapped his arms around me, pressing our bare chests together before his lips found mine once again. He moved his fingers up and down my back, clawing and scratching at my smooth flesh while I grabbed his ass and shoved our groins together. Hank's hard cock pressed against my erection, and I ground my hips harder into him.

Now that I had him in my arms again, I'd never *ever* let him go.

"We can continue arguing about this," he said in between kisses. "Or we can put our mouths to better use."

I grinned up at him. "I like the way you think, Mr. Burton," I replied while I undid the button of his jeans and then the zipper. Since he typically didn't wear underwear, Hank's blond bush and hard, pierced cock immediately sprang into view. It was the most beautiful sight I'd seen in far too many months.

As I knelt before him, I tugged his jeans down to his ankles. I took his throbbing shaft in my hand and delivered gentle kisses across its length before swabbing my tongue across the head.

"Holy fuck!" Hank muttered. He leaned against the door behind me. A crazed passion burned in his baby blues. "Do that again."

But I didn't. While he didn't remember how we had sex, I did. I was in control of his body. It was a lesson I was glad to teach him over and over again, so I gripped onto the base, slowly jacking his dick until I was rewarded with a milky pearl at the tip. I lapped across his slit, slurping up the sweet nectar his body produced while Hank tensed and shuddered.

"Okay. Do that, then," he mumbled.

I grabbed his ball sac and gave it a loving pull. Hank yelped, and he pushed his ass out. Whenever I got rough, he wanted to be drilled even harder and faster. "We do things my way."

Hank nodded. "Whatever you say." His breathing had turned ragged, and beads of sweat formed on his forehead.

"Good boy," I replied. I shoved my face in his bush, swirling my tongue through the hair while inhaling the scent of Hank's musk. The odor drove me crazy. I pulled harder on his balls while nibbling a trail up his shaft before taking his cockhead and piercing into my mouth.

Hank moaned and thrust his hip forward. "You want to take out the ring?"

I shook my head. Not this time. I opened wide and swallowed Hank's cock, jewelry and all. The tinny taste of the metal combined with the sweetness of his precum made me thirsty. I slurped at his slit, trying to funnel as much of his juice up from him as possible before I flicked my tongue across his cockhead and through the loop in the metal. Hank's legs began to shake, and his cries turned into whimpers.

"Oh, Santi," he whispered.

His cock grew even more rigid, and he leaked tons of precum. Hank was close to release, but it was too soon. I moved off his cock and stood up between his arms, which still leaned against the door. He panted and growled at the same time. "Why'd you stop?"

I answered him by tenderly kissing his lips while scratching my fingers through his beard. He released the door and drew me into his arms. He slid his tongue into my mouth, where I shared the taste of his body, which still lingered on my lips. He opened his eyes wide and pressed his mostly naked body against me.

"We need to get your clothes off," he said after breaking the kiss.

"Be my guest," I replied, leaning against the door.

Hank smirked down at me before he slid my shirt from my chest. After he undid the button and zipper on my pants, he pushed them past my hips until I stood there only in my underwear. When he returned his gaze to mine, I already knew what he was going to say. "Underwear? Really?"

I chuckled. He'd always hated that I wore briefs. "Just keep unwrapping your present."

"Too much wrapping," he complained. He dipped his fingers below the waistband. His fingers found my erection, and he wiggled them around the head before skimming his hands to my ass, which he cupped before diving back onto my lips. "I love kissing you," he said.

"Not as much as I love kissing you."

The smile in his eyes filled my heart with so much happiness that tears pooled along the corners. Hank backed up, wiping my tears away with his big thumbs. "What's wrong?"

I shook my head as I laughed. "Nothing. I'm just so happy. I've got you back in my arms again. That's all I ever wanted."

Hank pressed his forehead against mine. I don't know why that gesture always made me feel better, but it did. It expressed solidarity, that Hank and I were together in every aspect of our lives. "Do you want to know what I want right now?"

I had some idea. "What?"

"You out of these goddamn undies." He yanked the briefs from me, and they fell to the floor to join the pants around my ankles.

"Now what?" I asked, gazing up at him with as innocent a smile as I could muster.

Hank grabbed my cock and stroked it roughly. "I think you know," he replied with a smirk.

"I think I do too."

We made our way to the bedroom that was truly ours once again. I grabbed Hank's hand in mine and led him to the bed, where I had him sit. I walked between his open legs and ran my fingers through his hair while he gazed up at me. The love and affection was not only back, but it shone brighter than I'd ever seen, even before the accident.

I pressed my lips against his as I leaned him back against the mattress. I got up on the bed with him, straddling his groin as I wrapped my tongue around his and surfed my hands over the sheen of sweat that had coated his body. As I drank in his sweetness, I moved between his legs and guided Hank's legs around my waist.

"I can't wait to be inside you again," I whispered.

"I can't wait either," he said with a smile. "I know this isn't our first time, but, well, it kinda is for me."

I laughed. "I guess so, huh?"

He stared up at me as if he worried he said something wrong. "Is it okay for me to say that?"

"Of course it is," I replied as we scooted farther up on the bed. "How many people can say they've had two first times with the man they love? I consider myself lucky."

Hank traced his finger around my lips. "I'm the lucky one. To have someone as wonderful as you love me the way you do."

"It's easy," I said. "Because it's you."

He shook his head. "No. I'm the lucky one. You're the special one. How many people can say they've fallen in love with the same man twice? I might not remember the first time I did, but I doubt it was any different than what I feel right now. Being in your arms, feeling your skin against mine—it's like my body is light as a feather but on fire at the same time. I may still not be whole, but being with you makes me feel whole. If that makes any sense."

I nodded. "That's the way I feel about you. It's why I fought so hard."

"Thank you for that. Thank you for fighting for me and for us."

"I'd say any time, but I don't want to go through that again. That's why you're wearing protective gear everywhere you go from now on."

Hank frowned. "That's not very fashionable. Or sparkly."

"I'll bedazzle the shit out of the helmet. Don't you worry."

He reached between our sweaty bodies and grabbed my hard cock. "How about you bedazzle my insides instead?"

I leered down at Hank before kissing his lips. "Nothing would make me happier." I reached into the top drawer of the bedstand and retrieved the lube. I sat up on my haunches and thoroughly coated my cock before slathering a healthy amount on Hank's twitching center. "You're so beautiful," I said, tossing the jar onto the bed.

"That's because you love me," he replied as he grabbed his ankles and spread his legs for me.

I kissed his chest and then his cock before aiming my dick at his hole. "I do. Very, very much."

"I'm glad," he said. "Because I love you too."

I'd never take those three words for granted again.

I grabbed the base of my dick and guided it to his entrance. I pressed against him, and as I slid inside the body that I called home, I lay down on top of Hank. His blue eyes grew wide, and his mouth opened into a giant O as my cock made its way up his ass. "Oh God, Santi," he muttered once my dark pubes rested against his hairy blond butt. "You feel incredible inside me."

"And you feel incredible around me," I mumbled as I slowly began to rock my hips in a steady rhythm. I held Hank close, my left arm wrapped around his shoulders, keeping our chests together and our lips within kissing distance. Between pants and groans, our lips brushed together. He darted his tongue inside my mouth, and I suckled on it. Hank then coaxed my tongue in his mouth and did the same thing.

While I held him to me with one hand, I used my right to grab his firm bubble butt and knead it as I worked my cock in and out of his body. I pulled him up hard against me as I slammed with equal force down into him.

Hank made a noise that was part growl and part whimper every time I did that. He moved his hands to my back. I was hitting his pleasure button relentlessly, and he dug his fingernails into my back and scratched a fiery path across my flesh. The pain caused me to buck my hips harder into him.

"Oh, shit," he mumbled. He kept repeating "oh, shit" over and over again.

The sweat from my body dripped onto Hank as I continued to fuck him. He wiped the perspiration from my forehead and cheeks and rubbed it on his chest and his face. It was primal, as if he couldn't get enough of what my body produced.

And it turned me on. It made my cock rock hard and increased my desire to give him as much of the fluids my body made as possible, so I alternated between rough, powerful thrusts to slow and gentle deep probing. Hank moaned and continued to cry out when he wasn't trying to devour my face.

"I love you so much, my sexy man," I muttered. "And I want to come inside you so bad."

Hank gazed at me, a smile on his lips and a burning desire blazing in his eyes. "Yes, beautiful." He grabbed his cock and started jacking himself to the rhythm of my hips. "Do it. Please."

His pleading, combined with his powerful ass muscles, brought me to the edge. "You ready?" I asked.

He nodded enthusiastically, a loopy smile in his eyes.

I thrust one final time before my cock exploded deep in his ass. My cock spasmed seven times, and I moaned through each one as wave after wave of pleasure flowed through my body. As I emptied my spunk inside him, Hank pulled on his prick faster and harder. "I can feel it," he said. "I can feel you coming inside me."

And as the last volley of my semen spilled out of me, his body grew rigid before his beautiful prick erupted. Ropes of cum splattered onto his hand and chest as his body convulsed and his chest heaved. With each spurt, Hank's ass clamped down on my cock, squeezing even more liquid from my dick.

When Hank's breathing got back under control, I collapsed on his chest. His load and our sweat squished between us. It was a sensation I'd never grow tired of.

"That was fucking amazing!" Hank said. He kissed the top of my head.

"It always is," I replied. I rolled off him and lay on my side, my head against his pillow, and looked him straight in his handsome, tanned face.

"No one's ever made me feel like that before," he said. "And I mean it."

"I believe you. Especially since you've told me that once before."

He rolled his eyes.

"But I know what you mean. No one has ever touched my soul or my body the way you have, Hank Burton. You're a special man, and I'm lucky to have you. Again."

"We're both lucky."

I nodded. We were, but I still considered myself the luckiest man of all, because Hank might never remember our past, but he remembered our love.

And that was really all that mattered.

Epilogue

IT WAS hard to believe that two years had passed since my accident and so much had changed in my life. First of all, I wasn't Hank Burton anymore. I was now Hank Burton-Herrera, and Santi, my beautiful man, was my husband.

We had the wonderful wedding Santi had originally planned. We got married in San Diego on the grounds of the Presidio, and my father even gave me away. That was a harder blow to the noggin than the one that wiped the first three years of my life with Santi from my mind. Who would have ever thought that the man who kicked me out of the house for being gay would be the one to walk me down the aisle and give me away to another man?

I sure as hell didn't see that coming.

Or the fact that my dad and Santi were like the best of friends. They hung out together more than Dad and I did. But I wasn't jealous. I couldn't have been happier. Santi was my family now, and my family was his.

Although Santi wasn't as thrilled with how comfortable the Hag and Grandma had gotten with him. Being a part of their family came with endless nagging and constant bickering, but Santi took it better than I expected, even when they called him by his new nickname, Ripper. It was a nod to the unpleasant effects of my lactose-intolerant husband eating anything with dairy.

So many wonderful things had happened in our year of marriage. Although we still lived in Houston, we had moved out of the condo.

We owned a cottage-style house with the garden Santi wanted. It wasn't a huge house. It was cozy and rustic, and it fit our needs and those of our new English bulldog, Mags, who Santi bought for me shortly after we got married. She was a feisty little beast with a big heart. She never met a person or another animal she didn't like. She even made friends with cats, which was definitely not at all like her breed.

My business had grown so much that I now had an office staff. Gracie Designs was officially a hit in Houston, which kept me pretty fucking busy. Santi had just as much on his plate as I did. Once he and Wyatt ironed out their relationship, they actually created a pretty decent firm. The law offices of Perry and Herrera now had a total of five lawyers, and they'd managed to chisel out a respectable reputation for themselves.

We had thriving businesses, good friends, wonderful family, and a love I'd never thought possible.

That was precisely what we were all celebrating today on Santi's and my wedding anniversary, and it was why the house was in complete chaos.

"Where's the alcohol?" Mitch asked as he opened one kitchen cabinet after another.

I pointed to the liquor cabinet to the left of where he stood. "Where it always is, you hag. Why can't you remember shit?"

Mitch arched an eyebrow at me. "Really? This from the man who still can't remember parts of his life."

"Suck my dick."

He grimaced. "No, thank you. I'll leave that unpleasant task to your husband."

"What are you leaving for me to do?" Santi asked as he entered the kitchen carrying the bags of ice we'd need for the festivities later. Every time I saw his big grin, dark skin, and blazing brown eyes, I desperately wanted to get pregnant. It was a good thing we couldn't, or we'd be one of those families with more children than they could afford. I just couldn't get enough of him.

"Sucking my dick," I replied with a wiggle of my eyebrows.

Santi sneered before depositing the ice in the cooler and walked over to me. He gazed up at me with love far deeper than the vastness of space. "Yes. That's definitely my job."

I growled and gave him a long, deep kiss.

Mitch gagged as he opened a vodka bottle to pour a martini. "You two are disgusting."

"Who? Us?" Darren asked with his boyfriend Carmichael in tow. Carmichael had moved in with Mitch and Darren about a year ago, and he and Darren had fallen in love.

Mitch sighed. "God, all these happy couples are driving me to drink." He took a big sip from the bottle.

"You never needed an excuse before," Darren said.

"That's true, Grandma," Mitch replied after the long swig. "At least you and your man have the decency to save playing kissy face for the bedroom. Bubble and Ripper don't give a shit who's around when they paw all over each other."

Santi turned around in my arms. He rested his head against my chest and sighed. "I hate that name, you know?"

Mitch grinned. "Good. Then my job here is done."

The back door opened, and Mario and Jesse walked in with the tuna casserole Santi hated. Jill brought up the rear carrying the Kingfisher Premium Lager that she brought with her to every party.

"What's up, bitches?" Mario asked before he placed his dish in the fridge.

"Jildo!" I screamed before releasing Santi and heading over to her. She and I had become really close over the past two years. We went shopping for sparkly together.

"How ya doing, Butt Munch?" she asked before giving me a kiss. "You remember anything yet?"

I rolled my eyes. She was the only one to continually hound me about my memory. If anyone else did that, I'd pop a gasket, but I didn't want to take Jill on. She could be scary when she wanted to be. "No," I told her before smacking her ass.

"I *love* when you do that." She grinned.

I gave her one more smack for good measure.

"My turn," Jesse said, promptly presenting his ass to me.

"Sorry," I said, taking Jill's beer from her hand and placing it in the refrigerator. "Only Jildo and Santi get my smacks."

Jesse pouted.

"I'll smack the shit out of you," Mitch offered.

Jesse squealed in glee after Mitch popped him a good one.

Mario rolled his eyes at his boyfriend in pretend annoyance. "My love, the man whore."

"You wouldn't have it any other way," Jesse said before kissing Mario on the cheek.

Mario winked at him. "You know it."

Suddenly Mags ran into the kitchen, barking at everyone and wagging her butt. She'd been asleep on our bed upstairs, but all the commotion must have woken her. She hated to miss out on a chance to have as many people scratch her furry butt as possible. Everyone took their turn giving her some good loving before she sat at our feet.

"That's a good girl," I told her. She chuffed at me and shook her tan hiney.

"She's not a good girl," Santi said. He picked her up. "She's the best."

In response, Mags licked his face before settling down in his arms.

"She is getting heavier, though," Santi admitted.

"Don't talk about our granddaughter that way!"

We turned to the open back door, where my parents had suddenly appeared. My father loved Mags, and she had the biggest canine crush on him. As soon as she saw my dad, she wiggled her butt uncontrollably and practically leaped out of Santi's arms.

"Hold on already," Santi said before placing her on the floor.

Her feet were already moving before her paws touched the ground. When they finally made contact, she zoomed over to my dad, who bent down to spoil her rotten. He then produced treat after treat from his pants pockets.

"You're the reason she's gaining weight," I told my father before I hugged him.

"She's a growing girl," he replied as he gave her another Milkbone.

"You're fighting a losing battle." My mom kissed my cheek and patted my dad on the back. "He's turned into a big ol' softie."

My dad harrumphed before tossing Mags another treat. She swallowed it in one gulp.

"You're going to ruin her dinner," Santi said, pretending to be exasperated.

"I'm her grandpa. That's what I do."

Before my dad could give Mags yet another morsel of food, I said, "All right, everyone. I've set up the backyard for our dinner. There's drinks outside, and we'll be bringing the food out shortly."

"Are you kicking us out of the kitchen?" my mom asked.

Of course we were. How else were we going to get anything done?

"Not at all, Sharon," Santi replied. "We're just inviting you to take the party outside."

Jill nodded. "They're kicking us out."

"We just want our family to enjoy the wonderful summer day while we get everything ready," Santi said as he motioned for people to head outside.

Mags was the first one out. Whenever the door opened, she sprinted outside. Naturally my dad followed suit.

"Fine," Jill said. "Bring me a beer."

Santi curtsied. "Yes, Your Majesty."

"Cocksucker."

"Bitch."

Jill laughed before walking outside. Santi closed the door behind everyone and leaned against it. "What were we thinking? I love them, but they are going to kill me."

I walked over to him and caressed his cheek. Santi loved it when I did that, but I loved it even more. The feel of his smooth skin against my rough hands was like touching silk, and it soothed me. "You can't die. I love you."

He kissed my palm before resting his head on my chest. "Have I told you how much I love you?"

I smiled down at him. "Not in the last few hours."

"Because I really, really, really do."

"I'm glad," I said. "Because I really, really, really love you too."

Santi stared up at me as if he couldn't believe what he'd heard. "What?"

He shook his head and gazed off in the distance.

"*What?*"

"I'm just trying to remember the last time we said that to each other."

"That we love each other?" I asked before turning around to get everything ready. "We say it a dozen times every day. Now stop being a Silly McSillyson, we've got a shitload of things to do."

And then I suddenly saw Santi shaking my hand, his big, beautiful smile beaming up at me in front of Rich's. After that, his arms were wrapped around me as Picasso breathed his last in my lap. Then we were making out in front of the condo on my first night in Houston, and then rolling around on the floor after he proposed. We were at the Presidio on our first date, the Skyfari at the San Diego Zoo, and in Las Vegas for Darren's birthday.

The last image that flashed in my mind was looking down at Santi. He sat back on the pool lounge chair talking to me, and I was on the scaffold with Pork Chop right before my world suddenly turned topsy-turvy.

I spun around to face Santi. His lips had parted into the biggest grin of his life. I didn't need to tell him. He already knew.

"You remember, don't you?"

I nodded. "Everything."

Santi flew into my arms and I held him close. "That's the best anniversary present you could have given me," he said.

I gazed down into the eyes that had enchanted me since that first night at Rich's. "*You* are the best present in the world."

"Happy anniversary, my love."

I kissed his lips. "Happy anniversary." I grabbed Santi's hand and pulled him toward the back door.

"Where are we going?"

I smiled real big. "To tell the others. But mostly to let Jill know that my silly rhyming names are back. I know how much she's missed them."

Santi shook his head and we broke into laughter. We headed outside into the warm summer day, where our friends and family waited to celebrate.

And what a celebration it was.

JACOB Z. FLORES lives a double life. During the day, he is a respected college English professor and midlevel administrator. At night and during his summer vacation, he loosens the tie and tosses aside the trendy sports coat to write man-on-man fiction, where the hardass assessor of freshmen level composition turns his attention to the firm posteriors and other rigid appendages of the characters in his fictional world.

Summers in Provincetown, Massachusetts, provide Jacob with inspiration for his fiction. The abundance of barely clothed man flesh and daily debauchery stimulates his personal muse. When he isn't stroking the keyboard, Jacob spends time with his daughter. They both represent a bright blue blip in an otherwise predominantly red swath in south Texas.

You can follow Jacob's musings on his blog at http://jacobzflores.com or become a part of his social media network by visiting http://www.facebook.com/jacob.flores2 or http://twitter.com/#!/JacobZFlores.

3

By Jacob Z. Flores

JACOB Z. FLORES

Justin Jimenez has loved his partner, Spencer Harrison, for ten years. He'll do anything for him— including bury his feelings for a man he met while he and Spencer were separated last year. Justin never planned to fall in love, and he certainly never planned to tell Spencer about it—but when a phone call wakes them in the middle of the night to inform Justin that his former lover, Dutch Keller, has been in an accident, he doesn't have a choice.

Justin's revelation shatters the fragile relationship he and Spencer were trying to rebuild. The weight of his guilt—both for hurting Spencer and for leaving a heartbroken Dutch to find solace in a bottle—crushes him. But what Justin doesn't know is that Spencer and Dutch guard an explosive secret of their own. All three men are tangled in a communal web of lies, and unless they find the events in their lives that ultimately led them to friendship, passion, and betrayal, they won't see the love at the heart of the pain.

http://www.dreamspinnerpress.com

Being True

By Jacob Z. Flores

Jacob Z. Flores
BEING TRUE

Truman L. Cobbler has not had an easy life. It's bad enough people say he looks like Donkey from Shrek, but he's also suffered the death of his policeman father and his mother's remarriage to a professional swindler, who cost them everything. Now dirt poor, they live in the barrio of San Antonio, Texas. When Tru transfers to an inner-city high school halfway through his senior year, he meets Javi Castillo, a popular and hot high school jock. Javi takes an immediate liking to Tru, and the two become friends. The odd pairing, however, rocks the school and sets the cliquish social circles askew. No one knows how to act or what to think when Mr. Popular takes a stand for Mr. Donkey. Will the cliques rise up to maintain status quo and lead Tru and Javi to heartbreak and disaster or will being true to who they are rule the day?

http://www.dreamspinnerpress.com

The Gifted One

By Jacob Z. Flores

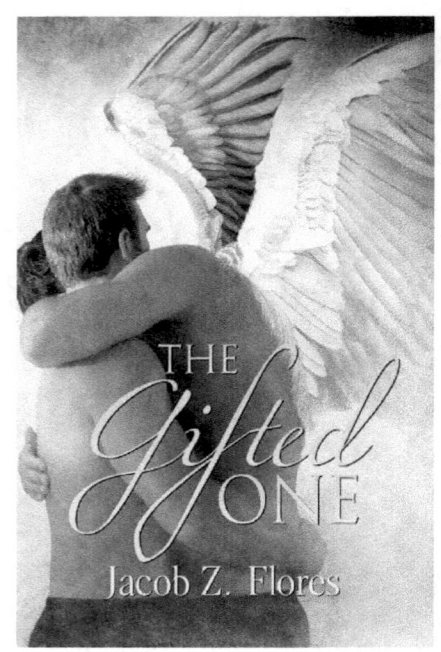

As his birthday approaches, Matthew Westlake fears more than just growing a year older. He fears never seeing another year at all. Each birthday brings a close call with death, leaving holes in his memory, recurring nightmares, and one more glimpse of his guardian angel. This birthday Matt must stand against ancient evils that have hounded him since birth, because he is a Gifted One—a seventh son of a seventh son.

Within Matt rests the unlocked potential of a force for good, but it also makes him a target. Being the Gifted One and dodging demonic attacks aren't Matt's only problems, though. He's fallen in love with his protector, the Archangel Gabriel, and Heaven will condemn that love to save Matt's soul. But Heaven doesn't count on Gabriel loving Matt in return, defying divine law and placing them in danger from demons and angels alike.

http://www.dreamspinnerpress.com

When Love Takes Over

Provincetown: Book One

By Jacob Z. Flores

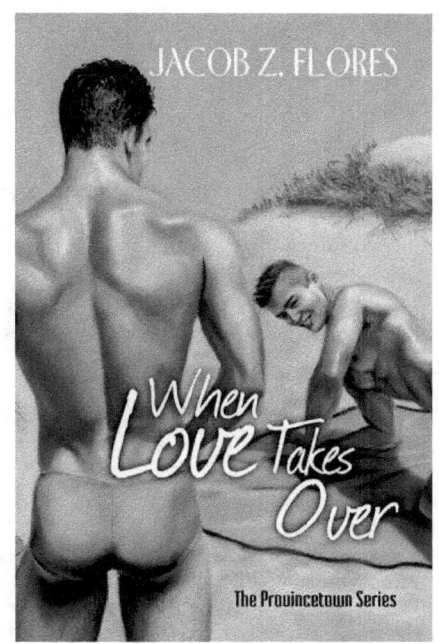

Zach Kelly's life is a shambles. His boyfriend of three years dumped him, and his writing career is going nowhere. On a whim, he heads to Provincetown, Massachusetts, to nurse his broken heart and figure out his next step. He's expecting to find rest and relaxation on the sandy beaches of Cape Cod. Instead, Zach meets a hunky porn star during a chance encounter at a leather shop he mistakes as a place to buy a belt that is definitely not for whipping.

Van Pierce is smitten when shy and inexperienced Zach crashes through a shelf of fetish gear. Though Van's got an insatiable appetite for men on and off the set, his porn persona, Hart Throb, hides a broken heart. He's struggling to find the reality the porno set doesn't offer, and Zach is fighting to find the fantasy that will set his writing on fire. The odd goofball and the suave beefcake may either find love amid Provincetown's colorful pageantry where summer never seems to end—or more heartbreak than either can imagine.

http://www.dreamspinnerpress.com

Chasing the Sun

Provincetown: Book Two

By Jacob Z. Flores

As a physician and prominent citizen of Victoria, Texas, Dr. Gil Kelly took a hard fall when his vengeful wife revealed his infidelity with other men. Closing ranks around her, the town's elite ostracized him, and his relationship with his children was nearly destroyed.

After spending his life focused on living for others, he has no idea how to live for himself. He wants to find love but now settles for anonymous sex that only further clouds his world with shame and guilt. Gil believes finding true love is an unobtainable dream, what his father used to call "chasing the sun."

Then he runs into Tom Martinez, his son's childhood best friend, who returned to town a grown man and offers everything Gil needs. But Gil hesitates to fall into Tom's arms, because after his high-profile divorce, the potential scandal of loving a younger man could separate him from his children permanently.

http://www.dreamspinnerpress.com

When Love Gets Hairy

Provincetown: Book Three

By Jacob Z. Flores

As vain as he is beautiful, Nino Santos happily lives life waiting for the next ferry full of fairies to bring him new conquests. As long as they aren't hirsute, he's all in. So he's shocked to wake up after a beach party he cannot remember with a hairy naked man lying next to him.

Teddy Miller doesn't remember the "Bear Week" party either, much less the Abercrombie & Fitch model wannabe next to him. Teddy doesn't give two cents about appearances, but guys like Abercrombie don't return the favor. That's why he prefers men with extra fur and padding over carbon copy clones of perfection—a type of man Teddy is far too familiar with.

When Nino and Teddy glimpse each other the next morning, it's loathing at first sight. Instead of exchanging phone numbers, they exchange insults and vow never to see each other again. In Provincetown, however, escaping a trick best forgotten isn't easy. Mutual friends and chance circumstances keep Nino and Teddy in each other's orbit. But are they fighting each other or the attraction growing between them? The answer lies amid Provincetown's windswept dunes and the night neither of them can recall.

http://www.dreamspinnerpress.com

When Love Comes to Town

Provincetown: Book Four

By Jacob Z. Flores

Brody O'Shea isn't looking for much, just a hot guy with a decent job, who is sane and doesn't have kids. The son of a former rock star, Brody has lived through the pain of bankruptcy and bad parenting, and he doesn't want to experience it again. As a reformed horndog, he wants the security and stability of a relationship. But almost every guy he meets seems satisfied with Mr. Right Now, and he wants to find Mr. Right—now!

The only men Eric Vasquez chases are criminals. As a deputy and single father, he has no need for a relationship after his last one ended disastrously. He lives for and through Maddie, his nine-year-old daughter. Everything else is a needless distraction, but distraction is what Eric gets when he comes to Provincetown to attend the wedding between his cousin Van and the man of his dreams.

When Brody and Eric meet, what they want and what they find conflict. An ocean of expectations separates them. If they cannot move past their reservations to reach each other's shores, they might miss the boat when love comes to town.

http://www.dreamspinnerpress.com

CANNING THE CENTER

TARA LAIN

LONG PASS CHRONICLES

http://www.dreamspinnerpress.com

FOR **MORE** OF THE **BEST GAY** ROMANCE

Dreamspinner Press

DREAMSPINNERPRESS.COM